THEY MAKE MONSTERS

COVETED KINGDOM, BOOK THREE

LEIA KING

THEY MAKE MONSTERS Blurb

Brutality is our legacy.
Pain is our lifeblood.
But family is everything.

Or it's supposed to be.

They've violated that time and again.
To our enemies, power is all.
They'll strike down their own blood to secure it.
They'll bury us all.

At least they'll try.

The chains have been broken now.
We'll cut down anyone who stands in the way.
They made us monsters.
And now they'll fall by their creations.

Author's Note

This is a Dark Mafia Reverse Harem Romance with scenes of M/M.

A list of TWs can be found at leiaking.com

There are *spoilers* for the VICIOUS THINGS series in this book.

Watch us rise.
Watch your fall.

~Nico~

My head was pounding as I came to.

I blinked past my blurry vision and struggled to get my bearings.

A burning pain in my skull drew my attention, and I looked to see my head was pushed against the driver's window, blood slicked across the glass.

I winced and pushed into an upright position, struggling to swallow down an intense wave of nausea that rose up from that small movement alone.

I brought my hand to the left side of my head and it came away drenched in blood.

Head trauma. Just what I didn't need.

A groan caught my attention, and I turned, a surge of adrenaline ripping through me when I found Caterina slumped in the passenger seat, her emerald eyes barely open, her face all cut up and bruised. Her seatbelt had sliced into her neck, and it was bleeding down to her shoulder.

I went to reach for her, only for a shocking spike of

pain to shoot through my right arm. My shoulder specifically.

Fighting to get control of everything, of the situation, it took me a few moments to realize that it was dislocated.

I looked out at Caterina in a battered state, my gut twisting, then I took in what had happened.

I remembered Angelo running us off the road.

Now we were at the bottom of the ravine we'd been driving alongside up above.

The car had landed upright, but it was mangled to shit, the bumper completely fucked and both our doors shot to hell. I tried mine just in case, but the metal was twisted and warped, just like Caterina's and it wouldn't open.

I managed to pull off my seatbelt and I glanced behind me, the rearview mirror smashed so unable to help me there, and I looked to see tree branches driven through both of the back windows and the rear.

The only way out was through the windshield.

I jolted as a bullet winged my mirror.

Angelo was still active.

Another bullet ripped through the back window, but its trajectory was obstructed by one of the mammoth tree branches, the thing thankfully embedding in it instead of where it had been headed—right for Caterina.

That luck would run out soon enough, though.

We needed to get out of here.

We were sitting ducks right now.

I finagled Caterina's seatbelt, having to twist to manage it with my good left arm, and she hissed as when I pulled it free, it aggravated her neck injury.

"So sorry, *principessa*." I studied the wound quickly. "It's gonna be okay. It's not too deep. Just a couple of stitches, I promise. We need to get out of here. Can you work with me? Are you mobile?"

Another bullet shot through the car this time and I jerked back just in time before it drove into the dash, narrowly missing me.

The screeching of tires caught my attention then.

The gunfire ceased.

A scream sounded, followed by hefty thuds and shouts of furor, before I heard the screeching again.

What was happening?

"Nico... something's wrong," Caterina whimpered.

"What? What is it?" I asked, urgency taking me over as I scanned her.

Her legs were crossed, her hand right beside them.

And as she removed it and she grunted with effort to uncross her legs, my breath caught in my throat as I saw blood leaking from beneath her black skirt and down her thighs. She turned her hand over and it was covered.

Fuck.

"No. No. No. No."

Tears welled in her eyes.

I shifted my weight and angled my right shoulder against my seat, then I roared as I forced it back into place. I couldn't do much without it in working order.

I forced myself forward, despite my head swimming in protest, searching the floor for my gun.

It was nowhere to be found. It could've ended up in the backseat, but with all the debris, finding it would be near impossible.

I instinctively reached for my backup, but it wasn't there, and I remembered giving it to Julian as an extra precaution. *Fuck it.*

"I can't find mine either," Caterina told me. Then she lurched, clutching her belly.

"Hold on," I told her frantically. "We'll get you to a hospital ASAP. Just... just hold on."

3

She murmured something in response.

I pulled off my leather jacket and draped it over her face and upper body. "Stay under here for a moment," I told her.

And then I reared back and smashed my boot into the windshield.

It didn't give way, pain radiating right down my fucking leg as a result.

Caterina's whimpers escalated, and it collided with the adrenaline and pain coursing through me like utter fucking madness, and I just kept fucking kicking.

Over and over and fucking over.

I finally made a dent and it cracked.

I stabbed at it with my boot and I was able to breach it, glass raining down and making me hiss as a couple of shards cut right through my jeans and into my calf.

I kicked out as much of the glass as I could, enough for me to get us through without sustaining significant damage.

"Come on," I told Caterina, before I hauled her up against me, my right arm screaming at me in protest. It could fuck the hell off. She needed medical attention and she needed it now.

"Argh!" I yelled out into the night as I dug the fingers of my free hand into the sleek metal of the car as I dragged us through onto the hood.

When I'd managed it, I pulled my jacket down to Caterina's chest, then carried her off it, my boots crunching in the brush and dirt as I moved us away from the car.

I laid her down on the grass, keeping her covered in my jacket because she was shaking. She gazed out at me, a grimace twisting her beautiful features. She was barely lucid.

"Nico," she breathed, reaching out to me.

I crouched down beside her and took her hand as I reached into the front pocket of my pants for my phone with the other. "We're out. We're okay," I told her, forcing a comforting smile that I really didn't feel.

That got worse when I pulled my phone out to find it smashed to shit.

I went to reach for her to see if hers in her blazer pocket had survived the crash, but then a rush of movement drew my attention.

I swung my head toward my left and sprung to my feet.

Had that fucker made his way down here intending to finish us off?

Was that why he'd stopped firing?

"Nico!"

I frowned.

Definitely not Angelo's voice.

"Rina!"

There was only one person who called Caterina by that name.

"Levi!" I called back. "Over here!"

A bright light filled my vision a few moments later and then we were bathed in the glow of two flashlights just as Levi came into view, bursting through the trees along with a bigger guy in a red Henley shirt I knew from my research on him to be Mason Hall.

As soon as Levi took us in, specifically Caterina, he choked and shoved a shaky hand through his black, curly hair. "Motherfucker," he said, rushing up to me with Mason just behind him.

Mason told me calmly and collectedly, "We ran them off, dropped two on the road. Our people are on their way to sanitize the area."

"Them? Angelo wasn't alone?"

"No. He had five others with him in the back of that thing. Military types, it looked like."

Fuck.

"Angelo?" Levi asked, eyeing me worriedly. "Angelo Simone? That predatory fucker who had his sights set on Rina?"

"The very one," I grunted.

Levi crouched down beside Caterina just as I did, on the opposite side.

He jolted when he lifted my jacket, instinctively trying to determine how badly she was hurt, and saw beneath. His eyes met mine. "She's... is she pregnant?"

I nodded, all I could manage as ice rolled through my veins with him putting the words out there, given the current state of her.

He looked at Mason, something passing between them. Mason winced and shoved a hand through his short, wavy brown hair.

"We've called for help. Paramedics will be here in minutes," he told me. "But we need to get her up to the main road. There are steps over to the west side that lead back up there."

"Levi?" Caterina groaned. "What's... how?"

He reached out and stroked her hair, but pulled back when he saw me looking.

I couldn't give two shits right now, honestly. All that mattered was her and our baby.

I gathered her into my arms and staggered to my feet, Levi staying close. He could obviously see what a fucked-up state I was in too, so he was there to back me up. He knew better than to pull her from me, though.

Mason led the way through the brush and heavy foliage with his flashlight illuminating the way, toward the steps he'd referenced, and Levi answered Caterina's question, telling her, "That motherfucker ran you off the road on the outskirts of our territory. I have eyes this far out and with you slated to come to us tonight, I was keeping an extra look out. We saw what was happening and headed out here."

"Oh," she murmured. "Good."

Levi grimaced, noting just how out of it that she was.

"Nico?" she rasped.

"Yes, I'm here, *principessa*," I said, gazing down at her in my arms.

"You… the guys… I love you. I *love* you… okay?"

My heart squeezed painfully in my chest.

"We love you too. That means you don't get to leave us. Ever. Do you hear me?"

Tears sprung to her eyes. "I'm… too… tired. So… tired. Sorry… so sorry, Nico."

Levi caught my eye, his emotion bleeding into mine.

I grimaced as I adjusted Caterina in my hold so I could stroke her face. "Stay with me, just stay with me. We're getting help. Any moment now."

Her tears rolled down her cheeks and her glazed eyes met mine, so much pain in them that it ripped me apart right where I stood. "She's hurt. She's… hurt… bad."

"We'll see to her. We'll help our baby. Almost there."

The last part wasn't true. Levi had said that we were at the border of Stonewell, which I knew to be a ways from a hospital. And we hadn't even made it to the fucking steps yet.

Levi spun toward Mason. "There isn't time."

Mason nodded, giving him the go ahead about something.

In the next second, Levi was pulling out his phone and dialing. "I need help. It's Rina. She's hurt. I'll fill you in later. For now, I need a medevac. I'll send you the coordi-

7

nates. Yeah. How quickly? Okay, good. Thanks, Dad." He hung up and told me, "I've got a chopper coming in. Ten minutes."

I'd barely taken in his words when Caterina cried that she loved me again, before her eyes closed and she slipped away.

"No!" I roared out into the night. "No, you don't get to leave us! Caterina! *Caterina!*"

2

~Emilio~

"What the hell is going on?"

I'd just finished up with Rocco finalizing the details for the enhanced security system that Nico had demanded, then I'd been on a call with Carlo updating him on the situation concerning Marco being MIA and Leo gathering forces. While I'd taken the call, I'd seen Julian leading delivery guys through the main doors and up the stairs near where Nico and Caterina's rooms were located.

I hadn't been able to do much about it while I'd been focused on reporting every pertinent detail to Carlo.

But I sure as fuck could see to it now.

Julian spun at the sound of my voice outside one of the spare rooms that was right beside Nico's. His eyes lit up with barely contained excitement as he told me, "A special surprise."

"What? Right now? After a home invasion?"

"I ordered this beforehand. I didn't know this shitshow was gonna play out like this tonight, *or* that all this stuff would arrive a couple of days early."

"*All this stuff?* What are we talking about here? You

know Nico's not gonna take well to you renovating the Manor without his approval."

"He just gets stuck in his ways sometimes and it's hard for him to accept anything different or spiced up. He'll have to get used to it with all four of us moving in here permanently soon."

That hadn't actually been officially decided upon.

He was definitely getting ahead of himself.

But that was Julian.

And, yes, he was obviously overcompensating too because of the state of everything right now—and the Angelo of it all.

Nico not being on board with Julian's *renovating* suggestions in the past hadn't been about him being stuck in his ways. It had been about Nico not being a fan of Julian's bold and often flamboyant style of interior decorating, his apartment being the ultimate testament to that. It really didn't mesh with Nico's much more toned down and somewhat minimalist and simple approach to the décor around the Manor.

Although, I did agree that a balance would need to be struck there if Julian and Caterina did move in here permanently.

"Besides," Julian went on. "I'm not renovating the Manor. This is something special. I've got a decorator coming in a couple of days as well to paint a mural."

What?

Before I could get a word out, two guys in navy overalls emerged from the room and told him, "Got it set up for you. Any questions, or you need anything else, we're one call away."

"Thanks," Julian said, slap-shaking with them.

They both gave me a polite chin lift, then headed on down the steps, where they were met by two of Nico's soldiers, then escorted out of the house, the doors sealing behind them.

"Come," Julian urged me. "Check it out!" he cried enthusiastically, disappearing inside the room.

I followed him in and came to a jarring stop just over the threshold as I took in the sight before me.

The room had been empty beforehand, but now it was boasting three new pieces of furniture.

A bookcase in the shape of a huge stunning tree in one corner, an oversized turquoise couch, and then, the feature piece being a golden crib against the right wall.

"Is that… is the crib—"

"Real gold? Yeah," he said gleefully, running his fingers over it reverentially.

Well, damn.

He pointed at the wall behind it. "We're gonna put a mural here of a mythical castle, like right out of a story-book. I've got a change table coming too, a shag rug, and I was thinking we could also put in a cozy area full of cushions and pillows for when the baby's a bit older and crawling around."

"Wow, this is… wow."

"Just the reaction I was hoping for. Do you think Cat and Nico will like it?"

I walked to him. "This is one of the most thoughtful things you've ever done. That's saying a hell of a lot, considering how many there have actually been, Sunshine. They're going to be touched. I have no doubt at all." I made a show of rubbing my chin as I looked around.

"What? What are you thinking?"

"A dragon, maybe? On the opposite wall?"

"A dragon? Hmm, well, I guess it will fit in with the fantasy theme. But only a friendly one, not a fearsome looking one. We don't want to scare our baby."

"Friendly dragon," I chuckled. "I can work with that."

"Maybe some knights? Cat's whole King Arthur thing?"

"Perfect."

"We could also bring in something from Nico's love of Roman and Greek mythology. Although, a non-violent element. That probably means Vikings are out and then—"

I pressed a kiss to his cheek, and it pulled him up short.

"What was that for?"

"Just being you."

I tossed one of his classic winks at him for a change.

And then I grinned and went to head out of the room.

But he snagged my arm, pulling me up short.

I turned back to him, raising an eyebrow.

The happy-go-lucky demeanor he'd been putting out there in spades had retreated, and he was actually showing me behind it, emotion swimming in his eyes. "Tonight was a lot, wasn't it? Cat being taken and thinking something had… that she'd been hurt… or worse?"

"It was a lot, yes. Especially on top of everything else that's already been a lot to bear as it is."

"Like finding out about Leo?"

I nodded. "Yeah."

"How are you doing with that? You haven't said a word to me about it."

"I can't risk processing it yet because of everything else going on."

"So Cat was right? Nico did teach you how to compartmentalize it?"

"He did, yes. Just temporarily."

"Until it's the right time to kill the asshole?"

"In a sense."

"You haven't said anything about the other thing either, you know? Not for a while."

I frowned. "You made it clear that me doing so and pushing it was causing you pain."

"It's not like you to back down. Not when it comes to this."

"I don't understand. Do you *want* me to push you to discuss it?"

"I don't want you hurting by worrying about me. I'm doing okay. For right now, I'm doing okay with it."

"Only because you're not processing it. When you broke down at the warehouses, I know that was you trying to purge it, fooling yourself into believing you could relieve enough of it to then shut down again without it being so much of a strain to do so. Then you've been operating as normal since, even being the architect behind us fucking together in the pool that night. You know as well as I do that Caterina blacked out that text from Angelo because what was beneath that was obviously about you, comments or threats toward you, yet you barely reacted. Santino is dead because she lost control, which means the power vacuum we were worried about has happened. Dante doesn't want it after everything that's happened and been done to him—the guy was tortured, for fuck's sakes—so Angelo is the likely candidate to take his place. That ill-equipped Capo, Elia, sure isn't ready for it. With that militia in play, Angelo also has a force at his back to steal that power. To be here and wield an empire, Julian, the son of a bitch who tortured and assaulted you. Yet, once again, you've barely reacted. Because you *can't*, can you? You've buried it, yes? Compartmentalized it to such a level that's beyond anything Nico's ever even done before, right?"

"Yes."

I started. Was he actually admitting to it? "Excuse me?"

"You're right on the money. All of that is true. I *am* shutting it down."

"Especially when factoring in your history with your father, doing that is incredibly dangerous and—"

"Just temporarily, like you." His eyes darkened. "Until I destroy him."

"My situation is very different."

"There's no other choice while we're caught up in all of this."

"Why not? Why can't you let me help you through this like I did last time? Nico and Caterina too? Why did you shut down with your therapist? She's trusted by you, she knows your history, the whole deal, and—"

"*Because!*" he yelled, tugging at his hair. "I can't function if I do any of that! Okay? I fucking can't! Not this time!"

"Sunshine," I uttered, reaching out to him.

He pulled away, shaking his head. "It's… it's too much. I was able to work through what happened in the past, but having this now on top of it… it's too heavy. And the way it happened with Angelo… the shame involved that he kept driving home to me, getting inside my head like that, making me… beg… I… it doesn't just make my skin crawl, it's like poison in my veins threatening to destroy me from the inside out."

He brought his hand to his face and turned his back to me, cursing to himself.

I walked to him and fingered the hem of his white tee. He jolted at the contact, but didn't move away.

I pushed his shirt up to reveal the angel wings tattoos decorating the expanse of his back. "Remember why you got these?" I asked, tracing the designs.

"Yes," he murmured.

"You're a survivor. But that's only part of it. You're beyond that. So far beyond that. You're extraordinary. Fucking truly. And Angelo managing to get inside your head doesn't change that fact. It never could."

He looked over his shoulder at me. "I thought… no, I was certain that after the past, that nobody could ever get inside my head again. Like my father with his *broken boy* comment."

Yeah, that was something that had haunted him for a long time.

"I mean, I know I was physically weakened at the time from the crash, but I still should've been able to withstand his torment, especially the psychological aspect."

"You did withstand it. This isn't about you failing or succumbing like you seem to think. You connected with Angelo."

"I… what?"

"I saw the footage. All of it, unfortunately. And there was a point where I saw you recognize that he'd been tormented like you had, been abused, then been lost when it came to his sexuality, the fact he was having trouble accepting what had been awakened in him, that he didn't know what to do with it. *You* do. You were always very good at embracing that part of yourself. You even really helped me to be able to as well. You recognized that you could help him. But he… that motherfucker used it against you. It was his way into you… into your head."

"But when I… when I begged him…?"

"You were delirious at that point. He didn't break you. You're rewriting that in your mind because you weren't fully cognizant at the time."

"You're saying I'm filling in the missing bits wrong?"

"In a way, yes."

15

He turned fully back to me, my hand slipping from his back in the process.

"Regardless, being *broken* isn't a permanent state. That's a misconception. So many have been broken by circumstances or others. But we remake ourselves, we rebuild." I reached out and stroked his hair. "We learn to fix our broken pieces. We go on."

He grasped my hand in his hair and brought it down between us, holding it tightly. "Once this is done, I don't want to be alone in this anymore. I don't want to keep it inside. I want to let you all in, let you help me. *But* for now, this has to be it, all we say about it. I hear you, though, I do. And thank you, Milo. *Thank* you."

"I'm just glad you let me in this much."

"I wasn't trying to push you away, I was trying to push *it* away."

"I know. But if your plan to hold it all off until this war is won becomes too heavy, I'm here, all right? We're all here. Don't let it get to the point of near self-destruction that it did for you the night of the Price takedown."

"I promise."

Relief sung through me. *Thank hell.*

"Come on," he said. "I want to show you the expansion plans specs I've been working on tonight before this delivery came in. I think Cat's gonna love that, too."

I followed him out of the room.

We'd only made it a couple of steps down the corridor, though, when my phone rang.

I pulled it from the back pocket of my jeans and took in the call display.

Unknown Number.

I came to a stop, and Julian noticed, spinning around and asking, "Is that Nico or Cat?"

"Doesn't look like it." I frowned, then took the call. "Milo. Who is this?"

"Levi."

"Levi?" I questioned. It had Julian tensing and coming right up to me. I put my phone on speakerphone mode and held it between us. A loud thrumming sound came down the line then, along with sirens piercing in the background. "What's going on? Is that a—"

"A medevac chopper. Yes. That's why I'm calling."

A shudder rolled through me.

"Nico and Caterina didn't make it to you, did they? They're hurt?"

"They'd reached the border when they were run off the road into the ravine."

"Christ," Julian choked, taking a staggering step back.

I swallowed hard and forced the next words out, "What's their status?"

"Mason and I arrived on the scene. We've had them airlifted to the nearest hospital and they're being seen to as we speak. Rina is unconscious and Nico… well, he needed to be sedated."

"So Nico was all right, but Caterina wasn't?" Julian asked.

"I don't want to make guesses. All I can confirm is that Nico suffered a dislocated shoulder and a head injury. Until they're checked out, I don't know how severe it is. As for Rina… it was worse, yes."

"Worse, how?" Julian demanded now, panicking and grabbing my hand around the phone, urgency blasting out everywhere.

"She was bleeding. Significantly."

"Bleeding? Where?" I pushed.

Levi's voice was unsteady as he responded, "It looks like the pregnancy is in trouble."

"No," Julian rasped. "No, that can't... no." He pushed away from me and started stalking up and down the corridor, pulling at his hair.

"Text me the address. We're heading down now."

"You need to know something before you do. And you'll have to approach covertly. They were run off the road by Angelo and the militia Rina was coming to me to help her track. We were able to chase him off, but he's still out there."

Julian stilled at that and then swung his head toward me, his eyes blazing with unadulterated fury.

"Understood."

"I'll be here when you arrive."

"Thank you, Levi."

"Of course."

With that, I hung up and sucked in a breath in a strained effort to keep calm.

"I need to call Rocco and Cassio and have them hold things here, then we'll head out."

Head out.

To the hospital.

To the hospital because Nico and Caterina had been badly hurt.

Fucking shit.

~Julian~

Jesus fucking Christ.

Having to take a roundabout route to get here in order to protect ourselves from a fucking madman—*the* fucking madman, as he'd become to us—had cost us precious time in getting down here to the hospital.

I'd barely been able to stand it.

Every additional minute that had ticked on by.

Every moment we weren't where we were needed.

With them.

With our loves.

It had me sick to my stomach as Milo and I burst down the hospital corridors after getting Levi's texted directions when we'd been ten minutes out as to where exactly Nico and Caterina were at in this maze of a place. Apparently, Levi's brother-in-arms, Mason Hall, had been here too, but then he'd had to head back to oversee the cleanup of the two bodies they'd dropped at the crash site.

We made a left turn and came upon a bench just a few feet down where Levi was supposed to be waiting for us.

"Where is he?"

"No fucking clue," Milo grunted.

But a moment later, we heard a commotion coming from one of the rooms further down the corridor.

We both rushed over there, voices reaching us as we drew closer.

"This isn't going to help anything, especially not her."

"I need to fucking see her. Right fucking now, Levi!"

"You already vomited three times on the way here because of the concussion you sustained. And on top of that, you lost your shit when Rina was led away to be treated, and the staff had to sedate you. While you had a fucking head injury, Nico. Do you think you'll be any help to her if you're killing yourself in the process of trying to get to her?"

"All that matters is her and our baby!"

"Do you think she'll see it the same way? Just let the doctors do their jobs. They're still seeing to her, anyway. They need space to do that."

"It's been too long already. You said I'd been out for a couple of hours."

"Yeah, you have. It actually should've knocked you out longer, but clearly not even heavy duty sedatives can keep you down in this state."

"You'd know a lot about that."

"You're right, I would, so I also know the downsides of it. And how it can negatively impact the people I love if I can't get a hold on that dangerous side of me when it's called for."

The door flew open just as we reached it and the both of us had to jerk back as Nico came bolting out, the speed and force he was using in his less-than-stellar state causing him to stagger.

He was only half-dressed, just his pants on, not his shirt or jacket, and he was barefoot too. His thick black hair was wild and mussed, his face and chest a map of bruises and grazes. He had his left arm in a sling. A gauze pad was taped over the left side of his head and as he shifted his weight, I noticed a limp in his right leg.

He jolted when he took us in and it cut into the intensity rolling off him in dangerous waves. He was in that worrying place between rage and pain.

Unfortunately, that surprise of nearly smacking into us only offered a brief reprieve for him.

And then he was trying to push past us, uttering, "We need to get to her now. Right now."

Milo blocked his path, a formidable wall of solid muscle forcing him to pull up short.

"Move," Nico ground out.

"Levi's right, we need to let the doctors do their thing," I told him, grasping his good arm, hoping the contact would help to soothe all that dangerous intensity, at least somewhat.

He caught me off guard as he grasped my arm back with an awful urgency, his voice unsteady as he uttered, "You didn't see her. You didn't see her like that, how badly she was hurt and… she said goodbye to us."

I jerked back at his awful words. "No. No, she wouldn't. She… she can't. She's not going anywhere. She's not leaving us."

A door down the corridor opened, and a doctor stepped out, white coat and all, her blonde ponytail swinging every which way as she searched around, before her gaze landed on Levi.

"Mr. Knight," she called.

Levi rushed over to her, with the three of us following, Milo supporting Nico's weight.

Levi gestured at us as we reached her. "These are her significant others. Next of kin listed."

Next of kin?

We hadn't done that.

He flashed his eyes at us. *He'd* done it, taken care of it.

The doctor nodded and stepped up to us.

"She's stable. She lost a lot of blood, but she was given a transfusion and she's responding well to treatment. She's in recovery and being closely monitored."

"Fuck," Nico breathed. "She's really okay?"

"Yes," the doctor said, smiling kindly. "She'll make a full recovery."

I stepped forward. "And the baby? She was pregnant and—"

"We're aware," the doctor said, shifting her weight in a way that I didn't like, a worrying fucking way.

"What? What is it?" Milo asked.

"Miss Leone suffered significant abdominal trauma. It caused a placental abruption. That involves the placenta being separated from the uterine wall prematurely. I'm so sorry, but there was nothing we could do for the baby at that point."

"Our child… you're saying… it's gone?" I croaked, struggling to process her words.

The doctor nodded. "I'm so sorry for your loss."

"Motherfucker," I heard Levi curse and saw him turn away and slump down onto the bench heavily.

A scream sounded from the room.

"She's just been informed, and she's having trouble processing the news," the doctor told us.

In the next second, Nico was pushing his way into the room.

Milo and I followed after him to find Cat thrashing in the bed and screaming, two nurses trying to calm her down, warning her that she needed to be careful, that she could complicate her recovery.

My gut twisted at the scene, at the tears pouring down her face, so much pain every fucking where.

And the fact that Nico just stood there staring, shell-shocked so deeply by it all that he couldn't move.

I couldn't keep it together, emotion spilling down my cheeks too and taking me in a brutal chokehold.

Milo was there then, pushing the nurses out of the way and wrapping his arms around Cat, effectively restraining her and hugging her at the same time with that superior strength of his. "We're here. We're here with you. Take it easy. Don't hurt yourself. Please, beauty."

His words impacted her, and she sank into him, burying her face in his chest and sobbing. "She's gone... our baby is gone... she's *dead.*"

I climbed onto the bed and stroked her hair and back. "We're so sorry, darlin'. So fucking sorry."

She grabbed my hand and squeezed it tightly, needing the comfort, the small comfort that it was in a moment like this.

A roar tore through the room and I looked out to see Nico completely losing it, having pulled from his intense moment of catatonia, now ripping all the medical equipment off a cart, then smashing his fist into the wall over and over, his pained bellow filling the room.

As the nurses called for security backup, Levi burst back in after hanging back to give us space. As he did, Nico staggered, then fell back into the wall, sliding down it onto the ground and burying his face in his hands. "No, no, no, *no.*"

Christ.

All I could hear were his sobs melding with ours.

So much pain, so much grief.

So much fucking loss lately.

But this was so much worse than anything that had come before.

A piece of us.

Our family.

Our *hope.*

4

~Emilio~

We were on the verge.

Right on the goddamn edge of cracking under the weight of everything.

The crash, the fucking tragedy of losing our baby that had come along with it… it had been the last straw. We'd been hanging on by a thread, to be honest, and this threatened to undo us entirely.

It had been a few hours since the doctor had told us that the baby had been lost and in that time, Nico had been sedated after his violent outburst in Caterina's hospital room. It hadn't ended with him slumping down onto the floor. He'd gotten a second wind where that was concerned. Julian had been sobbing his heart out, and I'd had to remove him from Caterina's room as a result, because she'd needed to rest. And, yeah, she'd also asked for some space, which had only made Julian more concerned. He was in with Nico now, trying to sleep for a couple of hours.

And I'd been taking point, getting Carlo, Cassio, Rocco and Tony up to speed. Levi had been keeping to himself and texting away the whole time, until I'd seen him get up while I'd been on a call, and head outside. Of course, I'd followed him. I was in heavy protector mode, and I had to make sure everything was okay. To achieve that, I had to be aware of the ins and outs of everything. Especially when it came to somebody who was technically an outsider, somebody I didn't know well.

As I stood blending into the shadows, I watched Levi approach a black Porsche that was pulling into a spot in the corner of the hospital parking lot.

A woman dressed in a pink plaid blazer and a matching skirt stepped out, her long, black hair blowing wildly in the wind.

He was there in the next moment, wrapping his arms around her, then nuzzling against her. "Thanks for doing this, *Wildflower.*"

"No problem. With Mason busy overseeing the sanitization at the border after the two of you had to drop those bodies, it needed to be me. Colt wanted to help, but he's not exactly well-versed with this sort of thing."

Levi chuckled. Then he gestured at the sweet car. "How did you get Mason to let you drive his beloved?"

"You know my powers of persuasion are unmatched. Plus, I promised to drive carefully, *and* ensure that I wouldn't allow *you* to get behind the wheel."

Levi slapped his hand to his heart. "I'm wounded, Brianna."

She rolled her eyes. Then she walked to the rear door and opened it, gesturing inside and telling him, "It's all here, just like you detailed."

"Including the spare phones?"

"Yeah, I completed the downloads." I saw her pull two phones from her blazer pocket and hand them to him. As he pocketed them in his hoodie pouch, she told him, "You should tell them that you breached their network, Levi."

"I don't want to stress them out. Besides, it's already done. I did what I needed to."

"I get that, but it's about trust and loyalty, especially right now for them when they're in the thick of all of this."

"All right, yeah. I hear you."

"How is Caterina?"

"She'll make a full recovery. But losing her baby is a whole other thing."

"I'm so sorry. I can't even imagine."

He scrubbed his hand over his face. "It's fucking brutal. It looks like she's shutting down, too. She doesn't want to see anyone in her room."

"Well, she's processing it. Have you talked to her yet?"

"No. It hasn't been possible with her guys hovering, and now her asking for space to rest. I also need to be careful not to intrude too much from a personal stand-point, especially with the way Nico is about it all."

"Because you slept with her once?"

He jolted. "How do you—"

"Please. I know _you._"

"She _has_ only ever been a friend. I was telling the truth when I told you that before. That one night, although sexual, was just between friends, trust me. And just as awkward because of that fact. It was more… clinical than anything else. For the both of us. A mission, basically."

"Yeah, I get it. She was the only person you could trust to go there with back then. It was an obstacle she helped you to smash through because you were traumatized when it came to sex after what you saw me suffer through when we were kidnapped."

"You're being really understanding about this."

"You mean mature?"

"Yeah, that." He slid his hands down to her hips and pushed her up against the side of the car. "I fucking love you, you know that?"

"It's been well established, *lovely.*"

He groaned and brushed his lips over the side of her throat, and it had her fisting her hands in the back of his hoodie. "Never gonna get enough of you calling me that."

As he pushed his thigh between her legs, she grasped his face. "Mason said no fucking in or on his car."

"*Fucking*? Who's being presumptuous? I'm just holding you."

"Your knee is grinding against my—"

"Your sweet cunt?"

"Levi!"

He chuckled. "What? It *is* so fucking sweet. In fact, get back in the car, spread for me, and I'll eat you up right here and now."

"Nice try, but no can do. Mason's car, remember?" she said, pressing her hand to his chest.

"Fucking cockblocker."

"Levi."

"Fine," he muttered before kissing her forehead sweetly, then pushing off her. "But when I get back, it's on. Hardcore with the four of us. I'm talking an all-nighter."

"I look forward to it," she said, beaming at him.

He gathered two large duffel bags and a laptop bag from the back, slinging them over himself, then shut the door.

"I know this is something you have to do, Levi, but be careful. Promise me."

"I swear it to you. My reckless days are behind me." Off her look, he added. "Fine, for the most part."

She leaned in and kissed his cheek sweetly. "I love you."

"I love you, too. Text me when you get back home safe."

"Will do."

With that, she slipped back into the Porsche, he shut the door for her, then she was driving out of the parking lot.

Levi sighed heavily, clearly emotional at staying behind away from her and his loves.

He went to walk back into the hospital, but I stepped from my position in the shadows.

"Motherfucker!" he exclaimed, jerking back. "For a giant of a guy, you sure can move like a fucking ghost."

"It's a honed skill."

"So, I assume you were watching the whole time, observing the private interaction between me and my woman?"

"It's not private when the contents of that interaction concern us."

"Ah, right. Rina mentioned that you're the paranoid one, the most distrusting of outsiders."

"She mentioned it, or you discovered it on your own?"

"You got me. I've been keeping an eye on her, yes. More so since that meeting that I had with Nico. I was concerned."

"Good."

He cocked an eyebrow, trying to gauge my reaction and where I was at when it came to him.

As I reached out and laid my hand on his shoulder, he tensed.

Nico was right. The guy *was* always expecting a fight.

Even though he was here busting his ass to help us. So much so that he'd had a medevac helicopter called in for Caterina and Nico, he and Mason had even murdered for us, and now he was about to do even more to assist. All because he was that undeniably and deeply loyal to our woman.

"Yes, *good*. She needs a friend like you in her life. And when this is all over, we should ensure that it's not so distanced and the contact isn't so infrequent."

He smiled.

"So, why did you breach our network? That was my only concern with what I overheard."

"Rina and Nico's phones were destroyed in the crash but Rina has a program that backs all their contents up every few hours, which I accessed to essentially replace said phones exactly as they were prior to the crash with all the corresponding data, everything. With what's happened, and Nico's position amongst the families, he needs to be reachable. And Rina doesn't like to be without her phone as a rule."

"Nicely done."

He handed me the two phones. "The black case is Nico's, the green is Rina's."

I placed them in my jacket pocket. "Thank you."

He nodded, then I stepped aside, and we headed inside the hospital together.

"So, how are you doing?" he asked, eyeing me as we walked side by side.

"Just keeping focused on what needs to be done."

He nodded. "I get it. And I'm so sorry."

"Thank you. We were really excited about this baby. It's… it's a lot."

"Yeah, it is. I'll help you find the cause of this tragedy tonight. Angelo Simone."

"He's been the cause of a lot of sickening shit," I ground out.

"So I've heard from Rina."

We made it to the elevator bay, and I was just about to

call one down when a rolling thunder pulled me up short, the ground reverberating beneath our feet, just a moment before the power went down.

Levi cursed and spun around.

Emergency power kicked in, whirring to life, but the elevators were a no-go.

"What the hell was that? It sounded like—"

"An explosion."

Chaos erupted all around us, an alarm blaring, security rushing all over the place, people in the waiting areas screaming and heading for the exits.

What the shit was going on?

Could this be Angelo?

I would've believed this to be too fucking bold for him before tonight, but after coming at Nico and Caterina like that and running them off the road, all bets were off where predicting his level of insane actions was concerned.

On our way down here, Levi had told me and Julian that he'd overheard Angelo screaming that Caterina needed to die for taking Santino's life.

Had he come to finish the job?

5

~Caterina~

Placental abruption.

Blunt force injury.

Abdominal trauma.

I hated those words.

I hated them all.

But they were the same ones swirling through my mind over and over.

Tormenting me.

Blaming me.

Our baby was gone.

And she was gone because of me.

Nico had almost joined her in that tragic fate, too.

And he still could. So could Julian and Milo.

Because of me.

I didn't understand why the guys didn't blame me too, why I hadn't seen or felt anything like that at all from them.

I was the one who'd lost control and murdered Santino, which had led to Angelo coming for us on that road.

And I wouldn't have been in a position to do that at all if the guys hadn't been so scared of benching me, of how I would react and lose all trust in them, and possibly even leave them if they'd forced me away into a safehouse somewhere.

I would've been safe there right now. Our baby would still be alive.

I'd brought this down upon us.

I squeezed my eyes shut and tried to get comfortable in the hospital bed, so I could fall asleep again, to get a reprieve from the suffocating grief and guilt that had such an unbearable stranglehold on me.

I brought my hand down to my belly, tears filling my eyes as I stroked it, stroked what was no longer there anymore.

"I'm sorry… I'm so sorry," I whimpered.

A sudden, violent rumbling had me jolting.

A thunderous sound inundated my senses, the whole room reverberating with it.

I strained to push myself up in bed.

In the next second, the power went out; the room plunging into darkness.

What the hell?

A whirring started up and the emergency power activated, casting a little light back into the room, but not enough to not have to strain to see clearly.

An alarm pierced through the place, making me wince.

Shit.

I dislodged the IV with a grunt then pushed out of bed, my body killing me with the strain of moving.

I'd just made it to my bare feet when the door flew open, startling the crap out of me.

As if the rest hadn't already been enough.

Adrenaline tore through me at the sight of two guys in

all black, wearing striking red and black hockey masks, bursting into the room, headed straight for me.

I went to spin into a kick to defend myself but, with the state of me, a brutal wave of dizziness assaulted me and I staggered back, smacking into the bed instead.

In the next second, one of them was on me, trapping me in a bear hold, while the other pulled a knife and approached me.

"You're to die the same way Santino did. But first Angelo wants you to suffer," the knife wielder rumbled.

I struggled against the hold on me, but I was too weak to make much of it.

Shit!

Something that I wasn't used to gripped me, something that made me shudder and made me fucking sick and ashamed at the same time.

Helplessness.

Just like earlier, when I hadn't been able to keep our baby safe.

Panting, all I could do was watch and struggle futilely as the knife wielder moved in close. "Let's carve this pretty little body up. He wants you sent to him in pieces."

I caught sight of more of the assholes outside and then the door slammed shut, being locked too, as a bunch of them stood guard, blocking the way so these two could take their time hurting me, like Angelo had clearly ordered.

The explosions I'd heard had to be some sort of distraction to send the hospital into evacuation mode, get security out of the way, the medical staff, everyone, basically.

There was a struggle outside that had the knife wielder pulling up short.

"Caterina!" I heard Nico roaring, followed by an agonized scream from somebody else.

"Destroy these motherfuckers!" Levi's voice followed.

"Cat!" Julian's voice came.

A bellow that I recognized as Milo's rang out, just before a hefty thud hit the door.

The guy holding me told the knife wielder, "They're making too much headway too fast. We'll have to speed this up. Kill her, then bring the body to one of the safehouses to carve it up for him."

Safehouses? One of?

I steeled myself as the knife scraped across the skin of my throat and I glared into the sadistic eyes of its wielder.

Just as he went to puncture my flesh, a violent crash tore through the room, the sound of glass exploding, wood cracking.

The guy holding me spun around with me still in his clutches, and I choked as I saw a very familiar figure landing in a deep crouch in front of the window amongst the wreckage.

His powerhouse form filled my vision. That brown buzz cut that, combined with the scar over his right eyebrow, gave him a very severe look. But as usual, when those amber eyes looked upon me, the gentleness and softening there transcended that harsh edge he always put forth to everybody else who he encountered. He was dressed all in black, in tactical pants and an aviator jacket.

Joe.

Without even taking a moment or disengaging the harness strapped to him, he pulled his Sig, fired off a shot through the fingers of the knife wielder that had him screeching, dropping the knife, and staggering back. The guy barely got in two steps before Joe put a bullet in his skull, and he dropped like a creepy rag doll.

The guy holding me screamed in the next split-second as Joe fired a bullet through his kneecap. And then Joe was there, using the chaos and agony that had the guy lurching forward to wrench his arms off me and haul him out through the shattered window.

Screaming rang out before it was silenced by a violent thud as the guy obviously met his demise when he landed three floors below.

"Just like you to make a dramatic entrance," I rasped, sinking back against the bed for support.

Mirth shone in his eyes for a moment.

But then it turned to concern as he took me in.

"You're barely mobile. As I feared."

He rapidly disengaged the harness, then holstered his gun and walked to me.

He wiped the trail of blood down my throat away.

"We need to get you out of here. They won't stop coming until you're eliminated. Angelo Simone has put a contract out on your life." He glared at me. "In retaliation for the murder of Santino, Caterina."

"Don't pretend you're not glad he's gone."

"Not like this, not at this juncture," he gritted out. He held up his hand. "Later. Now we must move. You need to disappear. But first, we need to give them something to chase, and that has to happen before the second wave arrives here."

"What are you—I'm not disappearing. I can't just—"

"You already lost your baby tonight. If you don't cooperate with me, you stand to lose more. All three of your loves."

I jolted at his awful words.

The brutal truth to the first part and the fear that had already been stoked in me where the rest was concerned, that I'd lose Nico, Milo, and Julian because of my actions.

He pulled his backpack off, then unzipped it, and yanked out a pair of tactical pants and a jacket.

"If you don't leave with me right now, they will all die. Every moment you stay here is endangering them." He held the pants out to me. "You need help?"

I snatched them from him as I eased myself away from the support of the bed, wincing at the ache through my abdomen. Emotion threatened to take me over as the awful reason for that hit me once again. Over and over, it kept doing that. And, *shit*, I couldn't stand to lose anybody else. I certainly couldn't take *me* being responsible for it again.

With shaking hands, I tried to put the pants on, but he ended up having to help me quite a lot. He pulled the jacket on for me too, top-of-the-line Kevlar, and tucked the hospital gown inside the pants and the jacket, then zipped it up for me. He even had a pair of boots for me that he helped me to put on.

He put the backpack back on and snatched up the harness, about to reattach it, when he told me, "This can take both our weights. Let's move."

I hesitated. "I can't just take off. I can't just leave them like this and—"

He startled me as he pulled my ring off, then tossed it on the bed.

"What are you—"

"I know there's a tracer embedded within."

"Leaving isn't—"

"This is a temporary situation, unlike what their deaths will be," he bit back at me.

I started at the harshness of his comment, especially in light of what I'd just suffered through.

"I'm sorry," he said, registering it. "You're emotional and vulnerable right now, more than I'd accounted for. I thought you'd be shutting down to cope with it. Not this. Not opening yourself up to the grief and despair at this juncture. I see your men have impacted your ability to do that." He shook his head, not happy about it in the least. "There's no place for that right now. Rationality needs to prevail. Emotion needs to be squashed. You can't allow it to complicate what needs to be done."

Something he'd drilled into me repeatedly when he'd trained me.

But that had been then. A lot had altered.

"If I just disappear with you into the shadows, especially right after losing the baby, it will break my men to pieces."

"That's an emotional reaction, one we absolutely cannot afford, Caterina." He loomed over me, glaring down at me.

And that was when the door flew open.

I looked out to see Milo bursting through first, someone's blood splattered across his cheeks and drenching his knuckles.

He misread the situation, as did Nico, judging by him snarling as he took in what Milo had, coming in just behind him, seeing a man with his back to them looming over me with a gun in his hand, the dropped bodies on the floor, the window.

"Stop!" Levi called out, coming into the room with Julian just behind him holding Nico's gun at the ready and shooting glances back and forth between us and the corridor outside, on high alert.

Joe grunted with frustration at the interruption while he was in mission mode and focused on getting me clear.

He pushed back from me and turned around.

"Stover," Milo uttered.

"What are you doing here?" Julian demanded. "How did you even get in and—" Catching sight of the debris around the shattered window answered his question. "Jesus."

Joe zeroed in on Levi. "Long time, Knight."

"A few years, give or take," Levi responded, tensing up because he knew Joe almost as well as I did. I saw him slip his hand to his back pocket, where I remembered he kept his collapsible bo staff. He also signaled Milo, warning him.

Nico's sapphire eyes were flaming with fire at Joe still standing so close to me. It was hard to pull off the intimidation factor when he was standing there in a sling, unstably too because he'd clearly just woken up as a result of the insanity while still having a heavy-duty sedative running through his veins. But Nico had that ability to do what he believed needed to be done, no matter what state he was in.

Joe told them, "I have solid intel that Angelo is sending another unit here as we speak. Caterina is the sole target. I need to remove her from the situation and use her to draw them away from here. They'll follow. I'll keep her safe. And the rest of you will be fine."

"That's not fucking happening," Nico growled.

"You're not taking her away from us," Julian bit back.

Joe wasn't the least bit fazed by their protests, eyeing Levi and telling him, "Concentrate on finding Angelo. I'll keep her off the radar, give her time to recover." He then looked at Nico. "You're needed back in Tolhurst. Your presence needs to be felt amongst your men and your enemies alike, especially at this critical stage where you've unofficially taken power, as well as the precarious situation with Leo Marchetti. Taking you all with us right now will undercut that and all your efforts, this war you've been raging. Caterina is the sole target of this hit. Like I said, I'll draw them away, have them follow us, take their attention. Return to your stronghold and we'll be in touch."

39

"Be in touch?" Milo scoffed. "And we're just supposed to trust that? Especially after your past manipulations?"

"Caterina," Nico spoke to me. "Do *you* trust in him?"

I stared out at my men, seeing their desire for me not to do this, not to leave. Levi was noticeably quiet on the subject, both not wanting to cross a line or intervene in the personal nature of it between me and my men, but also knowing Joe too well to believe there was any other safe choice right now.

And, yes, he also knew that with Joe adamant about this, he'd make it so, no matter what. He'd put them all down if he had to. And as accomplished as they all were, he was another level with decades of experience on them.

While I couldn't stand the idea of them getting hurt, of them suffering anymore than they already fucking had with all this madness we were caught up in, I also could bear the thought of being responsible for it.

So, it had me responding, "I trust in his strategy and his judgment where this is concerned."

"So that's it?" Julian asked, his voice cracking. "You're just going to leave?"

Nico scrubbed his hand over his face.

"It's only temporary," Milo uttered, as much to convince himself, it seemed, as the rest of them.

"It's not your fault, you know?" Julian told me. "Losing the baby is something that happened to you, not something you're responsible for, Cat. I promise. So if this is partially why you're choosing to do this—"

A beeping sounded, interrupting Julian's words that had me staring out at him, emotion threatening to get the best of me.

I looked to see it coming from Joe's watch.

He brought it to his eye level and tensed. "They're here. We're out of time."

Levi came forward. "Do what you need to," he spoke, before wrapping his arms around me, but I felt him slip something into my pants pocket as he did, using the hug as a cover. He gave me a chin lift as he stepped back.

"Caterina, you don't need to do this," Nico said, coming to me.

"I can't let you suffer because of me."

I stepped back and Joe blocked his path to me.

"That's not what's happening," he bit back.

"We're in this together," Milo said.

"And we still are."

"Caterina—" Nico started.

"This is the best solution for everyone right now, Nico. Please."

Before anything more could be said, screams and yells came from outside, down below at the rear of the hospital, followed by gunfire.

"We're out of time," Joe said.

"This is not happening," Nico told him, starting forward again, his eyes blazing with the clear intent to physically prevent it. Julian went to take aim at Joe.

Joe yanked me back, then pulled something from one of his pockets.

Too late, I saw it was a smoke grenade.

He activated it and tossed it toward the guys.

"Back up!" I heard Levi yelling, seconds before it went off.

All I could hear was coughing and cursing as thick smoke erupted, blocking our view of each other.

Joe took advantage of the distraction, reattached the harness, then grasped me in a sturdy grip and barreled out the window.

I heard the guys roaring, and I looked up to see them

rushing to the window in spite of the smoke, as Joe repelled us down the wall of the building.

"Fuck!" Nico bellowed. "Caterina!"

As we landed, Joe disengaged the harness, then rushed me toward a vehicle hidden by shadow and darkness in the far corner of the lot, as I took in the sight of the mercenaries rushing toward the hospital.

I jolted as I found myself staring at my Lamborghini, and Joe unlocking it with my fob.

"What's my car doing here?"

"We need to give them something obvious to chase. This is it."

He slid his fingers into his mouth and whistled.

It cut through the chaos and several of the mercenaries pulled up short on entering the hospital when they took in the sight of us supposedly trying to make a break for it.

In the next moment, they turned tail and came for us.

"Perfect," Joe said, then ushered me into the car while he hurried around to the driver's seat, firing off two shots to cover us and slow the enemy down as he went.

He rapidly started the car and turned to me. "Time to disappear, sweetheart."

6

~Nico~

"She was in no state to make that fucking decision!" Julian yelled, kicking the couch. "She was reeling from the crash, from losing our baby. You saw it, right? The guilty look in her eyes? She's blaming herself. The despair, too? She's beaten down, Nico. She wasn't thinking like the Caterina we know. She was compromised."

"Did you not see me try to stop her?" I ground out, as I paced back and forth smoking up a storm while I eyed my new phone, where I'd been waiting on another text from her for going on two hours.

Caterina: Safe. Evaded hostiles.

That was all she'd sent.

Nothing since.

Yes, there'd been a whole lot of relief for all of us when I'd reported it to the guys, but it wasn't fucking enough. It just wasn't.

She wasn't *here*.

"You mean, did I see you snatch my gun, barrel through smoke grenade resistance and nearly choke yourself to death, where you then took aim at Stover, about to take him out until Levi stopped you when he noticed the mercenaries headed for them, recognizing that if you'd killed him, Cat would've been done for, that she wouldn't have been able to fight them off in her barely mobile state? Yeah, I saw all that insanity. "

"Well, then."

"I meant beforehand when it was being discussed. We should have talked her down. We should have——"

I spun back to him. "It's *done*, J! It's fucking done!"

He stilled at my outburst. "I'm not blaming *you*. That's not what I'm saying. It's that manipulative bastard, Stover. He got in her head when she was compromised."

"You *should* be blaming me."

"What?"

I pocketed my phone. I couldn't fucking look at it anymore, waiting on another message from her, for her to make contact. It was making me fucking crazy. As if that needed any assistance with what had already happened in the last forty-eight hours.

I had a lot of other texts, emails, and missed calls that I needed to return. To my men, to Carlo, to a lot of people. But I couldn't, while my head wasn't clear. I needed to take a beat. I needed to find some semblance of rationality, to calm the hell down.

Somehow.

I pulled Caterina's ring from my pocket, thinking that could help.

But it did the opposite.

Knowing she wasn't wearing it, what had become a symbol of the love between the four of us… it wasn't right. It was all fucking wrong. Everything!

"Nico, what did you mean by that?" Julian pushed,

coming to me over by the windows that looked out over the Manor grounds.

I shoved my hand through my hair. "I made the call to keep her here in spite of everything, to keep her in the thick of the fucking fight. Milo was adamant about sending her away to a safehouse. But I didn't listen. And now our baby is gone and our woman is in the wind."

"You were respecting her choices, her agency," he said, his eyes darting to the ring and a forlorn look taking him over.

"But I didn't even try to strike a compromise with her. Because I was so afraid of losing her, if I pushed it even a little."

"And you were right."

"Right about what?" Milo's voice came as he strode into the room. "Chain smoking after ingesting all that smoke earlier? Nah, definitely not that, right, Nico?" he groused, sarcasm dripping. "Dropping ash all over the place when you hate mess, serving to demonstrate just how out of it you currently are? Maybe because you've been pacing up and down and, before that, raging, while suffering from a head injury and a dislocated shoulder because you almost died in a brutal car crash?"

I glared at him as I pocketed the ring and took another harsh drag of my smoke. "I can't worry about that right now."

He was there in the next second, ripping the cigarette from my lips and stomping it out on the floor.

He frowned when he saw that I didn't have a reaction to it.

"All right, you're going to bed. Right now."

"I can't just—"

"Things are stable. Stover's plan worked. Angelo and

the militia are focused on tracking Caterina. Levi has assured me that won't even be possible with Stover's skills in play. Leo hasn't made another move. You're in control of the Marchetti Syndicate soldiers—aside from Leo's one hundred or so—and most of its business operations. The rest we're working on. You can afford to get some sleep. You *need* to. You're being looked to as Boss now, even with it not being put in place officially while Leo is still at the mansion and bolstering his soldiers with these black ops shitheads. It's you they're looking to."

"We need to find Angelo. That motherfucker killed our child, almost killed me and Caterina, tortured—"

"We will. In fact, it's already in progress. Levi is setting everything up now, all his equipment he brought with him."

"And Cat?" Julian asked.

"We already discussed it on the drive home from the hospital. She's safer off the grid with Stover until we take out Angelo and nullify the hit," Milo told him. "So you raging about it to Nico really isn't helping."

"I can't just be okay with her not being here. Can you honestly say that you are?"

"No. Of course not. But she *is* safer right now. That's what we need to focus on. And it's also not such a bad idea for her to have some time away from being in the thick of everything."

"Now she's at a safe house," I muttered. "Too little, too late, though."

"What?" Milo asked.

I slumped down onto the couch. "I made a mistake."

"What mistake?"

"I shouldn't have shut it down when you were pushing for us to sequester her away."

He perched on the coffee table in front of me. "Well, there's nothing to discuss there. You were right, Nico."

I shook my head. "Come on."

"You were. If we'd done that, we would have lost her trust. It *would* have broken us apart."

"Instead, we lost our child. And her."

"First off, Caterina's not lost. She'll return. That's the plan and no matter what happens, Stover won't be fucking deviating from it. I know it and I also know that if worse comes to worst, you'll move heaven and fucking earth to make it so. It's what you always do—protect us at all costs. You always find a way."

"Why do you think I've been telling Cat that whenever I've needed to comfort her?" Julian said, coming over and perching on the arm of the couch beside me. "It's because of you. That's what you do, what you bring about."

Milo nodded in agreement, then told me, "What happened with the crash, losing our baby, that was all on Angelo. *He's* responsible for that. Not you and not Caterina."

It was easy to say that, but a whole other thing to accept.

I was the one who'd been driving.

I'd missed that shot that I'd fired at Angelo.

I wasn't... I wasn't used to guilt.

As I'd told Caterina, I did experience it sometimes. When the pressure became too much, I had to let myself feel it.

But it wasn't often.

And I could always shove it back down again at my will.

That was how practiced I'd become with it over the years.

But this was different.

47

The fact that I was exhausted physically as well as mentally right now really wasn't helping.

Fuck.

I pushed off the couch. "You're right. I do need to get some sleep." I looked out at the two of them as they rose with me. "You should as well. I'll go tell Levi the same thing."

"I already have," Milo stated. "He wants to finish setting up his equipment, which he says should take another hour, and then he's going to crash in the spare room next to Julian's."

"All right, good." I staggered in my step. Yeah, I really had overdone it since the crash.

So much physicality, so much rage, the fucking grief.

And now being separated from Caterina.

All of it was a mammoth strain on keeping my *feral* side leashed.

I'd already been holding it at bay for so long as it was.

My outbursts at the hospital had been just that—bursts. The grief and upset of it all had made it so, limited to only that. But the way things were going, and with having our foursome currently fractured without Caterina here, and with what we still needed to go up against to end this nightmare, I feared that it wouldn't be able to remain checked.

So many people were counting on me.

I was stepping into the role of Boss of the Marchetti Syndicate.

Unleashing like a monstrous entity geared toward utter destruction and brutal bloodshed was off the table.

If I couldn't get a handle on it, I'd become no better than Santino and Marco.

Me taking power was supposed to be different, to bring about a new era.

One of honor.

The days of unhinged men who mistakenly thought themselves gods would die with our enemies.

And I had to ensure I kept it that way.

I *had* to be better.

I fucking had to be.

7

~Emilio~

"Anything?"

Levi turned from where he was typing away furiously with one hand, and even then moving between keyboards and laptops themselves, while also somehow sipping from a coffee mug.

He'd set all his equipment up in the living room that we'd been using as a suite for Julian. Along with a few of Nico's soldiers, I'd had all Julian's stuff moved back to his actual assigned room in the house now that he was mobile and physically healed up.

The place looked like a command center.

"Not yet."

"What? You can't track her phone?"

"They're either in a dead zone intentionally or Stover's using a military-grade signal jammer." He turned on the swivel chair with his coffee in hand, took a sip, then eyed me. "What I can do is backtrack the signal."

"Pinging off cell towers, that sort of thing?"

"In a way. That's obviously time-consuming and I

really don't believe it's the best use of my efforts. Give it time. It's Rina. She'll find a way. Trust me."

"Stover told you to focus on tracking down Angelo."

"Exactly. I understand, though. If it was our woman in the wind, me and my boys would be hard-pressed to approach things rationally. *However,* this is a special case. Stover *will* protect her with everything he has and, believe me, that's a hell of a lot. She's safe with him."

I nodded, taking his words in. "It's where she should stay right now until she recovers. And until we take out Angelo."

"Speaking of, did you know about any of this?" he asked, turning back to face one of the laptop screens, and gesturing at it.

I walked closer and took in what he'd pulled up.

My gut was twisting in the next second when I found myself reading texts that Angelo had sent to Caterina just before the home invasion.

The full texts this time.

Blocked Number: *How's my pretty cock slut? He's definitely still obsessed with me, frantically trying to track me down, pretending it's all for revenge when he's really craving me. Not to worry, he'll be able to get his fill soon enough.*

Caterina: *Stay the hell away from him.*

Blocked Number: *No can do. And you, traitorous cunt, you've signed your death certificate. Your daddy knows what you did. He's gonna force you to return what you stole and then he'll do what he should have done a long time ago and bury you. Wish I could be there in person to see it, but I'll settle for spitting on your grave. Wondering how I was able to contact you? Let's just say I have some new friends. Better than the ones your boyfriends murdered. They were just a stepping stone to these guys. Bye, Caterina. I should warn you, it's gonna be painful. Santino promised me it would be. Can't wait until it breaks your boyfriends into pieces.*

I cursed under my breath.

"I'm focusing on the content about Julian. The rest, the threats toward her by that motherfucker, come as no surprise to me. From what Caterina told me, that's who Angelo is referring to, yes?"

"Yeah," I ground out, hating that it was the twisted truth of it.

"Well, there's clearly an emotional angle here. And not just with this text exchange. She has a transcript on file where she's highlighted certain elements of the audio she extrapolated from surveillance footage from when Julian was in captivity. She also has notes about a possible game-plan to work this angle, which seems more than feasible, especially when she's referenced that she's in possession of a tracking chip that's still operational. But then she's marked it as a no-go, completely discounted it."

"Because of what it would do to Julian."

"Yeah, I got that much. But it's still a viable angle. It could be used to draw him out, and to put him down ASAP, rather than taking the roundabout and time-consuming route of actually trying to track him."

"He'd need to be there in person," Nico's voice came from the door, and we turned to see him leaning against the doorframe, sipping from an espresso cup with his free hand, the other one in a fresh sling. It was also apparent that he'd taken a shower, and he looked wide awake now. A whole lot better now that he'd had a good night's sleep.

"What? No, we just need the chip."

Nico shook his head and pushed off the door, coming into the room. "Angelo is too sly for that. Especially now he's working with these fucking black ops bastards. He won't risk stepping out into the open and making his presence known unless he has confirmation that his obsession is actually there. Just bringing the chip and a decoy won't be enough." He eyed Levi. "And that's why we're not doing it, what Caterina obviously realized, and thereby ruled it out."

"All right," Levi said.

"I understand where you're coming from. The faster we take out that twisted fucker, the faster Caterina can return home, because the hit will be rendered inactive upon his death."

"Well, I also wouldn't risk one of my brothers, so I hear you."

I started as Julian's hand landed on Nico's good shoulder, startling him, too, before he came into view and rounded him into the room, walking in, just clad in a pair of his blue boxers.

His eyes went straight to the screen before Levi had a chance to shield it from his view.

He'd obviously already heard our conversation because he looked away without any visible reaction. "We should use me as bait. It's the optimal strategy."

When Levi turned back to the monitors, likely not wanting to involve himself in it from a personal standpoint, Julian looked between me and Nico, pushing, "Well, isn't it?"

"It's off the table," Nico told him.

"You're being too rash about this."

"Shawn Price takedown? Am I really being *too rash* about it in light of that fiasco?"

"That was then. I'm in control now."

"It's not happening."

"Nico—"

"We always find a way through, yes?"

Julian grunted. "Throwing those words that you know that I revere back at me? That's low."

"Whatever it takes to make you see reason here."

"Right back at you."

Nico stepped up to him and growled, "Off. The. Table."

I tensed as Julian glared right back at him, close to challenging him.

That was the last thing we needed right now. Fucking infighting.

Tensions were high with everything going on.

Caterina not being here really wasn't helping matters either where that was concerned.

But then Julian stepped back. "Okay. It's off the table."

"What?" Nico uttered, his surprise mirroring mine.

"We'll find another way, like you said. Fine. Let's do it then."

"On it," Levi spoke over his shoulder.

Julian nodded to himself, then told us, "I'm gonna take a shower. Then I have some Carver Group business to attend to."

With that, he smiled out at us, then walked on out of the room.

I frowned after him.

"Rocco will be here in a few minutes and we're finalizing everything regarding the upgraded security system together, but after that I'll have a talk with Julian," I told Nico.

"Yeah, that was too easy."

"Agreed."

"Security system?" Levi queried.

"Yeah," I confirmed.

"I'll need to ensure it's properly synced to Rina's system, so you'll need me there, too."

"Milo's got that aspect," Nico told him.

Levi cocked an eyebrow. "You didn't mention your capabilities in that area."

I lifted a shoulder. "You didn't ask. Plus, I'm used to keeping that on the down low, I guess."

"Just seen as Nico's guard, huh?"

"Pretty much."

"Underboss," Nico spoke.

I eyed him. "What?"

"If you want it, it's yours. There's nobody I trust more than you to fill that role."

I smiled out at him. "Wow, that's... that's a lot."

"What did you think was going to happen?" he queried.

"That you'd make me one of your Capos alongside Cassio and promote Rocco and Tony to that role alongside us."

"It's Underboss. Think about it. I know you might want out of the Marchetti Syndicate altogether, given everything that's happened, so take some time with it."

I gave his good shoulder a squeeze. "Thank you, brother."

"Of course."

My thoughts starting to swirl with the possibilities of it all, I walked out to grab some equipment that I'd need for this meeting with Rocco.

Emilio Bardi, Underboss of the Marchetti Syndicate?

Just like my dad.

It was a lot to process.

That seemed to be the theme lately.

━━

"JULIAN?" I called out, stepping into his room because the door was invitingly wide open.

"Bathroom!" he called back.

I strode through the room toward the ensuite, frowning

when I didn't hear the running water from the shower he'd said he was going to take.

I had been in that meeting with Rocco for a while, though.

As I opened the door, I located him over on the other side of the room in the large, round tub in the corner, bubbles literally up to his ears as he lounged back while playing on his phone.

He looked up as I entered. "I figured a soak in this sweet-ass bath would be more relaxing and calming. Centering, really."

"I'm glad. Sounds like a good plan."

His eyes shone with mirth as he gestured at the tub, the whole setup, actually. Candles everywhere around the edges and on the shelves, pot-pourri in the mix, then a champagne bucket in the far corner. "Cozy, huh?"

"It looks that way."

"Discover the proof of it for yourself. Take a dip with me."

I started.

After what had happened with that psychopath, Julian and I, we hadn't... gone there together, not on our own, like we used to. It had been getting it on as a foursome all the way. I'd figured there had been something about the intimacy and intensity of just the two of us that had unnerved him after what he'd been through, something that had perhaps even reminded him of his time in captivity and what he'd suffered through.

So I hadn't pushed it. I hadn't said a word about it at all, and I even tried not to think about it.

But I had missed it.

That much was driven home to me all over again from a physical standpoint when my cock thickened in my jeans just at the mere suggestion of me joining him.

At my hesitation, he went his usual brazen route—or what had been his usual way of doing things before everything had gone to hell—and he rose to his feet, water and bubbles dripping all down his sexy-as-fuck toned and chiseled body.

He put his phone down on one of the high shelves, then made a show of stroking his very hard cock, his piercings glinting in the muted light, the whole display sending a rush of desire straight through me. *Goddamn.*

He smirked at me as he sank back down into the tub, resting his head peacefully on the edge. "You really want a piece of this, huh?"

I rolled my eyes. "I thought we were retiring that phrasing?"

"Just bringing it out of retirement for this instance."

"Is that so?"

"Hell, yeah," he said, slicking his tongue over his lips in an intensely erotic way.

I ripped my tank over my head, and his gaze turned molten as he roamed his captivating hazel eyes over my torso.

I kicked off my shoes and yanked my socks off.

When I opened my jeans and started pulling them and my boxers down, my hard cock springing free for his viewing pleasure, his hand disappeared under the bubbles, and I watched his arm start pumping, the water sloshing as he obviously worked his beautiful cock.

He was fucking killing me.

I yanked my clothes the rest of the way off, and then I was sinking into the tub right beside him.

I'd barely settled when he climbed onto me, straddling my lap, then fisting his hands in my hair and yanking my head back so I was staring up at him. That mirth and flirtatiousness slipped away, and hunger laced with stark emotion bled into me as he uttered, "I need you."

"I fucking need you, too," I uttered, grasping his nape, then slamming our lips together.

His hands were all over me as we kissed, hot and heavy, the intensity stealing my breath away as much as the kiss itself, our lips clashing, tongues tangling, the both of us fighting to get as much of the other as we could, to fucking drown in one another completely.

He shifted his weight, and pushed his cock against mine, then had me groaning into his mouth as he started grinding along my shaft, those delicious piercings cranking the bliss-inducing sensation of it all up several fucking notches until I was rolling my hips and fucking my cock back against his, losing myself to it all.

I threw my head back, and he licked my throat, making me tremble with need.

"Sunshine... fuck."

He grasped my hand and placed it between his ass cheeks.

What the—

I lifted my head and stared out at him, cocking an eyebrow.

"Told you, I need you."

I couldn't believe it. This wasn't how we usually did things.

I watched him carefully as I peeled one of his ass cheeks back, then trailed two fingers down the crack of his ass.

Mixed signals came my way as he squeezed his eyes shut, but then bit his lip at the same time.

"Julian?"

"More... don't stop."

I teased his hole with the pad of my finger, and he squirmed, but then sank into me.

"Fuck," he breathed in rapture when I dipped inside a little.

I teased him, dipping in and out, then rimming his hole, titillating all the nerve endings, and it had him slamming his hips back and forth, then clutching my shoulders fiercely. "Deeper," he rasped.

I sank in further, groaning as I felt him clenching down around my finger.

He pushed back against me, so needy for more, that it had me drawing all the way out, then driving back in right to the last knuckle.

"Fuck!" he cried, digging his nails into my shoulders. "Yes."

I pumped in and out of him then, before adding another finger that had him growling, pre-cum leaking all over my cock. I was fucking dripping myself. This was something else to me, something I was really fucking getting off on, more than I thought possible.

Taking control, rather than him doing it, as was our usual way together, was empowering, all-consuming. And his reactions, being so overcome by it, just added another spine tingling element that had me beside myself.

Before I knew it, I was ripping him off me and shoving him down over the side of the tub with his ass in the air, his face smushed against the tile.

"Yes, lose your fucking shit, darlin'."

I spread his ass cheeks apart, then dove in, lashing my tongue over his exposed and vulnerable hole, eating him up, then thrusting inside and tonguing him.

It had him cursing out into the room, panting and squirming in my hold, losing his mind to it all.

"Sunshine… fuck," I choked when I came up for air,

then kept his cheeks spread as I slid my cock up and down between them, nudging at his hole in the process.

"Do it," he breathed.

I grabbed a fistful of his hair and wrenched him around to meet my gaze. "I need to see the look on your face as I sink inside your ass for the first time."

"Yes…"

"You need to feel the loss of control?"

He nodded, his eyes shining with more than need. Desperation. Emotion. "Please."

Fucking begging me? He had me. He fucking had me so deeply.

I pushed inside and he jerked as my crown sank into his tight hole.

I released his cheeks, then wrapped my fist around his cock, stroking, pulling, and pinching, and it had him pushing his delicious ass back, pleading for more.

His eyes shone at me as I drove deeper, another couple of inches, and squeezed his cock in the process. "Jesus, Milo. That fucking dick… ungh."

I sawed in and out of him with shallow thrusts, opening him up, moans spilling from him, until I then slammed all the way inside.

"Oh my fucking… *fuck!*" he cried, his thighs shuddering.

I didn't stop then, pounding into his ass, slamming my hips like a wild thing, hitting his sweet spot and zoning in on it until he was bucking in my hold, and slamming his fist down on the edge of the bath, struggling to take the intensity.

He dug his fingers into my ass, his glazed eyes fixed on mine, all fucking blissed out, mirroring my own state.

"Sweet fucking hole… gonna fill it with my cum."

His eyes rolled back in his head.

I jerked him closer to me, banding my arm around his torso, and he joined my hand wrapped around his cock, the both of us working to jerk him off.

"I want your hot cum spilling into my hand when I fill your ass with mine."

"Ungh... yeah... come in me... fucking come inside me."

"God-fucking-dammit, Julian," I growled. "You're driving me fucking insane."

He cried out as he jerked in my hold, then sprayed all over our joined hands, bucking his hips like a fiend, his ass clenching down around me fiercely.

A roar tore from my throat as I lost control and shot my hot cum deep inside his ass.

He trembled at the sensation, and I stroked his face, holding him to me, staring into his glazed eyes. "Okay, Sunshine?"

"More than," he answered, a sly grin spreading over his lips.

"You begging for that caught me off guard. I really wasn't expecting it."

"You got off on it, big time."

"Undeniable. And you? Was it what you needed?"

"Yeah, I just... thank you."

He didn't want to explain it, but I knew him well enough to get it, and I knew he'd been counting on that.

"I've missed this. I've missed being with you in this way."

"Me too," he said, nuzzling against me. "I'm sorry it took me so long to get back here, get back to *you.*"

"Don't apologize. Just be with me now."

He grasped my ass. "Don't pull out. Just stay with me like this for a while."

I stroked his hair. "Your wish is my command, Sunshine." I winked. "Or your begging is."

His eyes sparkled with amusement. "Shut it."

I chuckled. "Yes, Sir."

That had us both bursting out laughing, especially with the connotations involved with those two words.

And it felt really fucking good.

8

~Nico~

"Miss you as well, cupcake."

"How long are you gonna be, Lev? It wasn't the same sleeping in our bed without you these last couple of nights. Or at dinner. Or at breakfast this morning."

"I love you too, Colt."

"Love you. Mason sends his too. And Bree said she texted you."

"Almost as much as you've been texting me."

"Mason?"

"About a dozen messages."

"I knew it! He's been trying to hide how much he misses you, I guess for my benefit, but I fucking knew it."

"I'll try not to be too long, but they're in a shitstorm here. I can't leave until I've done what I can to give them an assist."

"It's okay. I get it. I know you need to help, especially because it's Rina. Is Nico still being a shit to you?"

"No, he's been fine. Welcoming even."

"Well, that's a change. I can't believe they lost their baby, though. It's so brutal. How are they all doing with that? I mean, if it was us —I know Bree's not ready for that, I'm just saying—I don't know how we'd get through it."

"*Together. That's how. Unfortunately, that's not what's happening here.*"

"*With Rina gone because of the hit on her?*"

"*It's not just that. I think she wanted to go. I saw the signs from her. She's blaming herself. She feels guilty around them.*"

"*She's doing that shutting down thing, you mean?*"

"*Seems that way.*"

"*Did you tell Nico that?*"

"*He knows her, too. I'm sure he's aware. I'm sure they all are.*"

"*It's so sad. What are you gonna do?*"

"*Help them with my skills and get her home here as fast as possible, so they can begin to properly process it all. It's taken her a long time to find what she has in the three of them. I might interfere a little personally, too, in order to make sure her guilt and grief don't have her fucking that up in a bid to protect herself.*"

"*Be careful, Lev, I don't want you getting yourself in trouble. I know you're there for Rina, but keep in mind that you're also delving into mafia shit by doing this. It's dangerous, and we just broke free from that sort of thing ourselves with all the danger we'd been in, our own war.*"

"*I promise, cupcake. I'll watch myself. And I'll be home with you all before you know it. Video call later? All four of us?*"

"*Sounds perfect. See you soon, then.*"

"*Bye, Colt.*"

I returned to sipping at my espresso as I heard Levi grunt when he finished his call. It was the crack of dawn, and he'd obviously thought that no one had been awake yet. Well, that certainly answered my concerns about him monitoring the surveillance system here too closely and possibly watching all of us. He wasn't doing that at all. And judging by the content of that call, he was with us more deeply than I'd realized.

As he strolled into the kitchen, he jolted as he saw me standing there leaning against the counter.

"Hey," he greeted, trying to cover up the fact that he'd been caught off guard. From my research on him, I was aware that it didn't happen often.

Although, now he was done with his own long battle, it was possible that he was relaxing into the peace of it all, so he wasn't as on the ball where that was concerned as he would normally be.

"Morning," I responded. "There's coffee ready," I told him, gesturing at three mugs sitting side by side, appealingly neatly on the island. "Just don't take the mug with the sorcerer on it."

He cocked an eyebrow.

"It's Milo's. It's got brandy in it. Helps take the edge off during stressful times."

He screwed up his face. "Brandy?"

"His father used to drink it. It's him carrying on the tradition."

"I see." He took one of the plain black mugs and eyed Milo's. "The mug is really something, too."

"It certainly is."

He smirked at me.

"What?" I asked.

"Just look at us being civil. I didn't know you had it in you, Nico."

"Well, I've seen behind the mask with you."

"Mask? No idea what you're talking about," he said with a wry grin.

"That antagonistic, bring-the-fight-right-to-my-door, and reckless image is far from all that you are. Although, I still do stand by my belief that it's not always going to be received as the deterrent you intend it to be."

"And believe it or not, I heard you. You're not the only one who's brought that to my attention. It can be viewed as a challenge and it can also invite a whole lot of trouble."

He took a couple of sips of coffee and slid onto one of the stools. "That image was necessary for what I was trying to achieve."

"Taking down Malcolm Lynch."

He nodded. "Something that's been accomplished now. So I'm learning how to move forward from how I used to be, to separate from that image, tone it down, if you will."

"I'm sure that's sent waves of relief through those who care about you. Especially Roman."

"No doubt."

"Delving into this war with us after just getting out of one yourself is no small thing."

He lifted a shoulder. "She needed me and I'm here. It's as simple as that."

"It's appreciated. Thank you."

He started at my open gratitude. A smile lifted his lips. "No problem."

An understanding passed between us, one that I hadn't thought possible not long ago.

How things had changed. Remarkably so.

He broke eye contact, clearly not liking the intensity, then told me, "Well, I haven't done a whole lot yet."

"You don't count saving Caterina from bleeding to death by calling in that helicopter *a whole lot?*"

"Seeing as though that was due to my dad's connections and ability to pull something like that off so insanely quickly, no." He shifted his weight, then told me, "*But* things are well underway toward me actually doing something and giving you guys the assist that you need. As you know, I have everything up and running, and I was honored to see that Rina's been making use of my facial recognition program, but I've also put other things in place. During my pursuit of Lynch, I developed a program that can pull a wealth of data and information, analyze it, and work to predict patterns of movements for those in our sights."

"That's ingenious."

"It is, yeah. It's just a time-consuming process, unfortunately. But with you not wanting to use Julian to draw him out, it's become the best way forward to tracking that sick bastard down. With him working closely alongside this black ops entity that's shrouded in a whole lot of mystery, we're now dealing with *their* security protocols. And these fuckers really know how to cover their tracks. The vehicle that ran you guys off the road was untraceable, not even fucking registered to a real person. Mason ran the DNA of the two we killed and it brought back nothing—they're fucking ghosts. They basically don't exist to the outside world. That was why there was no blowback from the hospital attacks, nothing that came back on you, because they covered it up, deleted surveillance footage, paid people off, a whole lot of covert shit to basically make it look like none of that ever fucking happened. Even the explosions they used as a distraction to move in and get to Rina."

I nodded, telling him, "I had my people run tests on the bodies of two of them that Caterina dropped at Santino's mansion too and it also came back with nothing."

He shook his head to himself. "I've never seen anything like it. The fact that they were able to penetrate Caterina's network is a hell of a feat in itself." He rose to his feet. "Speaking of that, now I have everything in place, the program running in the search for Angelo, I can get to work on investigating that, figuring out the details pertaining to the hack."

"What resources do you need from us?"

"Nothing. I'm all good. Focus on the Leo situation. I've got *this*."

"Breakfast will be arriving in the next hour. Make sure you eat."

"Arriving?"

I rolled my eyes as I had to tell him, "Julian has insisted on having his staff cater our meals for the next little while, as we're focusing on everything else. Apparently, some of us aren't getting the *necessary sustenance*."

He grinned. "You?"

"Right."

"You get into an obsessive mode, like me, huh?"

"It's been known to happen."

"Well, try to redirect some of that to figuring out how you plan to assuage Rina's guilt over what happened to the baby, and even the fact that she feels responsible for putting all of you in even graver danger because of taking out Santino."

I jolted at his words.

Of course, that had been his intent, to deliver it as something of a shock to the system to ensure they were heard and received in an undeniable way.

"She's engaging in victim-blaming, I'm aware."

"It's worse than that. It shook her. Really fucking badly."

Knowing her as well as I did, I was aware of what he was getting at, what he was worried about. I hadn't needed to overhear his conversation with Colton to determine it.

"She could be shutting down."

"And she could try to cut you out in a misguided attempt to protect the three of you. And herself." He folded his arms across his chest and regarded me. "I want this for her. Love and safety, but also people who really understand her, even the facets of herself that she used to previously be ashamed of. She deserves this. She's been alone for so long, I don't want her to go back to that. I might be overstepping as just her friend, but I needed to put it out there. *And* to also tell you that if she does try to cut you out, it's not through lack of care or love on her part. It's pain. A lot of fucking pain. The fact she's let the three of you in so deeply, that you're cohabiting together, and that she's even slated to partner on her expansion plans for Camlann Corporation with Julian, when she never lets anyone interfere in that, then that she wanted this baby with the three of you… it's an undeniable testament to how deeply she really is in love with you all."

I stared out at him, awestruck by his words.

The heartfelt sincerity.

The openness.

Even the vulnerability that he was putting out there.

Risking bringing all of this up when things were so volatile and also pained currently.

Trying to safeguard what we had in any way that he could.

All in the name of helping Caterina.

I couldn't help smiling. "You're a really good friend to her. I'll take these words to heart. And I can assure you that Caterina isn't going anywhere, or—"

Commotion coming from the main entrance had me pulling up short.

"No. You need to turn back around. Return all of this."

It was Julian, sounding frantic.

"Vin, come on. Help them get this out of here before Nico sees it."

Vin? He was enlisting my soldier to help with whatever this was? It wasn't in his assigned duties. He was running point alongside Mike on perimeter security around the Manor for the next couple of days until the changing of the guard beyond that timeframe.

And what didn't Julian want me to see?

I strode out of the kitchen and headed into the foyer.

And there Julian was, anxiously trying to usher two delivery guys back out of the door.

I frowned, taking in one of them carrying a shag rug that sparkled with gold. The other was hauling a giant plush panda that was more than half the size of the guy carrying it. There was also a box propped against one of the entrance doors with a picture of a... changing table?

My stomach dropped at the sight of it all.

Julian spun, registering my presence.

He held up his hands. "It's all good. I'm taking care of it."

"What is all of this?"

He grimaced. "I think you know."

"Obviously. That's blatantly apparent, Julian. But why? Why are you doing this?"

"I'm sorry. It was an accident. With everything else, I forgot to cancel this additional order and—"

"Additional?"

"Nothing. I mean—"

"J!"

His shoulders slumped, and he said, resignedly, "Come with me."

I gestured at Vin. "Get this gone. Now."

"Will do, Boss." The sympathy in his eyes hit me in the gut. Word had spread about the loss of our baby. "Don't think twice about it. Consider it done," he told me quickly.

"Thank you," was all I could manage before Julian then took my attention as he headed on up the staircase, gesturing for me to follow him.

I braced myself when he stopped outside the door of the room beside mine. It was one we didn't use. I hadn't ventured inside it in a long time.

Clearly he had because he then pulled out a key and unlocked the door, then pushed it open and stepped inside.

Bracing myself absolutely hadn't been enough, as was made clear to me the moment I walked inside and took in what resided within.

"Fuck," I choked.

A little nursery.

The crib, the bookcase, the… *motherfucker*.

I sank against the wall and hung my head.

"Nico, I'm so sorry. I didn't… I couldn't get rid of it. Not yet… I just…."

"It's okay," I murmured. "I understand."

I held out my hand to him, and he came to me.

As I wrapped my arm around him and he nuzzled against me, Milo walked on in, taking in the scene in his usual rapid-fire way.

He smiled sadly at us.

And then he was there too, throwing his arms around us.

"It's incredible," I told Julian. "Caterina would have loved it."

"Yeah," Julian uttered on a sob.

"Our child will be avenged," I ground out. I held them tighter to me. "And we'll rise from all these fucking ashes, believe me."

I fucking swear it.

9

~Julian~

My gloved fists plunged into the heavy bag with a ferocity that was therapeutic as fuck.

Talk about fighting shadows.

Or more like beating the motherfucking shit out of them.

I should've gone this route sooner, but I'd been stuck on trying to shut it down instead.

Until that talk I'd had with Milo a few nights ago.

The way he'd been, how he'd clearly been upset that I hadn't been dealing with it.. it'd had an impact. One I hadn't been able to deny.

And there was also something else pushing me along in this direction.

The search for the madman himself.

They'd declared that using me to draw him out was off the table, but things didn't always pan out in an ideal way. I would be foolish not to believe that there could be a chance where that would actually need to happen, that we would have to resort to that.

I needed to be prepared.

Christ, I had to be.

If that was the way it went down, I couldn't lose my nerve or let that fucker get under my skin again. The piece of shit had killed our child and nearly done the same to Caterina and Nico. He deserved more than death. He deserved our absolute worst, every monstrous part of us. I wouldn't fuck up again like I had at the warehouses. I'd keep my shit together and end Angelo Simone once and for all.

I wouldn't be the weak link.

I was better than that.

Stronger.

More resilient.

"You're a survivor. But that's only part of it. You're beyond that. So far beyond that. You're extraordinary. Fucking truly."

Milo's words had stayed with me.

He'd been right on the money.

I'd just lost sight of that with all that had happened.

But I never would again.

Especially not because of that psychopath.

"Want a sparring partner?"

I froze mid-strike, then pulled my fist back, and spun to see Levi standing in the home gym doorway.

"You don't like too much downtime either, huh?"

A knowing look sparked in his eyes. "Too much time to think, right?"

"Yeah," I admitted.

He rubbed his palms together. "So? Down for some sparring?" At my hesitation, he added, "Better than fighting shadows, right?"

I frowned. "Uh… yeah. How did you—"

"Been there, done that."

"Okay, yeah. Let's do it."

He smiled, then pulled his phone from the back of his

black cargo pants, and put it down out of the way on a bench in the corner.

I stepped away from the bag and into the center of the room, telling him, "There are some more gloves in that cabinet by the door."

"I'm good."

"You're good?"

He lifted a shoulder. "Street fighter."

"Huh. I thought I was getting a scrappy vibe from you."

He chuckled. "Yeah."

And then he took position opposite me, raising his hands in a boxer's fighting stance, his head and back leaning forward.

I assumed my own stance.

"Hit it," Levi said.

In the next second, I went to surprise him with a roundhouse kick, but he reacted before I'd even followed all the way through, and dodged the blow easily.

"What the——"

He grinned. "You were taking a Muay Thai stance, indicating you were gonna go for a kick from your back leg right off the bat."

"Huh."

He crooked his finger. "Again."

I threw a punch, but he caught my glove in his hand.

"Let me guess, you knew I was gonna do that too?"

He released my glove. "To overcompensate for the first kick going awry."

"That's not——"

"You're fighting emotionally. It's compromising your impressive ability that I've heard about from Milo. The way you can read people so incredibly well. And if you're looking to fight somebody who evokes a lot of emotion in you as you also do to them, you're gonna need to employ that skill, have it transcend the rest. And use that emotion against them in the process."

"You're talking about Angelo?"

"Isn't that why you came in here? Why you've been here for the last few days, supposedly fighting shadows?"

"Yes," I admitted. "I know it doesn't seem to make sense given Nico's stance on the matter of not putting me on the front lines where that bastard is concerned, but—"

"It makes perfect sense to me."

"What do you mean?"

He dropped his hands. "The hardest part for me to get over wasn't the powerlessness or even the despair. It was the shame."

I started.

He went on, "The shame that I couldn't stop what happened to me, what they did to me, or Brianna. Fuck, especially Brianna. Shame that they were able to make me a victim, able to... do a lot of fucked-up things. I couldn't accept it. I couldn't move on. And I became obsessed. That shame drove everything for me. It risked a fuck of a lot, too. Even the people I love."

"How did you purge it?"

"By taking back the power that was stolen from me. I had the main perpetrator incapacitated beneath me, then shoved a gun down his throat and blew his fucking head off. I destroyed his entire organization while I was at it. I took everything from him, even his life."

"Whoa... that's... intense."

"It was, yeah."

"And it worked? It gave you the peace that you'd been searching for, wiped away the shame?"

"I was too far gone at that point from years of utter obsession to find that motherfucker and destroy him, so it couldn't have been any other way for me than it playing out that brutal way. Because I let rage drive me. I wouldn't deal with it. I wouldn't let myself see that the shame wasn't mine, it was theirs. *They* were responsible for everything that happened. It wasn't my fault. I was essentially victim-blaming myself. But it was something that happened to me, not something I'd brought about. If I'd recognized that sooner, allowed myself to, it would have saved me years of fucking pain, in all honesty."

He stepped up to me, intensity rolling off him. "And you're not me. The brutality you engage in is a product of what's happened to you. It's not who you are, is it? You don't relish it for the sake of it? Only as a means to put down an opponent, to protect yourself and those you care for? And as I've heard, you're a fan of the adrenaline rush. Just not the violence on its own?"

"That's right."

He laid his hand on my shoulder. "Don't let your pain and this shame turn you into somebody you're not. Because, believe me, it's not always possible to go back once you start on that path. It twists you faster than you can imagine until you're warped into a foreign version of yourself." He squeezed my shoulder. "The shame is *his*. Not yours. All right?"

"I hear you, yeah." I grasped his hand on me. "Thank you."

"If I can use my fucked-up experiences to prevent somebody else from suffering as I did, I will."

"It's just… it's easier said than done when it comes to the shame of it all.

He stepped back and folded his arms across his chest. "You know, Rina told me you're a breath of fresh air through all of this darkness the four of you are caught up in."

"She did?"

He nodded. "When she called me up asking me to give her an assist, she laid out the situation, and she told me about her relationship with the three of you. Being able to be *that* through all of this is no small thing. It's fucking striking. It's more than even strength and resilience, it's another level. Don't let Angelo take that from you. Don't let anyone."

"I won't," I uttered unsteadily, the emotion of it all getting to me.

I wouldn't let him take anything more from me.

Levi unfolded his arms and assumed a fighting stance again. "You still want to do this?"

"It might come to it, right? Me going head to head with Angelo?"

"It's a possibility," he admitted.

"Last time I had a chance to put an end to him, I fucked it up. I got emotional."

"Coming face to face with your abuser is unnerving as fuck," he said. "But there's an emotional aspect on his end, too. He's obsessed with you. He wants you as his. That can be used to his detriment. *You* have the power to use it against him. You see it, right? *You're* actually his weakness."

I… was?

I thought about it for a few moments while Levi looked on, giving me time to process.

The bits and pieces running through my mind, all of it… I started putting them together.

"Beg me, Julian. Fucking beg me already."

It had been more than him wanting to teach me a lesson, to break me and own me from a pure domination perspective. It had been more than even him being in pain and lashing out at somebody else in a bid to purge it.

He'd needed that from me.

He'd wanted it. Desperately.

He'd wanted *me*. And he'd wanted me to want him.

"I'm his weakness," I breathed, as the realization rolled over me.

There was power in that.

Control.

Over *him*.

I stepped up to Levi and assumed a fighting stance. "Again," I said, tossing him a wink.

He went first this time, and I blocked his blow, then deflected another, bringing my knee down when he also went in for a kick.

He smiled as he realized that I was doing what I did best—reading the fuck out of somebody.

We met blow for blow, moving rapid-fire, until sweat was pouring off both of us.

I was growing tired, faster than him. I guess his extensive street fighting experience gave him an edge where stamina during combat was concerned.

He managed to snag me in a headlock, and he swept his leg at the back of mine, making me crash to my knees as he held me basically incapacitated.

"Damn," I chuckled against his grip. "Holding back, weren't you?"

"Maybe a little," he said, releasing me, then giving me a hand-up. "I fight to decimate, but we're just sparring."

His phone buzzed over on the bench, cutting into our conversation.

In the next moment, that buzzing was joined by a piercing alarm coming from it.

"What's that?" I asked as he darted over there.

I rapidly pulled my gloves off and tossed them aside as I rushed over there to see what the fuck was going on.

He scrolled for a few seconds, then swung around to tell me, "There's been a breach."

———

THE THREE OF us stood hovering around Levi in the living room, as he sat rigidly in front of his command center setup, his fingers flying across one of the laptop keyboards.

"It's the same people as before," he reported.

"Shut it down," I told him.

"No. I need to trace the hack. This is the optimal opportunity."

"What about the security breach factor?" Nico questioned.

"Not an issue. Rina's got a poison pill in the—it means anything they obtain will be destroyed the moment they access it. Meanwhile, let's see what they're after."

He was stopped from doing that when something suddenly flashed up on the screen.

A black, shattered circle with cracks of red and green light breaking through, kind of like an eclipse, really.

"Goddammit," Milo exclaimed.

"What the shit is that?" I asked.

Levi stilled, his face paling. "Motherfucker."

"You recognize the symbol," Nico realized.

"What is it?" Milo pushed, grasping the chair and leaning in.

"Erebus," Levi choked.

I saw something spark in Nico's eyes. And then he told us, "In Greek mythology, Erebus was the personification of darkness, a god from the dark part of the underworld. The son of Chaos."

"That definitely doesn't seem to bode well," I uttered.

"It really doesn't," Levi spoke. "I've come across these guys before. In my crusade against Lynch." He stared out at us, a haunted look in his eyes. "They're nowhere and everywhere. They're above the law and in the darkest recesses of the underworld. They're ghosts and demented gods. They're fucking *death.*"

10

~Caterina~

"How are you doing?"

"I'm fine," I bit back.

I grimaced as that came far more petulant than I'd intended.

I'd always been mature for my age, a result of my fucked upbringing, and I'd carried that with me into everything that I did. *Except* when it came to Joseph Stover.

There was just something about him, or about our dynamic, where it brought something else out in me. Something that I didn't care for.

"You're mad at me."

"Whatever gave you that idea?"

And there it was again. What *was* that?

"You've barely spoken to me in the last few days that we've been cooped up in this safehouse."

I finally looked up from my plate of grilled cheese and eyed him across the small two-seater table that was situated in the corner of the miniscule kitchen.

"I thanked you for bringing in those trays of food when

I was recuperating from the miscarriage over the first little while."

"I don't need your thanks. But, to be clear, those were more along the lines of grunts, rather than actual words." He put down his knife and fork—that's right, he ate his grilled cheese with utensils—and regarded me shrewdly. "This is about me neglecting to tell you that I'd ensured your marriage to Nico Marchetti was a falsity?"

"As you can imagine, I don't exactly relish being a puppet in your fucked-up masterpiece theatre."

"That's not how I view you, nor what I intended, Caterina."

"And yet," I said, rubbing my finger, the place where my ring had been. Until I'd had to leave it behind, so we couldn't be tracked. Until I'd had to leave the symbol of my connection to my men behind.

"I knew you didn't want to be forced into that marriage. *I* was in a position to ensure that wasn't the case. You weren't at the time. So I did what was needed."

"You also made us all believe that it was real. Because you wanted me at the Manor. You skewed our perception. You manipulated a whole fucking lot." I shook my head at him. "You've spent so long in the shadows, making moves, taking out ruthless pieces of shit, that you've lost a lot of your humanity along the way. People are just pawns to move around on a board for you. Even *me.*"

"Others, yes," he admitted in that usual matter-of-fact way of his. "But not you. Never you."

"Then why interfere at all where the marriage was concerned? That was a personal move. Why would *you* go that route?"

"Because your mother would have wanted me to."

I scoffed. "Come on."

"Come on *what?* That's not a good enough reason?"

"I don't believe it's a viable one, not when it comes to you taking action. Extremely dangerous, multifaceted, and complicated action, to ensure the marriage was bullshit."

He stared at me. "You don't think you can trust me. Hence all this focus on the marriage, something I know you're actually relieved about."

"Of course."

"Look, I *did* manipulate things. I admit that. It *was* to put you in that house with Nico and your boyfriends. *Because* he was considered off-limits at the time. Due to Marco's insistence that he not be harmed, nor that those he cared for be harmed. And I was aware that it had come to include you."

"Marco's insistence to who? Santino? That seems more than just a little unlikely."

"Santino was the least of it. There was much more at play. There *is* much more at play."

"You're referring to the black ops creeps who Angelo has involved, who he seems to have lent out to Leo Marchetti now as well?"

"It's worse than that." He sighed and leaned back in his chair. "Your mother reached out to me when she discovered that Santino was delving into human trafficking. She rightly concluded that he'd taken a much darker turn, and she was afraid. For herself, for you, and for the family as a whole. So I looked into it. That was when I also discovered Marco trying to make that arms deal with Malcolm Lynch's *Osiris.* The timing of them both venturing down those dangerous roads was more than a little suspicious to me. So I investigated. I discovered that the initial human trafficking buyers, and Lynch, even Price, were connected. Santino and Marco had allied with a specific entity that controlled all of that, that provided those opportunities and connections for them."

"What? How did I miss this?"

"Because they're ghosts, Caterina. The best of the absolute best." He pushed out of his chair and started pacing back and forth as he went on, "They call themselves Erebus. Their goal was to gain control and influence in the city. Between the Marchetti Syndicate and the Leone Family, they could provide access to key infrastructure for them, like the Marchetti Holdings ports and smuggling systems, drug trafficking routes and systems, along with influence over key city officials, politicians, judges. They could also offer them *safe zones* for their operations on Marchetti and Leone territories, something they've wanted for a while, so they don't have to continue to be constantly on the move. And on the families' end, they wanted access to Erebus' connections, military-grade equipment, along with their technological and hacking expertise that rivals even yours."

As I took his words in, it all began to fall into place.

He went on, "Angelo didn't kidnap you that night to send you off to a sex slave buyer like he'd claimed. That was the cover to protect Erebus' existence. The goal was to bring you to their HQ and have you turned to become an asset. And failing that, to kill you. They'd identified you as a threat. A significant one because of your skills."

"So this hit isn't just Angelo seeking vengeance for me killing my father?"

"That's what he's using it as, but from Erebus' perspective, it's to eliminate a threat."

I cursed under my breath.

"Santino being killed this early has now led to Angelo being tapped as Boss. Erebus is also currently bolstering Leo Marchetti because he doesn't have support, as Nico has everyone's loyalty in the Family now. But then their next move, after killing you, is to officially install Angelo as head of the Leone Family. I've intercepted communications between Leo and Angelo recently, wherein they've pledged to work together going forward. Soon, the two families and Erebus will be irreversibly intertwined. They'll run right over the city, and then they'll even expand from there."

"Hold on. Knowing this, specifically about the hit not just being a case of Angelo using these assholes to carry it out, means that having the boys search for him to put him down while you keep me here off the grid makes no fucking sense. It wouldn't stop the hit at all."

"Correct."

Adrenaline thrummed through me at his admission.

I rose from my seat, noting that the nasty ache and pain that had been there a few days ago with any sudden movement had now lessened a great deal.

At least bringing me out here had enabled that to happen, basically forcing me to take the time to work on my physical recovery.

"What the hell are you playing at, Joe?" I demanded. "Why do this, then? Why create this layered charade? Why take me from my men?" I slammed my fist down on the table. "You used my less-than-stellar state and my grief to manipulate me, to make it much easier than it ever would have normally been to convince me to actually leave with you."

"All true. I did take advantage of your weakness at the time. I had to. You wouldn't have allowed yourself to be parted from them otherwise. Even in spite of the guilt you were feeling toward them regarding losing your child."

"You're shameless. You know that?"

"What I am is equipped to do what needs to be done for this mission *and* for your wellbeing."

"The first part we were handling ourselves. And the latter, you have no right to."

"You were operating with merely pieces of the overall puzzle. Because you needed me and what I know, what I can do."

"I'll find another way. Me and my men will."

I went to walk out of the room, but he called out, "I know who controls Erebus!"

"What? I thought they were ghosts?"

"They are, but their leader no longer is. Not to me. His name is Nathan Donahue. We served together years ago. It's why he's targeting Tolhurst, because of my connection to it. We had a falling out when I exposed him for the disgusting side deals he was making while we were deployed overseas. Since then, he's grown this vast network. Now he wants to settle with Erebus, instead of staying in the shadows. And, as a fuck-you to me, he's chosen that first place as Tolhurst."

"Shit, Joe."

"I need your help to track him. But that can't happen safely until the herd is thinned, so that the contract on your life is no longer a main priority, until they can no longer afford it to be."

"Thin the herd? How? What have you done?"

"I have an asset in place back in the city. He'd just required a little more time to gather what we needed in order to see to this phase of the plan. Something he now has. He'll be making contact with Nico any time now."

"If you're putting my men in danger to pull this off—"

"I wouldn't do that to you. I know how much they mean to you."

"How can I trust that? How can I trust any of this?"

"I've looked out for you with the hit and—"

"You just admitted you had other reasons for doing

that. You need me as a resource. You need my skills to find Donahue."

"I trained you for months to protect you, to give you the means to survive, to become an exceptional combatant."

"A killer, you mean?"

"It served to protect you either way."

"And you did that at my mom's behest, because you were still emotionally involved with her at the time."

"I didn't just train you, or care about you, because of Bianca."

"Give me a reason, a concrete fucking reason to trust you, or I walk right now."

11

~Joseph Stover~

This wasn't how it was supposed to be.

I hadn't wanted to encounter Caterina again in this manner.

Under these circumstances.

With this grief and pain she was now carrying with her.

It was tainted now.

Especially with what I had to tell her.

I should have already revealed what I'd planned to, the first night I'd brought her here.

The truth was, I'd wanted to do it much sooner.

From the get-go, actually.

But it would have risked far too much. It would have put her life in jeopardy. Her mother's too.

Things had shifted, and they had now opened the way to me being able to do this at long last.

Just… other circumstances weren't ideal.

She was suffering.

She was struggling.

The idea that this *intel* could complicate or possibly

even worsen all of that for her didn't sit well with me in the least.

Once this was done, once she no longer needed my assistance, though, I couldn't stand the notion of disappearing back into the shadows without her knowing the truth.

Especially now that she was settling down and clearly looking to build a family with her boyfriends as well. She'd need to know, and she obviously deserved to know.

The bottom line was that it was now safe for her to know.

She and the boys had upended the system, and they were on the verge of casting out the detrimental elements entirely and cementing their power. Once we conquered this last obstacle together. A significant obstacle, yes, but conquerable, nonetheless.

It would be their reign going forward.

The old guard would truly be no more.

There was a place for this truth now to exist out in the open, to finally breathe freely.

"Well?" she pushed, that fiery aspect of her finally coming out after days of her recuperating in bed, grieving the loss of her child, and reeling from being kept from her boyfriends.

I pulled my phone from the pocket of my tactical jacket and unlocked the files I'd had prepared for this.

Files that I'd had for a long time.

Too long.

"Here," I said, handing it over to her.

"What is this?" she demanded impatiently.

"Read and find out." I gestured at the chair she'd vacated. "You might want to take a seat again."

Uncertainty and wariness spread over her face and her demeanor as a whole.

She narrowed her eyes at me, but then actually took my advice, and sat back down in her chair.

I leaned against the counter, adrenaline thrumming through me, as I watched her start reading and going through the folder of documents that I'd opened for her.

"Data pulled from military databases, hospitals… for what?" she murmured to herself, as she continued reading away.

"These records no longer exist anywhere," I told her. "I scrubbed every trace once I got the confirmation I'd been searching for."

"Your DNA… mom's… mine." She choked then as she took in the undeniable proof I'd laid out before her.

Her gaze flicked to mine. "It can't be."

"You know it is. It's right there. Incontrovertible."

"You're—"

"Santino wasn't your father. *I am.*"

———

CATERINA LOOKED on dazedly as she followed me into my room, and watched as I unlocked a trunk I'd pulled out from underneath the sleigh bed.

She hadn't said a word since I'd told her the truth of her paternity.

I rummaged inside for a moment before placing a scrapbook on the bedspread, along with several news clippings and investigative documentation.

I perched on the edge of the bed and opened the scrapbook, flipping through the pages and showing her all the photos and knickknacks that I'd put together of her childhood.

She stared for a moment, then sat down on the bed

and started looking through the book herself. "You did all of this? Made this?"

"I did."

"It's a masterpiece."

"Well, I might have taught myself how to scrapbook at some point."

She raised an eyebrow at me, clearly seeing a new facet of me.

More so than just her trainer, her mother's ex, and most recently, the person who'd manipulated her life.

She spent some quiet time with the book.

And then she moved to the news clippings that consisted of things like any time she'd been in the paper for her achievements over the years, including the award she'd recently won, as well as a few mentions during her college years.

I tensed when she picked up the thick document next. I'd debated on whether to actually include that amongst the rest. Because, to be honest, it was invasive.

"Jeez," she uttered. "Doctors' records, even hospital records of the time I'd been admitted for breaking my arm when I'd fallen out of the tree in the Leone Estate backyard when I was a kid, the recent… incident too." She kept looking. "My high school and college transcripts, legal documents and contracts for my properties, assets, business deals. And a whole shitload of surveillance. You even got my numerous storage facilities." She started. "Fuck, and the location of every go bag I have around the city."

I braced myself for her to make her displeasure known in no uncertain terms.

But then she actually surprised me when she grinned, giving a shake of her head. "You're certainly not a normal *dad*, by any definition, are you?"

"That I'm not, no."

"All this, it makes so much sense. Especially in light of the strange dynamic between us. It was a father-daughter dynamic all along. I guess, I just couldn't recognize it because of the twisted way Santino had always been with me."

"I was also trying to keep an emotional distance, which would have made it very difficult for you to actually correctly identify it, anyway."

"Why? Why didn't you tell me sooner? Why have me believing all these years that the monster that was Santino Leone was my father?"

"You were conceived when I was on leave, and I came to Bianca one night when I'd found out she'd gotten engaged to Santino. She told me she'd built a life for herself and that the night we spent together was just a goodbye. I left, and we didn't talk for years. When I discovered that she'd had a child, I did the math. So I had those tests done that I showed you. When I told Bianca that I'd discovered the truth, she begged me to leave it be, to stay away. I was halfway across the world and I was also involved in some dangerous shit at the time. That was no life for her or a child. I didn't exactly take well to what she wanted, but I did it because it was what she needed. I delved deeper into a whole lot of high-risk black ops shit as a result, a way to cope with it. Of being without her and our child."

"And later on?"

"He would have had you both killed, Caterina. To protect you, I would have needed to remove you from the city and everything you knew, and drag you into the shadows with me. That isn't a life I would wish on anyone. You would have been stifled and you never would have come into your full potential or even had much of a life at all. You've built an empire now, and you're successful and respected in the business world."

"That empire came at a cost. A steep one."

"I know, and I'm so very sorry."

She shoved her hand through her hair. "This is a lot to process."

"I have no doubt." I shifted my weight. "For the record, I *am* actually happy, and also proud of you, for eliminating Santino. It's just the fallout that concerned me with the timing of it all."

"Yeah, definitely not a normal dad. Proud of me for murdering someone. Wow," she said, with a twinkle in her eye.

I lifted a shoulder. "Normal is highly overrated."

That actually managed to get a little laugh out of her.

When it faded away all too quickly, she had me tensing as she said, "I don't know how to do this... this thing between us... you being my biological father."

"We do it how we approached your training. One step at a time."

"What would the first step be, though?"

"How about you tell me about these boyfriends of yours?"

She screwed up her face. "I don't think that's a good idea."

"They're clearly smitten with you. And you're most definitely in love with them. They're important to you and that's important to me. I'd like to know."

"Here, I thought you already knew everything," she said, gesturing at the documentation.

"Touché. Although, as you know, there are many things you can't obtain from distanced investigation. It lacks a personal touch."

"All right," she agreed.

"Yes?"

She rose from the bed. "Although, let's do it while we're eating. I was actually really hungry before we got into everything."

"Certainly. Whatever you like."

She smiled out at me. Although it was definitely restrained, it was a start.

A really good start.

Something I'd never thought I'd have with her.

Not as her father.

Yet now, here we were.

Here *she* was without the lies and fakery between us.

My daughter.

12

~Nico~

It had been a week.

A week since Caterina had been spirited away from us.

A week since we'd had to let her go, even temporarily.

A week since we hadn't been able to see her, hear her voice, feel her.

"I'm undeniably, obsessively, and dangerously in love with you."

My words to her hadn't been hyperbolic in the least.

They'd been the raw truth, through and through.

And when I wasn't with her, that obsessive and dangerous aspect tended to rise up.

Just like it had with our war after I'd first developed a connection to her.

Now, though, that connection was so much deeper, something that invaded every fiber of my being, that consumed me even in my stronger and more rational moments.

Things didn't work without Caterina.

Right now, I was trying to sublimate.

One of the ways I was doing that, and one that was also helping Julian and Milo to do the same where she was concerned, was through re-reading the encrypted communication that Levi had intercepted from her two nights ago.

Just needed to let you know that I'm doing well. Healing up and mobile again. Getting stronger. I miss the three of you so much, though. So fucking much. Know that I love you, and that will never change. I can't wait to get home to you. Love always, Caterina.

We'd read between the lines with the tail end of her message. It was her telling us that she was also working through her grief concerning the baby, particularly the guilt that she'd felt, which we'd all worried would keep her away. Apparently, that wasn't the case, though.

And she would come home to us.

When it was safe.

After Levi's report on Erebus, that safety was definitely an issue.

They were more than just hired guns that Angelo was currently using to try to take out Caterina for killing Santino. A lot fucking more.

And they certainly weren't run-of-the-mill hitmen either. Their skills were dangerous beyond belief, even in respect to our world, and so was their reach and resources.

That said, this wasn't exactly the first time that the odds had seemed stacked against us. Taking down the two families had been viewed as near impossible by many.

But we'd found a way through.

This would be no different.

While Levi was working to generate leads on Angelo's whereabouts, as well as actionable intel where Erebus was concerned, I was dealing with things on our home territory. Angelo thought he could use these black ops shitheads to claim power? When I was done, there would be nothing left to claim.

After our strikes, Santino's murder, and Angelo being

in the wind working with Erebus, the Leone Family was reeling.

Carlo and I had ordered Dante Rivera to take advantage of the uncertainty and chaos, wherein he'd been covertly instilling a whole lot of doubt into Leone soldiers.

He'd come to me yesterday with insider intel concerning Elia, the remaining Leone Capo who was still in the city. The fucker was working and coordinating with Angelo from a distance, and they'd decided to call a closed-door meeting with their soldiers to *reinforce their commitment* to the Leone Family. In their sadistic terms, that meant making a brutal example out of those they'd identified as losing faith in the Family. Basically, they were going to torture, then murder them in front of everyone else, and maintain control by fear and force.

The fools had unwittingly provided me and Carlo with a significant opportunity.

Elia and Angelo were so overconfident that they'd written Dante off as nothing even resembling a threat. All Dante had needed was some support, to be bolstered, and he'd been able to demonstrate just how capable he was. He'd even been able to ascertain the location of this supposedly covert meeting, along with specs concerning the building itself and security protocols.

And now I was putting the final touches to the tactical strike that Carlo and I were going to launch jointly within a few days.

I looked up from the plans laid out on my desk, as Julian barreled in, not bothering to knock, as was far too common of an occurrence with him.

At my grunt, he held up his hand. "I know. But you're gonna love this."

I rounded my desk and leaned against the front, folding my arms across my chest. "I'm listening."

"The task you gave me is completed."

"Already? It's only been forty-eight hours since I laid out the strategy to you."

"Yeah, it's done. I've convinced the majority shareholders in Leone Realty of just how unstable things are now, in light of Santino's death. I showed them proof of the human trafficking activities as well, highlighting that it would come back on them all and spook investors in a major way." He grinned. "They're selling the company to me, where we'll then dismantle it piece by piece, effectively destroying the Leone Family's flagship business."

"I'm impressed."

"Well, I'm just that good. Some of that may have gotten lost lately with everything that's happened, but believe me, I've still got it."

"I never doubted it, Julian. None of us did."

He smiled. "Finally, some good news, huh?"

"Absolutely."

"With Caterina holding Leone Family funds hostage, they'll fall from a business perspective. In a few nights, when you deal with their soldiers, they'll be decimated, Nico."

"Except for the Erebus aspect."

"Yeah, speaking of that," he said, shifting his weight uncomfortably. "I think you should reconsider having Levi tracking Angelo the way he currently is."

"He's not just tracking Angelo. Given that the fucker is working with Erebus, he's also tracking *them*."

"We should draw him out, and use me to do it," he told me, point blank.

"Julian, the dangers of doing that—"

"I know. Believe me, *I* know better than anyone. But the outcome would be worth it. Lure Angelo out into the open and this group he's allied with. We could even use those of them swarming around Leo at the Marchetti mansion to do it."

"Those *swarming around Leo* haven't made a move for a reason."

"What are you talking about?"

"I have eyes on them through my soldiers. They're waiting on something."

"Like what? Their leader? Succeeding in their hit against Caterina?"

"They're on the hunt. We've tracked them venturing throughout the city. Levi and I believe they're searching for something or someone. Something instrumental here in Tolhurst to their plans. Something that has the means to usurp those plans."

Movement at my office doorway pulled my attention.

I looked past Julian to see Levi standing there.

"We now know what that something is," he announced. He walked into the room, his phone held in his hand, the screen unlocked. "I was able to discern what they came for when they hacked into Rina's system. It wasn't the Leone funds. I've actually determined that the way she's hidden them makes them untraceable, no matter how skilled or technologically advanced these assholes are."

"If not the funds, then what?" I asked.

"These individuals. Politicians, city figures, a whole lot of influential people who Santino had in his pocket for years, many of whom he acquired recently through the power increase that the Leone-Marchetti alliance seemed to promise."

He held his phone out to me, and I took in the names, recognizing every single one of them.

I eyed Julian. "These are the people we severed from the Leone Family the night of the strikes. We relocated and hid many of them at the time. Following Santino's death, I've had my soldiers hide others who've come to me wanting protection in exchange for dropping their support of the Leone Family."

"So Erebus is trying to find them?" Julian spoke.

"Yeah," Levi confirmed. "It coincides with the places Nico's soldiers have tracked them to over the last little while—all those locations and people have connections to these influential people. It's clear they were hoping that they'd find the safehouse locations on Rina's system. But she was smart. She kept all of that offline, so it could never be ascertained via a hack."

"This doesn't bode well," Julian uttered. "It suggests they're not just here for a temporary assist or being hired by Angelo and Santino and now apparently also Leo, that they're actually here to stay and they want to cement their position here in the city and use the influential figures that Santino had in his pocket in order to strengthen that."

"Now we have this intel, we move from reconnaissance to annihilation," I told them.

"Have your units of soldiers tracking them when they're moving outside the mansion and into the city, and put them down going forward," Levi surmised.

"And in bits and pieces so we can cover it up, so there's no outright massacre to worry about," Julian said.

"Precisely," I confirmed.

I handed Levi his phone back.

I went to pull mine out to connect with Carlo. Given our alliance, I had to ensure I ran an operation like this by him, rather than making a dangerous, unilateral move. I wouldn't make the same mistakes that my father had made.

But before I could make the call, Julian's phone started ringing.

He pulled it from his pocket and answered, "Carver here. What? Hazel? Who are you talking about? What do you mean you can't say? Are you in danger? Okay, yeah. Christ. Just try to stay calm. We'll be right there. It will all be okay. I promise. All right? Yeah, good."

He hung up and shoved his hand through his hair. "We have a situation."

"That much was just made clear by your end of the conversation," I said. "There's something wrong at one of Caterina's businesses?" He was overseeing everything for Caterina while she was still off the grid.

"Not the operation of the businesses themselves," he told us. "It was Hazel, Cat's assistant. She's at *Luster* and she has a visitor. A visitor who's aggressively and threateningly insisting on seeing *you*, Nico."

"Who?"

"I don't know. She wouldn't say. Or, more like, she wasn't allowed to say. It sounds like she's under this person's influence and control right now."

His phone buzzed and he swiped it open. "Uh, definitely on the control part." He showed me the screen, and I took in the sight of Hazel bound to a chair, her eyes bulging with a whole lot of fear. From what I could make out, she was inside Caterina's office and it was actually *her* desk chair that she was bound to. Words were scrawled across the photo. *Come alone, Nico.*

"Surveillance footage is offline at *Luster.* Looks like it went down a few minutes ago," Levi reported, eyeing his phone.

"If something happens to Hazel, it will kill Cat," Julian told me.

As if I didn't already know that.

Hazel was an integral staff member of Caterina's, a highly trusted assistant. She was somebody who'd worked for her for years, somebody she trusted to work that closely with her. When it came to Caterina—or how she had been until she'd let the three of us into her life—that was a rare thing. It had basically been her assistant and Nova Henderson, Caterina's architect.

"Not to mention, *Luster* itself could also be under threat," Levi pointed out.

"Respond. Tell whoever it is that I'm coming down. In the meantime, get surveillance back online."

"Take a unit of your soldiers with you," Julian advised me.

"He's right," Milo's voice came from the door. He stood there, his arms folded across his chest. "I'm coming, too. We'll wait in the wings, have this shithead believing you are coming alone, but you'll actually have backup nearby."

I nodded. "Let's do it."

⊏⊐

THEY WERE ALL WORRIED.

Having the Boss on the front lines made everyone nervous as a rule. In the past, they'd always been heavily fortified. Marco, Santino, Carlo. They didn't walk into volatile situations alone. Hell, they didn't really venture anywhere alone.

But things were more intense now, the concern deeper than it normally would be, because of how much they were counting on me to spearhead this new era, to push out the bad and rotten, and bring about a new reign.

I wasn't used to being coddled by security, like Marco and Santino had been.

I'd come from years in the field, getting my hands dirty.

Waiting for security to be shored up around me felt more than a little claustrophobic.

But I also wasn't a fool. I recognized the risks. And I also understood that those under my charge needed reassurance at this juncture.

It was just something I would need to get used to.

A lot about being Boss of the Marchetti Syndicate required such adjustment.

My earpiece buzzed as I entered *Luster* covertly through one of the side doors, my Sig Sauer at the ready.

I tapped to answer, and Levi's voice came down the line. *"I pushed out interference from the club's security system. Wouldn't have had to do that if Rina was using her own setup, instead of outsourcing it to a security company."*

"She didn't want anyone to know what she was capable of, Levi."

"Yes, I'm aware. But still."

"Your point about the actual mission at hand?"

"Right. I also recovered footage that showed a figure sticking to the shadows, their identity shielded by an overhanging hood, entering Luster *an hour ago. Alone. You're dealing with a single individual."*

"Got it. Thanks."

"Remember, Luster *opens in less than two hours, so you're gonna have to move fast to deal with this. According to Julian's calculations, if the club fails to open for a night, Rina stands to lose—"*

"I know what the loss would be. I'll handle it."

"Emilio and a unit of your soldiers are waiting in the wings. Although, I agree with your intent to deal with it without them, given what an insane amount of damage them storming the place could pose to the club."

"Just keep me posted if reinforcements for whoever this mysterious bastard is show up."

"Will do. I'm monitoring the immediate area."

With that, I tapped my earpiece, ending the communication, because I needed to concentrate.

Especially when I didn't know *who* I was dealing with, or why this individual was determined to meet with me, and going to these lengths in order to make it so.

Either way, there would be no negotiation. Not with somebody using these tactics.

As I made my way through the darkened club floor, sticking to the shadows and approaching strategically, the lights suddenly went on behind one of the bars to the left, a couple of hundred feet away.

I heard the clinking of glasses a moment later, followed by the sound of liquid being poured. What the—

"Holster the weapon, Nico."

That voice.

Absolutely distinctive to me.

It had me pulling up short, and even doing a double take.

Of all the scenarios I'd imagined, this hadn't come close to being one of them.

"You're not in any danger from me. Neither is Caterina's employee," he called again, when he got no response from me.

My earpiece buzzed with an incoming transmission. I tapped it and Levi's voice sounded again. *"The facial recognition software has identified the gait and key mannerisms of Marco Marchetti. Also, he's pouring you a drink at the main bar. What the fuck is going on?"*

"I'm aware. He just spoke to me."

"Another reason why Rina should be using her own surveillance capabilities, then there'd actually be sound."

"Thank you, Levi, I'll take it from here."

I disconnected and responded to my father, "Yes, let me just foolishly take you at your word."

"The assistant isn't hurt in the slightest. I just needed to get your attention."

"My attention for what?"

"I have information that you need. Joseph Stover sent me. He can't pass this on himself while he's off the grid."

How the fuck did *he* know about Stover or his part in this?

In the next second, two Berettas slid across the floor toward me.

"I know you're a killer. I made you into that long ago. But I believe there is a line for you. You're not ready to murder your own father."

Son of a bitch.

I pushed from the darkness and strode over to him at the bar.

"This is about the intel you claimed to have. Nothing else," I grunted, as I took him in, sitting on a stool at the bar and knocking back some bourbon right from the bottle.

There was a glass poured beside another bottle, this one Johnny Walker Black.

An oversized, dark hoodie hung loose on him, the hood up and hanging low over his face, a few strands of his layered black hair spilling out. He was wearing matching sweatpants, too. It was a world away from the man I'd known, from the impeccable image he'd crafted and maintained over the years. The designer suits, being perfectly put together.

I stopped at the edge of the bar.

He gestured at the drink he'd poured for me.

I shook my head.

"That's a shame."

"What?"

He turned to me, angling himself so I could get a

proper look at his face, those deep brown eyes of his burning into mine with an intensity I wasn't used to from him. With emotion. "It's our last drink together, Nico."

"What does that mean?"

He sighed heavily. "I didn't intend for it to end up like this. I didn't want any of this. This... insanity."

"You lost control of the Family."

"Worse. Leo took it from me. I allowed that reckless fool to take it from me." His voice dripped with thick emotion as he said, "I didn't handle your mother's death well. Not like you. You processed it and came out on the other side."

I secured my gun and holstered it. "She was sick for a long time before she passed away."

"Perhaps that should have made it easier, to expect what then came to be... her leaving us. But it didn't for me. I know to you she was a shell of her former self for years before she died, so it had given you time to already say goodbye to her. But for me, I didn't accept that change in her. I wouldn't allow myself to see that *shell* of her that you were able to see."

I ground my jaw. I didn't like talking about this at the best of times. I made my peace with things and I moved on. Or I compartmentalized things. I didn't dwell, and I didn't wallow, not even when it came to this, something that I'd put behind me years ago. Dredging it all up now really wouldn't do me any favors, especially not when there was already fresh grief that I was trying to process, that I *couldn't* shove down because Caterina needed me not to. She'd need me and all of us to be emotionally available when she returned, so we could help each other through the loss of our baby.

I couldn't have *this* on top of that.

I hadn't said a word to the boys, but holding back and

not tearing into the Marchetti mansion and waging a fucking bloodied massacre for the ages had been a fucking strain like no other. Not letting loose and unleashing my *feral* state in all its destructive, blood-lusting glory had been taking a shit-ton of self-control. Focusing on the fallout of doing such a thing, and how it would absolutely come back on us all, and draw the attention of the law in an irreversible way, either forcing us into hiding or behind bars for the rest of our natural lives, was helping to stop me from giving into the part of me.

There was another way through, another way to go about this.

And we were doing that, working toward it.

I just wasn't doing well with the time-consuming nature of it all.

Somewhere along the way, I'd lost my patience.

And least, internally. I wasn't projecting that outwardly, fortunately.

They needed me not to. They needed me solid and rational. They needed to trust in me.

All those who'd had the courage to pledge their loyalty to me deserved my best, because they'd risked their lives by going against the Marchettis and the Leones.

True loyalty wasn't forced or even a given, it was earned.

"Get to the point," I ground out.

"In the throes of my grief, I gave Leo too much power. I gave up control when I should have held on tight to it. And by the time I came up for air, he'd done the unthink-able. He'd tied us to Erebus."

I jolted at him mentioning that name.

He read my reaction. "Hmm. Props to you for discov-ering that already." A glare from me had him pressing on.

"Leo made deals in my name. One such deal was with them."

"Hence the Malcolm Lynch deal."

"Yes. Something you engineered the destruction of." Before I could get a word out, the corner of his mouth turned up. "Impressive."

"If you knew, why didn't you strike against me? Officially remove me as Capo?"

"Because you were doing what I couldn't."

"You want me to believe that you didn't want any part of this?"

"It was too late to undo it. The deal with Erebus, the despicable alliance with that depraved demon, Santino. When I realized the turn everything had taken, I pushed you out. Partly to keep you safe, but also to keep you at a distance so you could make moves under the radar." He smiled proudly. "Which you did. Very well. You actually exceeded my expectations."

"And what of Leo? You left and disappeared into the ozone—until tonight—and simply handed over power to him, despite claiming you didn't want things going this way, that you didn't approve of the decisions he'd made?"

"I didn't hand over power because I chose him as the optimal candidate for Boss. I did it so I could assist you, pass on this information to you, so you could end this."

"What?"

"It's your turn to take power, Nico. I choose *you*. But my word and tapping you as Boss isn't enough at this juncture, given the chaotic nature of everything. *Or* given the fact that Leo is now working very closely with Angelo Simone."

He scrubbed his hand over his face. "It's too late for me. Our soldiers have pledged their loyalty to *you*. You have support that I will never have again, given what I've allowed to happen, how I lost complete control over it all. The respect they had for me is long gone. And it's also not safe for me anymore. Disappearing like that has tarred me as a loose cannon, as a threat. They'll come for me." He took a large pull from his bottle of bourbon. "I'm leaving tonight. Joseph has facilitated it with some of his connections. I'll be untraceable." He shook his head sadly. "I'm sorry, son. I'm sorry for all the pain that this has caused you, how you thought I'd discounted you. I never had. I never will. I have absolute faith in your ability to take my place, and to do better than I did, to achieve what I could not." He took another gulp from the bottle. "I'm also so very sorry about your child."

I looked away, biting back the emotion that his words had wrought. *Fuck.*

He slid something across the bar top toward me, and I took in a flash drive.

"This contains a complete list of all the safehouses that Erebus is using within the city. Many of them are being provided by Victoria Munsen at Angelo's request. Take these in synchronized assaults, use Marchetti Holdings transportation to move the bodies out of the city, then bury them. They're all ghosts. You can bury the evidence of their murders without drawing the attention of the law. You'll need to ensure there's no collateral damage that could expose you, though. No arson, no blowing them to hell. You'll have to do it the hard way. Just keep in mind how well-trained these bastards are. Although, the soldiers you had under your charge as Capo have been trained well at your insistence, so they should be able to win out in these scenarios. Carlo also has several skilled combatants among his soldiers." He took a beat, then told me, "You do this, take out these safehouses and those residing there at the optimal times indicated on this drive wherein they'll be there and not at the mansion, and it will violate the terms of the agreement that Angelo and Leo have with them of providing *safe zones* for their operations throughout the city. It will also be enough of a blow to redirect their focus from pursuing both Caterina and the influential individuals they're currently hunting. It will cause the destabilization that you'll need and what they're most afraid of—exposure. Light being shone on their operations."

"All right," I said, pocketing the flash drive.

"Concerning Angelo Simone, he's currently being protected by Erebus. When you cause this chaos with the safehouse takedowns, that would be the optimal opportunity to see to him. Given what Joseph has told me about Erebus—some of it limited because that covert bastard can't stand not holding most of the cards—they'll pivot once they get word of those takedowns. They'll use resources and their men to try to dig their heels in and obtain more *safe zones* with the help of Leo, who's become one of their men on the ground here. Angelo will be moved somewhere secure in the meantime because they still need him. But at that point, you need to draw him out." He grimaced. "Unfortunately, you know as well as I do the most optimal way to do that. Obsession makes puppets out of us all, Nico. That is certainly true where Angelo is concerned."

I clenched my fists at his suggestion of putting Julian in danger.

Not just the suggestion itself, but how strategically sound it was.

"I need to know who the leader of Erebus is."

"I don't know myself."

"And Stover?"

"He must know at this point. Perhaps that's why he's taken Caterina and hidden her away. Not just to shield her from the hit, but also because he needs her to locate this bastard. From what I can gather, the way they're set up, if this leader of theirs falls, everything collapses. He's an egomaniac. He won't give up control to anyone. Meaning he doesn't have a line of succession. He believes himself an untouchable god."

I couldn't let this opportunity go by without asking another question that had been weighing on me. One that Milo needed me to ask.

"What about Enzo and Rosa Bardi?"

He cursed under his breath and shifted his weight.

"What the fuck happened?" I pushed.

He sucked in an unsteady breath. "Rosa wasn't supposed to die that night." He screwed up his face. "Leo lost control. He took it too far."

"I'd say that putting a hit out on your own Underboss was taking it too fucking far to begin with. Talk about flying in the face of loyalty, honor *and* brotherhood, all in one shot."

"It was a mistake."

I scoffed. "A mistake? I'd say so."

"No. I mean evidence had been presented to me that incriminated Enzo. Proof that he was working with the Leones against the Marchettis. We were at war. It was a mammoth act of betrayal and I couldn't have one of my own, especially not somebody in his position, being a fucking traitor, Nico."

"Enzo was no traitor."

"You're right, he wasn't. That proof was falsified. I didn't find out until years later. It was Leo. And he was also the one who'd actually been working with the Leones at the time. I discovered it shortly after your mother's death, when I was in a really bad place. And that was when Leo revealed that he'd made those deals with Santino and Erebus."

I slammed my fist down on the bar, jarring the glass and bottles. "So much would have been avoided if you hadn't trusted in Leo!"

"I know. I know, Nico." He laid his hand on mine. "I'm sorry, so very sorry."

I jerked my hand free and moved away. "We're done here."

"Wait!" he cried, grasping my arm before I pulled away entirely.

With his other, he reached inside his hoodie, then pulled out some rolled up documents. "Here."

I took them from him and flipped through the thick documentation, determining what the hell this was all about.

I choked when it became all too apparent.

"I had another reason for wanting to meet before taking off. Of course, part of that was to see my son one last time."

"Stop," I bit out.

He held up his hand. "All right. Listen, I've been meeting with my lawyers discreetly. Marchetti Holdings is now legally and undeniably yours. You have enough on your plate without having to fight to claim that, which you *will* need when you become Boss."

"You're just handing this to me? Just like that?"

"Not *just* handing it to you. You've earned it." He smiled. "And I couldn't be more proud of the leader that you've become."

"If only your pride in me still held any weight."

His smile fell, and he gestured at my Sig. "It's never been done where a Boss has been left alive after a coup. Let's face it, they're always the first to go in order to take power. You must have also assessed the risk of me remaining alive. That I could return bolstered by more resources and try to reclaim my seat. I can tell you that I have no intention of doing so, but to trust in that is still a risk."

"I'm aware."

"I told you this was our last meeting. I was prepared for that when I walked in here."

"So your claim that you were certain I wouldn't kill you was bullshit?"

Just like so much else.

"I wanted to put it in your head for when this meeting came to a close. For your own good, Nico. It's what needs to be done."

"That's your assessment of the situation. It's not mine."

"What are you—"

"Go. Disappear into the ozone. Get away from all of this, the ashes of your former reign. This is your second chance to rebuild yourself into the man I barely remember now. A chance to do something positive with your life, to make *her* proud and honor her memory. But that will never be around me again. It can't be. This *is* our last interaction, Father."

"Nico, I—" He reached out to me, but I stepped back. Emotion welled in his eyes, something so rare for him that it was hard to stomach, and even harder to process.

And I didn't want it.

"Go," I told him. "Before I change my mind."

I didn't want it to infect me any further than it already was.

I didn't want him to see that there was an impact on me, that losing him in spite of everything was actually cutting at me.

He didn't deserve to know that.

He nodded and without another word he rounded me and walked off in the direction I'd come in.

I watched him leave the guns he'd relinquished earlier, then disappear through the door.

Disappearing from my life forever.

He was a shadow of the man he'd been before. The man I'd once looked up to and respected more than anybody else.

His role as head of the Marchetti Syndicate and the weight of the tragedies that had befallen him, his bad fucking decisions… it had all broken him. Twisted him. Changed him into a man I barely recognized as my father. It had made him a monster.

It wouldn't let that happen to me.

Not just because I'd will it so, nor because I planned to do things differently.

But because I had people I could trust implicitly in my corner.

Something he'd never really had, especially in Leo.

I had a family in our foursome.

And everything began and ended with that for me.

Marco Marchetti's fate would never be mine.

Because I had *them*.

~Julian~

"How's it going?"

I looked up from the wealth of documents, financial reports, shareholder agreements, tenders, and project management reports concerning ongoing developments, all spread out over the kitchen island.

Nico was striding into the kitchen, eyeing me.

"It's coming along. There's a lot to reconcile regarding the mess that is Leone Realty."

"With those other deals that Santino had in the works, he's let this slide?"

"It's taken a hit, yeah. There are also a lot of people involved here, from architects, project managers, to construction workers, skilled laborers, who are slated to lose their jobs if I dismantle Leone Realty the way we intend and merely leave it at that."

"So what are you thinking?" he asked, rounding the island and heading for his go-to espresso. Milo had just made him one a few moments ago, but Nico had been on the phone with Carlo Benzino discussing what Marco had revealed to him a couple of nights back. He'd taken that time before telling Carlo to have Levi analyze its viability and to also have me confirm that the paperwork involving handing over Marchetti Holdings to him had been legit. And it all had been. Marco hadn't been playing him. He'd actually been trying to help. Nico considered that help too little, too late.

And he hadn't said much else about it.

He'd been grunting around the Manor ever since.

That was kind of the beginnings of him processing that sort of thing.

I was proud of him for handling the processing of the miscarriage a lot better. He'd been talking about it with us and especially me, something I'd needed. I figured it was him trying to make sure he was ready to do the same to help Cat with it when she returned.

"J?" he pressed.

I blinked out of my thoughts. "Right. Sorry. So, I could bring in the innocents involved who are just a part of it for a paycheck and an honest day's work, rather than being caught up in the *mafia* of it all. They don't deserve to lose their jobs and suffer for all of this."

"Bring them into what? Carver Group?"

"Specifically, the expansion that Cat and I were in the process of planning. When the Brimbank Waterfront development is finally announced, we'll also need to expand our workforce, and these people already fit the bill. They're highly skilled, many with years of experience in these fields."

"That's an inspired plan. Very honorable, too. It would clearly be much easier just to sell off the pieces of Leone Realty, rather than work to save all those jobs in the process and to reassign everyone."

"Yeah?"

He frowned. "You're very good with this sort of thing. Why are you hesitant?"

I shifted on the stool. "Time is of the essence. I'd have to put some moves in place now."

"Ah, you're worried about Caterina."

"I don't want to make decisions without her. Camlann Corporation would be directly impacted by this, just as much as Carver Group."

"She'd love it, Julian."

"How can you be so sure?"

"Because I know her. And so do you. You're just playing devil's advocate. Also, don't forget that I was obsessively watching her every move for years. I'm very well aware of how she operates from a business perspective."

"But to make this choice for her? Not having her input?"

"When she left, Camlann Corporation was put in *your* hands. She trusted you with it. If she hadn't, believe me, as difficult as it may have been to do so, she would have put things in place to the contrary and kept you out of it if she didn't trust you with it."

"Yeah," I said, as I took his words in. "You're right. Of course you're right. I'll take care of it."

"Good," he said, taking some big gulps from his espresso.

I frowned. "All right, N?"

"Just keeping on top of everything."

"It's a lot of pressure, huh?" I winced as he gave me a look. "I mean, obviously it is. But you've got it in the bag. Let's face it, you were born for this shit. And these last few years of us covertly going it alone with our brotherhood has also prepared you for all this subterfuge and doing things in this roundabout, complicated way in order to come out on top."

"Yeah," he murmured, nodding to himself. "Exactly."

This was about more than the pressure bearing down on him, then. "You miss her. You're feeling the weight of it, especially when there's any downtime."

"I am," he admitted. "But it's more than that." He finished his espresso with two more big gulps, then put it down, and leaned against the counter. "When she's not here, when there's something separating her from me, it risks me becoming dangerous."

"That obsessive and possessive edge of yours when it comes to her. The latter must be hardest to hold at bay because she left when she was still hurt. And straining emotionally."

"Brutally put, but yes."

"This is why she sent that message. She knows how we are, and how we'd each struggle with the loss of her."

"It's not enough."

"Then, until we can have her back with us, I'd suggest you unleashing your *feral* side to take the edge off and to keep your head clear, which is vital right now."

"As demented as it is, I like that about you. I like it even more that we share that. The thirst for violence, for domination of our enemies, of tasting that power." That was what Cat had told Nico a few months ago the night she'd assured him that she accepted that messed-up side of him, the same thing that raged within her. Unlike Cat, though, Nico hadn't been able to let it out at all lately. He'd tried to tame it because of taking on the role of leader, knowing so many were counting on him. Unfortunately, it *was* a part of him, one that couldn't be denied for long, no matter how much he might wish for that to be the case. Milo and I had seen him try numerous times over the years and he'd never succeeded in killing that darkness that lurked within him. It was here to stay, and it needed to be let out every now and

then. Even with things changing, we could still find ways for him to do that without it impacting his role as leader or the people under his charge.

Just like what I was about to suggest right now.

"I agree with the reasoning. But how?"

"Unleash during the Elia mission. I know you wanted Milo to take your place with leading that because you were concerned about that happening, so you relegated yourself to dealing with the Victoria Munsen aspect of the safe-houses takedown operation. Take point on the Elia mission instead. Have Milo overseeing the safehouses op alongside the units of your soldiers and Carlo's, and *I'll* take Victoria Munsen and her bodyguards. I know you're worried about doing it this way because it's gonna be a split of Benzino soldiers and yours, like the safehouses takedowns, but I think you're seeing it the wrong way. It could be framed as a positive thing. You bring a lot of power when you're in your *feral* state. The fact that you've taken on the leadership role now and it's hitting so deep with you could also help to streamline it and enable you to pull back from that state when it's needed—to maintain control, basically."

"I hear what you're saying, but—"

"Nico, it's a part of you, one you haven't been able to shake. So you need to find a place for it with this new state of things, with your role as Boss. *This* is the perfect opportunity to do that."

He thought for several moments, analyzing and taking everything in.

And then he smiled out at me. "I'll make the necessary alterations to our plans."

"Even the part about *me* being in the field?"

"Yes."

I cocked an eyebrow.

"You've been training with Levi and it's been going

exceptionally well. He's told me as much. Besides, I want you to get back to doing everything you used to do, to be yourself all the way. And this is a part of that. I need to run it by Milo first. He needs to be on board, as he'll be running point on the safehouse takedowns connected to Munsen. First, I need to see how he's doing with what I revealed to him from Marco about his parents."

Yeah, since then, Milo had just been retreating to his room alone whenever there was a break with planning these upcoming assaults, beseeching us to leave him be and allow him time to process it all.

Levi burst into the kitchen all of a sudden, his attention snapping to Nico. "I need to talk to you," he said, urgency *and* a whole load of stress coming off him.

His curly hair was wild as fuck and the dark circles under his eyes spoke of his obsessive determination to get the job done, where tracking Angelo *and* discovering more about Erebus was concerned.

Before Nico could get a word out, Levi reported, "I can't pinpoint that fucker. No matter what I do. I mean, I've placed him at two locations, but he's been moved so quickly. My program can't even anticipate his projected movements, either because these Erebus fuckers aren't moving in any sort of pattern. They'll backtrack, then move forward, then backtrack again, but by several steps and—"

"Like leapfrogging?" I asked.

"Sort of. But not in a systematic or logical fucking pattern. They're moving completely nonsensically."

"They must know about your program, then," Nico suggested.

"It's a possibility, I guess," Levi agreed. "I mean, I did use it to find Lynch, and he was connected to Erebus at the time."

"Come," Nico said, wrapping his arm around him in an actual sweet, supportive way. "Show me what you've got so far. We'll talk it out, analyze everything. It can help to have somebody to bounce things off. Especially when, despite our insistence, you haven't taken a proper break in hours upon hours." Nico looked out at me, torn with all the responsibilities upon his shoulders.

"I'll talk to Milo," I told him, so he didn't have to actually ask me.

It was probably better that it was me anyway, given that Nico was the one who'd had to give Milo the bad news before. Well, twice now. And I was also separated from it, unlike Nico, with his involvement through his father. Basically, his father had killed Milo's. It was fucking brutal.

Nico gave me a chin lift, then headed out to the living room—or the new temporary command center—with Levi.

———

AT AN AFFIRMATIVE CALL FROM MILO, I opened the door to his bedroom and stepped inside.

I found him over on the far side, sitting at his worktable and painting his fantasy figurines.

"How's it going?" I asked, going for an upbeat and casual air, trying to set the tone.

He eyed me over his shoulder briefly before returning his focus to the task at hand. "Almost done with this one entirely."

"Wow," I breathed, coming up to his side and taking in the figurine. From his robes, that were so intricately detailed to the purple hair that wasn't just a single dollop of color, but layered with different shades and detailing that actually made it look like real strands, it was a work of art. "This is amazing."

"Patience and precision, Sunshine."

"Patience and precision, huh? Are you planning to practice that beyond this pastime?"

He craned his neck to look at me again, his mouth curving slightly. "You're not exactly being subtle."

"I figured I'd try a rip-off-the-Band-Aid approach and see how that landed. Considering you're a fan of people calling things as they are, it stands to reason that you'd respect that, even where this difficult subject matter is concerned."

"You'd be right."

"And?"

He carefully stood the figurine up and put down his brush, then turned to me on his swivel chair. "*And* I'm fine with waiting for the right time to end Leo. That hasn't changed just because Nico recovered more information about what happened back then."

"Really? Even though—"

"Even though we now know that my parents were murdered because of Leo's fabricated lies about my father being a traitor? And because Marco was fool enough and so out of touch as to believe said claims, ignoring years of loyalty for supposed *proof* shoved in his face?"

"Yeah... that," I answered, grimacing as the brutality of it was put out there once again.

"You don't need to worry. And you can definitely tell Nico that, too." He took my hand and looked up at me, earnestness rolling off him as he told me, "I'm controlled and patient, Sunshine. I approach things carefully but with a strategic lethality. I'm not going to let what happened *or* those motherfuckers responsible change who *I* am, or change the way I plan to do things. That would be a form of victory for them. They thought they'd achieved that by killing my parents. But they haven't. In fact, that despicable action was one of the first steps on the road to their ruin. They'll fall. They'll have their day of punishment. Marco has already lost everything. And Leo and Angelo will suffer a far worse fate than that soon enough. That's what I'm focused on." His eyes brightened as he said, "But not the only thing. Knowing this has provided a sort of clarity for me. I was on the fence about becoming Underboss. For obvious reasons. But now I see that doing that will be a way to honor my parents, my dad especially. And as worried as I actually was about Nico taking power, fearing that it would be akin to him being trapped in this life forever, it's now clear to me that this is the chance for him to rewrite his legacy and a chance for all of us to once he's officially in position and our enemies have fallen. It's our chance to rewrite our twisted and brutal pasts with our futures determined by no one else other than ourselves." He gave my hand a squeeze. "I think my dad would be proud of me for stepping into his role in this way, with Nico at the helm."

I smiled out at him. "I have no doubt that he would be. And this is a fantastic way of framing things."

"Well, we can't allow any of them to change who we are. Right?"

"Now, who's not being subtle?"

He rose to his feet. "I've seen you getting back to yourself, seen it also coming through a great deal in your sparring sessions with Levi. When I heard about it, I thought it was gonna be just a one-shot deal for you, but I'm glad it wasn't. You can't do it with me because of our agreement about all that, our size difference and my fighting style being too dangerous when slammed up against yours, and Nico has needed to refrain from any physical activity so he can ensure his arm heals in time for our strikes, so I'm glad you've had Levi to do it with."

"Funny you should bring this up, because Nico's noticed my progress too, and he's offered to put me in the field during the operation to takedown the safehouses. I'd be relegated to the Victoria Munsen aspect of it, but it would still put me back in the fight, in actual combat again. He's gonna discuss it with you, but seeing as though we got to talking about the rest, I figured I'd lay it down now."

"I think it's a good idea."

"You do?"

"It's part of who you are—or who you were before all this shit happened that served to weigh you down so much."

"The adrenaline-junkie aspect?"

"The guy who lived life with a whole lot of thrills and excitement."

"Ah. I see."

He smiled and wrapped his arm around me. "Come on. Let's work out the reconfiguration of the op with Nico."

We made our way out of his bedroom and down the hall.

As we reached the living room, Nico's voice rang out.

"Are you fucking kidding? You were so torn up about the Angelo task, yet you were doing this as well? This is an impressive feat, Levi."

We walked in to see Nico had pulled up a chair beside Levi at the command center, and he was studying diagrams of what appeared to be an electrical grid.

"What's going on?" Milo asked.

Nico looked out at us, while Levi was scribbling down what looked like formulas and a whole lot of high-level math on a notepad. "Levi has found a way to give us an edge concerning our assaults on the safehouses putting up Erebus members in the city. He's going to launch a synchronized set of localized disruptions to the power grid that will impact the safehouses themselves and the immediate areas surrounding them."

"You can actually do that?" Milo questioned, looking mighty impressed. "On your own? Without help?"

"I can, yes," Levi answered distractedly. "Just working out the specifics now."

Nico told us, "He was also able to identify the vehicles belonging to our targets, and he's going to employ an additional distraction technique wherein he'll activate their alarms in a bid to draw some of the tenants out into the open, to split them up so our teams can take them in pieces."

"Jesus," I breathed. "And, Lev, there you were earlier getting down about the Angelo of it all? While you were putting together this phenomenal shit? Seriously?"

"I don't… fail," he uttered, finally looking up from his notepad at the three of us.

I started.

Milo and Nico had told me that Caterina had expressed something virtually identical when she'd been running up against roadblocks searching for me before.

The three of us exchanged an amused look.

"What?" Levi asked.

"You sound just like Caterina," Nico informed him.

"That makes sense. We're the people called in to achieve the impossible, something we have the skills to do. But even with my workarounds, I can't get a lock on one fucking man."

"You've pinpointed him twice. Given what we're up against, that's a hell of a thing," Nico reminded him. "Also, it's no longer *one man* that we're tracking. It's not his movements that you're trying to track. It's those of Erebus," Nico told him.

I cut in, "Who you, yourself, have stated is an organization made up of black ops ghosts."

As he started to give a nod of acceptance where that was concerned, one of his alerts went off.

He accessed it via one of his laptops, then told Nico, "Your doctor is here to give you the checkup you wanted to ensure your shoulder is healed to the degree needed to carry out the Elia op in a couple of days."

"All right," Nico said. "Finalize the technical details of the safehouse takedowns, Levi." He eyed Milo. "You and I will conference with Carlo and the teams to reconfigure things to include Julian."

"Sounds good," Milo said.

With that, Nico headed on out of the room to meet his doctor.

I sucked in a breath, a mixture of excitement and adrenaline rolling through me.

The unfathomable had happened.

They'd agreed to allow me back into the field.

And I wouldn't fuck it up this time.

14

~Emilio~

I had a lot of fucking concerns, and overseeing this mission was just one of them.

Julian was out in the field for the first time in a long while. Although I was glad that he'd reached a state where he was ready to take that on again, it still had me on edge. I was used to being there with him, too, so that added another layer of worry to it all as well.

Nico was going to unleash his *feral* side on the Elia mission tonight. It was something he hadn't done fully for a long time, either. Worse than that fact alone, was that he'd been actively repressing it for some time. What if he lost complete control? And this time I wouldn't be there to force him out of it, to make him pull it back.

And then there was all the worry I had about Caterina coming back to us. What if the results of ripping these *safe zones* out from under Erebus didn't result in what we were hoping for? What if it didn't redirect their focus from the hit?

And there was still the issue of Angelo.

Levi was working on another strategy and reworking

his program to try to cut through Erebus' misleading way of doing things, so he could obtain a lead and pinpoint Angelo's position for more than an hour at a time. Enough for us to get there and take the fucker out.

My focus was split in several different directions.

Given that I was overseeing synchronized raids on eight different safehouses right now, my concentration being split even more so than the nature of the mission itself already entailed wasn't fucking acceptable.

I just had to see through the shitstorm of it all to keep my eye on the prize. Not being there as their protector... it got under my skin. It made me fucking queasy... unsettled. But what I was doing tonight had to be shoved to the forefront of all the rest. Success with this operation would be a massive step on the road to ending all of this.

As the confirmation came in from the final team leader that they were in position, I switched frequencies to Levi.

"Cry havoc."

"Copy that," he returned, dark amusement in his tone.

I scanned the building that *my* team was targeting, taking everything in for the umpteenth time.

Despite being known as a slumlord, Victoria Munsen did own and rent out other properties that weren't total shitholes. In the case of these, Nico had delved into Munsen's records and discovered that she was offering these without so much as a fee. She wasn't fucking charging these shitheads. Either it was out of fear for what Erebus was, or Angelo had offered her something greater, like a massive piece of the pie for when he returned and took power over us all—his foolish and highly unrealistic belief that something like that would actually be able to come to pass. His insanity operated on several different levels.

This particular safehouse was the largest of the eight,

hence why I was taking point on it.

It was a classic villa design taking inspiration from Mediterranean architecture, the walls with stucco finishes, a terracotta roof, along with a couple of terraces and a fuckload of columns and arched windows. The spacious courtyard had some impeccable landscaping, along with manicured hedges. It had an elegant charm that stood in contrast both to the purpose the place was currently being used for by a bunch of hyped-up mercenaries, as well as the three ugly-ass unmarked black vans parked out front in said courtyard.

The whole situation from start to finish since we'd decided to wage war against the two families had basically been a clusterfuck of insanity.

And only two things had kept *us* sane through it all—the promise of what victory would mean *and* each other.

The lights suddenly shut off as Levi had obviously cut the power.

In the next few seconds—and I didn't know how the hell he was doing it concurrently like this with barely a breath to see to it in between—the alarms of the three vans were set off, blaring out into the night as we watched from the cover of the surrounding trees.

Confirmations rang in my ears again, all seven other teams confirming that the same had happened at their target locations.

Then Levi's voice sounded again.

"Over to you. Let slip the dogs of war."

I smiled to myself.

With pleasure.

I communicated with the leaders of the other seven teams spread throughout the city at the other safehouses, including the likes of Tony Amato and Rocco Barone, and ordered them to move in and take the fuckers.

Then I focused on my own team, the nine soldiers that I had with me here tonight. I had three positioned at the rear of the villa, ready to infiltrate via the back door and the kitchen over in that area. Another four were poised to scale the two balconies at the front of the building. And I had two with me who were going to engage in my *wrecking ball* approach and cover me in doing so.

When, as what we'd predicted happened, and two hostiles came barreling out of the front doors to check out the car alarm situation, the distraction was in place to make the op a go.

I tapped my earpiece and transmitted my command along our frequency. *"Move in. Neutralize all enemy targets and retrieve any devices that you can."* That last part had been at Levi's behest. He wanted to see if he could use them as an in to crack Erebus' communication systems.

Standing with two of my soldiers at my back, I watched as four others made it up onto the roof, then moved to the two balconies either side on the front face of the villa, then two each dropped onto either balcony.

The moment they breached the doors and headed inside the house, I made my move with the two at my back, guns at the ready.

Two well-aimed shots from my guys dropped the hostiles by the vans.

I broke into a run with my backup flanking me, and I fired at a hostile rushing through the front door, blasting his brain matter all over the formerly pristine white wood.

I stepped on his fresh corpse and burst into the living room as five guys were getting up from where they'd been hanging around watching TV on an antique, fancy-ass couch, while two others had been playing cards at a table just off to the left.

My two soldiers fired off two chest shots, taking out the

card players on the sidelines, which cleared the way for me to pull my *wrecking ball* and launch myself at the remaining shits.

A brutal push kick from me sent one of them hurtling into the couch, the thing toppling at the force I'd used.

Then I snagged the other two with either arm by the collars of their black muscle tees and took them down to the floor.

They choked from the impact, slowing their reaction times, which allowed me to beat on them with fists of fucking fury, utterly decimating them as my superior weight and muscle trapped them there at my mercy.

I pushed off them when they were pummeled unconscious, bloodied macabre figures of their former selves. I crushed one of their skulls beneath my boot, and my backup shot another through the throat.

Commotion coming from the kitchen in the distance and upstairs took my attention, and I ordered, "Back up the other two units."

Just as they headed off to do that, I picked up movement in my peripheral vision of the guy I'd downed with the couch. This time I was highly alert and at my best, so I didn't miss it as I had last time when Caterina had needed to step in to save my sweet ass.

I spun just as he came at me with a knife—a knife to the fucking back! There really was no honor with these shits and anyone connected to Angelo and motherfucking Leo.

I snagged his wrist and jerked it to the side, making him grunt as a telltale snap sounded, indicating that I'd broken it in one vicious shot.

Demonstrating his training, he managed to move past it, and he even extricated himself from my hold with a series of rapid-fire moves.

The knife was still in play as a result.

He went for me again, and I dodged it, but it was clearly what he'd been counting on, because he was then in the perfect position to roundhouse me into a column. It smashed my gun right out of my hand with the precision of the kick.

As my back jarred hard against the column, another hostile broke free, hurtling down the stairs, clearly having gotten past my team. Between them, they kept me forced against the column, each of them holding me on either side with all their strength.

"Fucking beast of a guy," the knife-wielder grunted to the other as they struggled.

The other guy told him, "Take him out! Now!"

The knife-wielder went to do just that, going for my throat, but I managed to twist harshly at the last second, and it plunged into my right shoulder instead.

My roar that was more indignation than pain startled them and the guy without the knife made a mistake of shifting his weight.

It was all I needed to use it to my advantage and haul around with him holding onto my other arm, essentially tossing him into the knife-wielder.

They were fucking shocked at that, because not a lot of people had the ability or strength to pull off ripping a grown man off their feet and tossing them away with just one fucking arm available.

But their superior training showed again as they recovered quicker than most people would have been able to and came at me.

Either side of me, I fought them back and forth, their rapid-fire blows slamming up against the hefty powerhouse nature of mine. Every time one of my hits connected, it jarred them considerably, serving to slow them down.

I got in a shot at the new guy's throat that had him reeling back.

Then I ducked and rolled over to the table.

In the next second, I was snatching up one of the wooden chairs and smashing it into the knife-wielder. His knife went flying over near the door as he, himself, took a hit to the face.

I was there in the next second, wrenching him up by his shoulder, then slamming my knee into his face. As he reeled back, blood spurting from a clear broken nose, I dropped him, jammed my knee into his gut and, as he instinctively doubled over, I smashed my elbow into his back. That knocked him to the ground, sprawled out on his back.

Before I could finish him, I picked up on the other guy coming at me in my peripheral vision and I snagged him just before he hit and tossed him into another column.

I located my gun and dove toward it.

I managed to snatch it up just in time as the fucker bounced back and came for me, and I spun on the ground and fired off a shot right through his throat.

He choked as blood erupted like a fucking geyser.

Unlike Nico *and* Caterina, I didn't care for that sickening sound, so I pushed back to my feet and pistol-whipped him, knocking him out so I didn't have to hear the sounds of his brutal death.

Then I put a bullet in the back of the knife-wielder's skull, ending him as well.

In the next second, I was bolting across the vast space and into the kitchen, throwing the door open to see all hostiles down and my team gathering their devices.

"Nicely done," I told them.

I headed back out to the living room and started for the

stairs to check on the progress of the others up on the second level.

But before I'd even made it a single step up, one of my guys came barreling down, reporting, "All down, Emilio. We're good."

"Excellent job. Drag the bodies down here for transportation. I'll call in the truck."

He gave me a chin lift, then set off to carry out my order.

I placed the call to the truck and to the cleanup crews.

And then I tapped my earpiece and reached out to Levi.

"Lev, I need eyes on Julian."

"I thought you might. It's already in place. Go to the link I just sent to you."

"Thanks."

I pulled out my phone and accessed the link, which I quickly realized was access Levi had obtained to the security cameras inside Victoria Munsen's house.

I took in the sight of five of her bodyguards dropped. The two soldiers we'd sent along to back up Julian were cuffing them for transportation out of the city. It took me some time cycling between the different feeds until I caught sight of Julian in Victoria's bedroom, executing one of his flying kicks and sending the final bodyguard across the room.

As the guy struggled back to his feet, Julian was there already with those fast moves of his, trapping the fucker in an impressive chokehold, while also ripping his feet out from under him with a sweep to the back of his legs.

As he was doing that, Victoria burst from the bathroom, screaming when she saw the last of her protection was in the process of being taken down.

She made a break for the door, but Julian was at his

best, and he pulled a throwing knife and tossed it at her. It cut through the air like fucking lightning and drove through the arm of her robe, missing her skin, but pinning her to the door.

"Fucking cunt!" she yelled at him. "That's what you are, you know? Angelo told me as much. Actually, he even showed me the footage of your kidnapping."

Goddammit.

I saw Julian flinch at that.

But he didn't release his hold on the guy.

"I'm sure you had a sick viewing party. Trash like you *would* enjoy something as demented as that," he told her in a calm, yet eerie tone.

He finished choking the guy out, kicked him in the face for good measure, then approached Victoria.

"I did enjoy it. Immensely," she told him nastily. "And so did you."

No. No. No.

My fingers tightened around my phone as I watched Julian clench his fists, a hiss of indignation escaping him.

He was fighting himself, fighting what had happened, fighting for his fucking life.

This was the first time that he'd come up against a direct, brutal reference to what had happened to him with that motherfucker. Especially in this way, being thrown in his face.

"You can deny it all you want, but I saw it. And so did Angelo. He knows the truth."

She was a fucking demon of a woman. *Irredeemable piece of shit.*

Julian stepped up to her, but I saw his fists unclench. And when he spoke, all I heard from him was calm. "There's a difference between a physical reaction being elicited—or forced in this case—to actual enjoyment being had. To consent being had, to wanting it. Or wanting him. The two of you are cut from the same cloth, so I wouldn't expect your warped minds to understand that. It was sexual abuse, forced degradation, and torture that I was subjected to. And the shame of that isn't mine, nor something I'm going to allow myself to take on any longer. The shame was all Angelo's. What he did to me was horrific and most definitely unwanted. No amount of attempted emotional manipulation from either of you is going to reframe the reality there."

I smiled.

He'd done it.

As she went to speak, Julian cut her off, telling her instead, "And just so you know, unlike your bodyguards here, *you* aren't being transported outside the city and merely removed from the situation. We're dropping you on the ADA's doorstep. You had a second chance when you were released from jail early on good behavior, but you didn't take it. You even delved into more sinister activities. Suffice to say, with the proof of said activities, along with Remo's close relationship with the ADA, you'll never taste freedom again."

She started screeching, and fighting to escape her pinned position against the wall, cursing him out, the whole nine.

At that point, two of our soldiers strode into the room and removed her.

I watched as Julian stepped back uneasily and slapped his hand to the wall, then scrubbed his hand over his face.

He took several beats, and then he straightened and walked out of the bedroom with his head held high.

My Sunshine.

15

~Nico~

Elia Volpe had certainly let the illusion of power go to his head.

Abuse of power didn't even cover it where he was concerned.

I shot a glance at Dante Rivera, who was standing beside me, shaking his head with a disgusted expression as he took in Elia's repulsive antics from our vantage point on the catwalk high above the torturous show taking place below.

Dante's revulsion and loathing of Elia was such that he'd insisted on being a part of this operation, needing to see the trumped-up Leone Capo fall.

I was tapping my fingers on the butt of my gun in my right hip holster as I waited for the confirmation from Remo and Cassio who were leading the other two units of our soldiers on this op, which was a collaboration between Marchetti soldiers under my charge and Benzino soldiers. Combined with the safehouse takedowns happening at the same time tonight, these operations were the first of their kind—two families merging their soldiers and resources as one for a mission. Given how easily Carlo and I were able to work together, how our strategies aligned well and our temperaments, values, and outlooks on key things meshed exceptionally well, I doubted this sort of thing would be a one-off. It was the beginning of a close-knit alliance that would serve to bolster both families and ensure a smooth working relationship going forward.

Seconds ticked on by, which felt a hell of a lot more like minutes, as I waited for the other two units to take position.

I'd never been so anxious for that to come to pass before.

I'd never really had to wait like this before, or concern myself with the lives of so many, of a multi-pronged and complicated operation like this.

I'd spent a lot of time as Capo getting my hands dirty, either Milo and I going it alone, or with a trusted few.

But times were changing, even beyond the scope of this operation.

And in this particular case, it was more complicated.

While the safehouse takedowns when combined together were essentially a massacre, those Erebus targets were ghosts, so their deaths would go unnoticed. These Leone soldiers gathered here didn't fall into the same category.

If we simply took them out by blowing the warehouse to hell with them all contained inside, or even took them down in a hail of gunfire, we were talking more than three hundred deaths to cover up. It just wasn't feasible. And it would end up bringing my new version of the Marchetti Syndicate down with it, alongside the Benzinos as well.

Besides, there were soldiers present here who'd already lost faith in the Leone Family and were disgusted and abso- lutely not on board with the way things had come to be.

They wanted out, and we had evidence that showed several dozen of them were already in the process of moving their families and planning their escape. They didn't need to die for Carlo and me to succeed, for the Leone Family to fall.

Both Elia and Angelo had become so delusional and severely overestimated their power to such a degree that they'd really believed pulling this shit tonight would keep their soldiers intact and reinforce their loyalty. They thought they were untouchable. The fact that both Elia and Angelo's soldiers had gathered here tonight under one roof was foolish enough and clear proof of their level of delusion.

With Erebus' support, they considered themselves beyond interference from enemy forces, namely me and Carlo.

When, in fact, they'd just made it that much easier for us to end the Leone Family here and now. With the exception of Angelo, who was being bolstered by Erebus forces, like Leo was. But they would be dealt with soon enough, too.

I tried to ignore the screams echoing hauntingly through the warehouse as Dante and I relayed instructions to the other two units getting into position, on who to put down hard, and who to extricate once the operation got underway.

Twenty-five Leone soldiers were being tortured in the clearing near the entrance of the warehouse down below as Elia held court, uttering a whole load of bullshit about loyalty and treachery, words he clearly had no true comprehension of, given what he was doing to his own men—and Angelo's at his orders from afar.

Several of the victims he was taking it out on were bound to pallet racks naked and on display to everyone, some of them being cut into with blades, others having fucking power drills driven into their thighs. There were half a dozen also bound to metal chairs, their knuckles and kneecaps being shattered to shit. The ones strapped to worktables, also on display for the crowd gathered around to see, were being forced to deepthroat the fists of their torturers, while money—coins and balled-up bank note—were being shoved into their asses as they squirmed, bucked and screamed.

Elia was clearly taking a leaf out of both Angelo and Santino's books.

As if that wasn't enough, there were five naked soldiers hogtied, having the cocks of their torturers—the soldiers still loyal to Elia and Angelo—shoved down their throats.

Elia would pause every now and then in his speech, flip his brown mohawk, then take part himself, fisting their hair so brutally and taking his pleasure, his cock hanging out of his leather pants as he moved from one to another, before then getting back down to his pathetic speech.

"I can't stand much more of this," Dante whispered to me.

I acknowledged what he was saying, and I was having a great deal of trouble myself, and I looked down the line at the fifty soldiers with me hidden in the shadows up on the catwalk above, seeing the same reactions from them. These were hardened fucking men, too. That was how horrific what we were witnessing actually was. How truly demented Elia was.

My earpiece buzzed, and I finally got word from both teams, one after the other.

They were in position.

There was a team located at the rear of the warehouse, C-4 all set to blow the door, create a distraction, wherein they'd then storm inside.

The other team was positioned at the cargo bay over to the west of the warehouse, ready to move in at my word.

And the fifty soldiers I had with me were crouching low on either side of the catwalk, twenty-five to my right to take the metal steps with me, and the other fifty to the left of Dante to take the other set of stairs.

I gave Dante a chin lift, and he started moving his men right to the edge of the steps.

I signaled mine, and then I sent the command via my earpiece, *"Move in. Hard and fast. No fatalities. Elia is mine."*

In the next second, all hell broke loose.

From our perspective, controlled chaos.

The explosion from the rear door had Elia jolting, and his torturers pulling up short, the crowd looking all around, startled.

Those in the crowd were unarmed. Another way for Elia to ensure he held all the power.

But the torturers were armed to the hilt, obviously making them priority to take down.

As my team targeted them, I fired off a shot at one of them holding up a drill; the bit covered in flesh and blood. He shrieked like a little bitch and dropped the drill as the bullet drove through his clavicle, making him feel a mass amount of pain that he could barely handle, that most could barely handle. It was nothing less than he deserved for what he'd dealt out to his victims under Elia's sick orders.

Another pulled his fist from a victim's throat, making the guy vomit all over himself, and as he turned, our gazes clashing, I fucking kneecapped him with another bullet, his screams adding to the cacophony of battle swirling all around.

My team worked well alongside me, disposing of the others strategically.

Dante's team was tasked with extricating the torture victims and getting them medical assistance once they were clear of the immediate area, and I watched them heading across the warehouse floor toward them to do just that.

Our team at the rear door burst on in and so did those entering through the cargo bay.

Bullets zinged through the air, plunging into kneecaps, or delivering flesh wounds, anything to put them down and out of the fight without outright killing them. Not that they'd be anything resembling a threat once we were through with them. They just needed to remain breathing, technically alive, but that still gave us a lot of leeway where taking them down and incapacitating them was concerned.

I caught sight of Elia panicking in all the chaos.

He made two of his torturers cover him, and he tried to make a break for safety down one of the aisles.

That was my opening.

I ensured everything was going to plan, watching as Dante's team worked to get the torture victims out of harm's way, while mine disposed of the torturers. The other two teams took out those we'd identified as still being loyal to Elia, while also extricating those who were no different from the torture victims, being forced to follow those they no longer had faith in through fear of death— or worse, as we'd just witnessed.

It was under control, things progressing according to plan.

Now it was time to let loose.

I wasn't used to doing that around so many witnesses.

And, even though I'd prepped our soldiers, I still didn't know how it was going to go over once I unleashed and let that *feral* state take me.

But I *did* know that I needed to let it out.

And I needed to know more than anything that I could pull it back now.

There was too much at stake for me to have this dark, twisted, and brutal side of myself existing without a means to control it.

Too many people were counting on me.

Even when the war was won, with me taking the helm of Boss, that wouldn't alter.

I *had* to be able to reconcile that part of myself with the rest.

And this was as good a test as any, where it mattered that I both unleashed *and* kept control.

No small feat.

Then again, none of this had been.

But we'd still come this far. *So* far.

I wouldn't falter now.

I sprinted for the aisle that Elia had disappeared down.

When I was just a few feet out, I caught sight of a door to an office over on the right side of the aisle. Although there was no exit this way, it looked like Elia was intending to barricade himself inside the room and hide like the true coward that he was, and leave these two guys with him to defend his position. His two torturers who were doused in the blood of their victims. Victims whose utter agony I'd watched them take pleasure in.

There was about to be some major role reversal.

I went to that headspace, focusing on the violence of the battle raging all around, the blood soaking their jeans and tees, the sadistic expressions on their faces as they'd tormented their own. But most of all, and the thing that had triggered this state for me in the first fucking place, the powerlessness they'd levied upon their victims. Taking away their agency, their choices, depriving them of hope entirely.

And then a snarl was escaping me as I stormed down the aisle.

It caught their attention, and Elia spun while in the process of being ushered toward that fucking office.

"Nico," he sneered. "You're making a big mistake. You won't survive this."

"Your perception is deeply flawed." A growl rumbled from me. "This is your execution."

A dark thrill rolled through me as fear broke through some of that heavy delusion of his.

"No. We're the Leone Family, you can't just—"

"There's no more Leone Family. Once we're done here tonight, that will be an absolute certainty."

"You doing this, working with the Benzinos too, bringing in the disgraced Leone Underboss in Dante... it's an act of fucking war!"

I stepped ever closer. "We're beyond war. This is utter decimation."

His eyes widened, and he even trembled, unable to conceal it. His true colors were showing. The real weak bastard beneath the façade and all the muscle he'd been too fortunate to have bolstering him.

"Take him the fuck out!" he raged at his two guys.

As they came at me, Elia made a dash for the office door.

I reacted lightning-fast, drew a tactical blade, then lobbed it toward him.

It cut through the air rapid fire, then drove through his upper left arm, and into the frame of the door behind him, effectively pinning him to it.

His shrieks just fueled the intensity taking me over as I sank deeper into my *feral* state.

And, as the first of his men reached me, I reacted, firing a bullet through the center of his right hand that had him crying out and dropping his automatic weapon instantly.

As it clattered to the ground, I bolted forward and kicked it away, back the way we'd all come.

Then I snagged the guy by his bloodied hand, digging my fingers into the wound for good measure that had him shuddering and screaming in my hold as I hauled him into the other torturer. The impact sent them both crashing to the floor in a heap of tangled limbs.

The guy beneath the wounded one shoved him off with a bellow of indignation, then sprung to his feet and charged me.

I caught him by his tee just as he hit, spun, and slammed him into one of the pallet racks. My hand closed around his throat as he struggled against me, cursing and trying to break free from my hold.

I snarled down at him, the ferociousness of it that I couldn't hold in check while I was like this, making him shrink away—or try to. I squeezed his throat, watching him gag and fight for air.

In my peripheral vision, I saw the torturer with a hole through his hand scrambling to his feet, looking to go to Elia and remove the knife that I had keeping him from running.

At the same time, two more of Elia's soldiers turned down the aisle, slipping past the battle to come to their Capo's aid.

I shoved my gun into the guy's temple and pulled the trigger, blowing his skull to shit.

As I released him, blood and brain matter splattered on my face and neck, my pulse pounding in my ears, that primal part of me taking the lead.

The remaining three assholes were closing in a moment later.

Everything was a blur of violent furor as I unleashed on them, tearing into them with a blade, countering their blows as my own snarls and roars of ferocity echoed hauntingly in the air all around me, fueling me, and punishing them. The snap of bones, their screams, blood splattering, all collided into a spectacular bout of aggression and violent intensity.

"Jesus fuck," Elia choked.

My head jerked in his direction as I shoved my boot into a screaming soldier's skull, silencing him as it knocked him out cold.

And then I stormed up to Elia.

I ripped the blade out, and he shrieked and convulsed against the door.

"Please!" he cried, as he watched me spin it in my hand right in front of his face.

"Isn't that what your own soldiers begged you for? A shred of fucking mercy?"

"That was... I made a mistake. I... I'm sorry. Please. *Please.*"

"There's no mercy for a piece of shit like you. You're beyond repentance and you fucking know it."

"Nico, listen——"

His words ended on a shriek as I plunged my blade into his gut.

I didn't stop there.

The monster in me that was seeking some form of retribution, that needed to deliver punishment, wouldn't allow it.

I cut into him, slicing up, then out, tearing him open as bloodcurdling screams filled my ears.

Only when they ceased because he'd passed out from the agony did I stop.

And then I drove the blade through his heart, sending him straight to hell.

I stepped back, breathing heavily, and looked out at what I'd done.

Bloodied, disfigured bodies covered the floor, blood pooling all fucking over.

But aside from Elia, I'd managed to leave them alive.

Even while I'd been in the throes of that state.

More than even that, I'd pulled out of it on my own, once the job had been completed.

I'd achieved control that had previously eluded me.

Cheers and clapping caught my attention, and I looked up, blinking rapidly to fully return to my normal state, to see my soldiers and those of Carlo's gathered at the end of the aisle, the battle having come to an end. They'd clearly seen my *performance*.

And they weren't reviled by it.

They weren't even judging it.

Nor were they displaying the least bit of concern.

Instead, they were reveling in it.

In the power that I'd demonstrated, the ability to protect those under my charge.

That, combined with the control I'd managed to muster this time, was a hell of a thing.

I smiled to myself.

The doubts that had been plaguing me finally eased off.

I had this.

I'm ready.

16

~Caterina~

"It's not your fault, you know? Losing the baby is something that happened to you, not something you're responsible for, Cat. I promise."

"We're in this together. We're a team. I have your back just like the three of you have mine."

"This is what it means to be ours, principessa."

As those thoughts swirled around my head, it had my fingers flying across the keyboard of the military-grade laptop Joe had provided me a few days ago.

Thoughts of my men and the intense need to get back to them were spurring me on, firing me up, making me push harder and faster.

It had been two and a half weeks now.

Too long.

The four of us had been living under the same roof, intrinsically linked and bound together on our mission and in love for so long now, that I hated being away from that, away from them, away from what we shared.

And as I kept coming up against the same obstacles over and over again in my technological aspect of the fight

148

against Angelo and Erebus, all of that just fueled my frustration to an unbearable degree.

This organization… *fuck*… to say they were technologically advanced didn't exactly cover it. They were also using military-grade encryption.

While it wasn't my first rodeo where either of those things were concerned, I had been running into a shitload of roadblocks that I wasn't actually used to—at least, not to this extent. After making it through the arduous task of decrypting, all that time and effort had been proven fruitless when I'd discovered Erebus had a network of redundant servers. There was no way I could break in with that in play without being detected.

Son of a bitch.

Movement across the small living space had me jerking my head up from my laptop just as the front door of the small cabin opened. Instinctively, I snatched up the gun that Joe had left for me before he'd headed out earlier.

I quickly cocked it and took aim.

A split second later, *he* came into view.

As I lowered my gun, he shook his head at me. "You were slow on the draw there."

"Well, I was distracted by the task at hand," I said, securing the gun, then gesturing at the laptop on the coffee table before me.

"Hmm," was all he said.

"Was there an issue?" I asked him.

"Issue?" he queried as he shook off his tactical jacket and hung it on one of the hooks beside the front door.

"You're back early. Did you even have time to communicate with Carlo?"

He frowned as he walked over to me on the couch. "I've been gone for four hours, Caterina."

"You have? Wow, time really flew on by then."

"I assume that intense focus means you've made some headway?"

I closed the laptop lid and sank back against the couch. "I'm up against redundant servers, several layers of technological subterfuge, including cryptographic keys, and military-grade encryption." I shoved a hand through my hair. "To crack their system, I'd also need to hit multiple servers at once, which would require synchronized precision. The bottom line is that I can't do this on my own because of their complicated, multi-point security. I need to work with Levi."

"You want to leave here," he murmured. "Hmm."

That *hmm* with him never boded well. It meant he was resistant to what I was suggesting. And *that* meant that I had a fight on my hands.

"As for trying to track Nathan Donahue directly, I've generated two sightings of him in the last five fucking years. There's absolutely nothing recent. He's clearly been underground this entire time. Our only chance is to access their communication systems and obtain a location on him from there. Obtain all intel about these fuckers. The locations of their servers, their operational hubs, upcoming operations, physical locations and systems."

He perched on the edge of the coffee table. "Your boys have carried out two successful joint operations with Carlo Benzino that have resulted in the decimation of all the *safe zones* that Erebus was using within the city, while also eliminating said targets, as well as removing all remaining Leone Family soldiers from the equation."

"Wow, that's… that's amazing."

"It is, yes. Erebus will be suffering the fallout of it shortly."

"So this is when we make our move. Sneak me back into the city so I can work with Levi and get this done, while Erebus, Angelo and also Leo, by extension, are reeling."

"While this is a blow, it won't have them reeling for long. One of Erebus' strengths is being able to pivot and recalibrate."

"As is ours. And by *ours* I mean all of us collectively. It's time we pulled together on this, time *you* did. No more lone-wolfing it. Even all the leads and personal intel you gave me via your insider knowledge on Donahue haven't panned out. He's a true ghost like you. So you'll need more that *you* to accomplish this mission. You'll need all of us."

He smiled.

"What?" I asked, off the indecipherable look he gave me.

"You've come a long way, is all. From a lone wolf like me, to an adamant team player."

"Well, you made sure I could operate as a lone-wolf, but circumstances forged a different path for me in order to both survive and thrive in this war."

"And you've also made connections that remain strong, despite your time away."

"Did you think bringing me out here would alter that?"

"I suppose part of me had hoped that it would. The truth is that I don't want you having anything to do with that lifestyle, the mob, any of it. Especially now the tide has turned, and there's actually an opportunity for you to escape it. You could set up somewhere else, yet still use your reputation that you've garnered in the city so it wouldn't be completely starting from scratch."

"Leaving my men is not an option. We're a package deal, Joe."

He sighed heavily.

"I spent my life alone and they've altered that. They've become my *family*. I won't turn my back on that. I can't."

I saw my words penetrate, the hurt all over him, as my statement was put out there.

He was leaving me little choice.

I needed him to understand.

There was no other way forward for me than with Nico, Julian, and Milo. They'd earned that devotion from me several times over.

"If you'd like to be a part of that, for me to keep you in my life beyond this brief safehouse interlude, a great step toward that would be you accepting them and respecting my decision."

His eyes lit up. "You'd actually want that? Beyond this *safehouse interlude*, I mean?"

"To get to know you as my father?"

He nodded.

"I would like that, yes. But, given everything that has happened, and how I know you to be, it has to be on my terms."

The corner of his mouth turned up. "I suppose after all you've suffered, all that training I put you through, expecting you to live a normal life devoid of danger, is a tall order, yes?"

"I'd say so. The die has been cast there, I'm afraid."

"Okay," he said, rising to his feet. "I accept your terms. However, you need to accept my condition. And it *is* non-negotiable. For your own wellbeing, Caterina. This isn't me being stubborn or overprotective. It's a necessity."

Here we go. "What's this condition of yours?"

"You take me down and we'll leave."

"What? You actually want me to fight you?"

"You didn't have a problem doing that beforehand."

"I was undergoing training then. A really brutal training program, I might add."

"What you're asking me to take you back into will

require nothing less than being able to live up to that brutality."

Damn him.

"Besides, I'm sure there's some residual anger toward me that this will enable you to work out."

"I don't know how *residual* it is."

He grinned. "Indeed."

I pushed off the couch and rounded the coffee table. "You don't think I'm ready, do you?"

"It needs to be a certainty. You've healed physically, but let's not pretend that what happened didn't shake you."

"Something I've been processing since we've been here. And, while we're talking about this, it's something I can't completely process without my men. We all lost our child, we all went through that, and we all need to work through the grief together."

"It's doubtful there will be time to entertain that much joint processing when we return, so I need to ensure that you're combat-ready, and clear-headed to do what needs to be done, even in spite of that."

"Some things never change. You always have a rebuttal for everything."

"As do you. You're welcome. You got that from me."

I rolled my eyes. "You do know that I have the ability to disable all your security protocols in and around this safehouse, and leave without your agreement?"

"And *you* know that I'll give chase. While your skills are next-to-none when it comes to the hacking and cracking of it all, you're not at the same level as I am when it comes to fieldwork."

Damn him again.

"Fine." I squared my shoulders. "Let's do this. I'll show you that I'm good to go."

Here goes nothing.

I GRUNTED as I hit the grass hard.

Again.

Before I could recover, he was there going in for a kick.

I managed to roll out of the way in time, and I used the momentum to come up in a primed crouch.

"You're not afraid to hurt me. You got past that during months of our training. So you're afraid of getting hurt? Is that it?"

"No," I told him. That would be a hell of a lot easier to conquer.

He dropped his fighting stance and frowned at me, at a loss, something definitely rare for him.

But there was no way he could deduce this, what was really eating at me in this situation. He didn't know about it, he didn't know the violence he'd taught me had slammed up against the violence of the world I'd inhabited for so long and had created a... monstrous entity within me.

I pushed from my crouch and back to my feet, straightening as I told him, "With everything that's happened lately, something that was formed in me years ago, something I'd tried hard to deny, has risen up and become more prevalent. A dangerous, depraved and monstrous side of me. When I'm in combat, it unleashes. It's what happened the night I was kidnapped by those three Erebus soldiers at Santino's behest. It was also in that state that I murdered him."

"You're talking about bloodlust?"

"In a sense. But it's also more than that."

"Are you referring to the state that Nico lapses into when the need for violence arises?"

I started. "You know about that?"

"I've had eyes on him since he inserted himself into your life with your *war* several years ago."

"Your invasiveness knows no bounds."

"Not when it came to protecting you and ensuring you were well." Off my look, he added, "But with how things have shifted, I'll try to curb the intensity where that's concerned." He smiled. "For the good of our new father-daughter relationship that we're trying to build."

Well, that promise would do. At least for now. So long as it wasn't just a fleeting thing, and I saw him actually trying to keep it.

"So, is that what we're talking about with you as well?" he pushed.

"It's similar, yes."

"As I understand it, Nico likes entering that state. It's very much bloodlust to him. How about in your case?"

"It's triggered. By fear, indignation, the sense of power-lessness."

"Everything that Santino and the world he created around you incited."

"He was a major trigger, yes. No doubt."

"It could very well just be a product of circumstances, then. And that's something we're working on changing, that we will change."

"I haven't let it out since that night I killed him. I haven't wanted to. Not just out of concern that I could lose control, as I most often do when I unleash like that, but because I haven't felt the need to. There's been no pressure building up to do so, like there usually has been. So it could be better, or at least easing off now that he's dead, that I've finally conquered that fucking demon in him."

"But you're concerned that may also not be the case and that it'll come out through our battle here and any that you involve yourself in back in Tolhurst?"

"Yes."

He rubbed his bristly jaw. "You're certain you want this *monstrous* part of you gone?"

"It's uncontrollable. It has me losing my grip on rational thought. I've also hurt Nico during an episode before."

"It's triggered by desperation, fear, and the sense of hopelessness, you said. That means you believe it gives you more power being in that state."

"Undoubtedly."

"Then I'd suggest learning how to control it, instead of repressing it. Learning to obtain better control will also take away your fear of losing yourself to it. Nico understands it, so you can work together. And I'll help you both."

"Okay, yeah. I mean, I'll have to run it by Nico, but on my end, I'd like that. I trust you as a trainer, after all, so there's a solid foundation there."

He smiled, then assumed a fighting stance. "And, for right now, try to put me down without bringing it out. Let's see how that goes."

"It will give us a baseline," I realized.

"Exactly."

I readied myself and crooked my fingers at him. "Come at me, old man."

"General rule of thumb, Caterina? Don't antagonize your opponent."

"I've actually found that to be helpful. It gets under their skin."

"Touché. Although, you know well that it won't work with me."

"Either way, I should warn you that I've learned a few things since we last trained together."

"I can't wait for you to demonstrate them."

"Then make your move. Let's do this."

A thrill ran through me as he did make his move, coming at me.

And for the first time in a long time, the thrill of the fight, the empowering sensation of being able to hold my own in combat wasn't overshadowed by pain and negativity, by something bearing down on me through every moment of it.

No. This time it felt different.

Freer.

17

~Julian~

There was a lot to celebrate.

We'd eradicated the *safe zones* that the foolish Marchetti-Leone alliance had provided for Erebus. That nasty woman, Victoria Munsen, was behind bars. With Carver Group's resources, I was now in the process of assisting those tenants of hers who she'd victimized. All Leone Family soldiers had been disposed of in one way or the other. Elias had been killed. *And* Nico had managed to pull back from his *feral* state without assistance or being forced to by the might of Milo. Not to mention the power he'd demonstrated when he'd been in that zone during the operation at the warehouse had imbued another level of respect, pride, and trust for him in both his own soldiers and Carlo's.

We were so close to ending all of this now.

Normally, we'd celebrate such major victories.

But it didn't feel right doing that without Cat being here with us.

Carlo had tipped Nico off that Stover had reached out to him asking about our progress back here. He'd reported a whole lot of positivity. But we still hadn't heard anything from either him or Cat herself.

We still didn't know when she was coming home.

I mean, it was supposed to be when the hit had been eradicated and Angelo had been taken out. But, given that he'd been impossible to find, we'd hoped that taking out the *safe zones* and the Erebus operatives within, and thereby causing some major destabilization to their organization *and* their plans here, would have forced them to recalibrate, making the hit much less of a priority, or nullifying it altogether. It should have also shaken their faith in Angelo. He had no fucking power here now. None of the Leones did. They were gone. All that was left was Leo Marchetti, those soldiers at the mansion, and the Erebus operatives bolstering him.

I sighed as I leaned back on the patio lounger by the pool and tried to keep my mind focused on the task at hand.

I'd already posted some pool shots for my IG, and since then I'd been working on sorting out a celebratory surprise for whenever Cat returned home to us.

Milo and Nico were in a meeting with their soldiers, and Carlo and Remo. Meanwhile, Lev was finally getting some rest after ending up being awake for nearly forty-eight hours straight. Not being able to achieve the impossible when it came to tracking Angelo and Erebus had really been getting to him, and he'd dipped into an obsessive state. Fortunately, our victories and how instrumental he'd been in all of that had pulled him out of it enough where he'd finally been willing to take a break. And Nico getting his loves—Brianna, Mason, and Colton—on the phone to push him to chill had also helped out and clinched it.

As my mind started wondering to what Cat might be

doing right now, I forced it back on track to my celebration plans I had in the works.

I was fully immersed in it again when a text notification flashed on my screen.

Blocked ID: Miss you.

Hope sprung, and a huge smile spread over my face.

Cat was contacting us again!

It had to be happening then, really soon. She had to be coming home if she was able to reach out in this way, instead of in the covert way she'd had to last time.

Although, why was she keeping her number blocked and hidden?

And last time she'd sent a message for all of us, not individual texts.

It had me frowning.

Julian: Cat?

That brief spark of hope died a sudden death when the response came in.

Blocked ID: No, tesoro.

I jolted, almost dropping my phone in the process from the shock of it.

A chill ran down my spine. That and a surge of adrenaline had me shuddering, my hands shaking.

It was him.

Blocked ID: Well? Does my pretty little bitch miss me, too?

When I just stared at the message and didn't respond, he texted again.

Blocked ID: I know you do. You've been looking for me. Just like I intended, you're being drawn back to me.

Blocked ID: I've been thinking. How about I let you fuck me next time? I've been fantasizing about what it will be like. That jewelry and your sexual know-how... fuck, it'll be another level.

What was happening?

Blocked ID: Julian, I know you wanted it and wanted me. Your denial is bullshit. So this is my deal. You come to me agreeing to try again and build on this thing between us, agree to be mine, and I'll call off the hit on Caterina. I'll redirect my friends' efforts to taking the city and recruiting more Leone soldiers to replace what Nico took from us, rather than bothering with the four of you.

I swallowed hard and finally responded.

Julian: Where do you want me to meet you?

Blocked ID: Ah, there you are. Fuck, I really have missed you.

Julian: Where and when?

Blocked ID: You agree to be mine? To stop your bullshit denial at long last?

I gritted my teeth,

Julian: Why would I be asking how you want to arrange this if I didn't?

Blocked ID: I fucking knew it. Tomorrow night, as soon as the sun goes down, head north outside the city on the main highway. I'll give you instructions when I deem it's safe and that you're actually alone.

He would be tracking me via the chip he believed had gone unnoticed and was, therefore, still buried in my fucking body.

Julian: I'm on it. See you tomorrow night.

Blocked ID: Can't wait. You don't even know how much I've been craving you.

As if that wasn't enough to make me gag, he sent another message.

Blocked ID: XOXO.

Jesus Christ.

It was another level.

He was another level.

Demented beyond belief.

Beyond all reason and logic.

Beyond all sanity.

I hurried off the lounger, and strode back into the house, rushing through the kitchen, scanning every which way, and hoping like hell that the guys were done with their meeting, and that Levi had almost finished his nap.

I made a sharp turn out of the kitchen, intending to head to Nico's office, when I ended up smacking into Levi instead.

We both jolted to a stop at the impact.

He was the first to react, steadying me with a hand to my chest, before he then stepped back and regarded me, concern quickly sparking as he took me in. "You look majorly spooked. What's happened?"

My fingers tightened around my phone at the question.

Of course, he noticed.

"Julian?" he pressed gently.

Pressing but carefully was his whole thing with me, particularly when we were sparring. It was because he was a tough and seasoned son of a bitch, but he also understood what it was like to be horrifically tormented and abused, to have your hope stolen and your power ripped to shreds at the hands of contemptible people.

We'd built an enjoyable and strong rapport since he'd been here. I liked having him here with us, and that was only undercut with the knowledge that he'd have to leave at some point soon and return to his own life, his own foursome.

I opened the most recent text conversation and handed him the phone. "This is what happened. Just now." I knew I didn't really need to add the *just now* part because he'd see the timestamps for himself, but I figured it was me needing to ensure no one thought I was keeping secrets like I had last time, which had led to me risking that entire Shawn Price operation by heading up there behind everybody's backs.

Levi read over the messages, his eyes narrowing, and a growl escaping him. "Angelo Simone," he seethed.

"Yeah."

His eyes met mine and his expression shifted to fierce and resolute. "He may have just made a fatal mistake."

"What are you—"

The next thing I knew, he was spinning and telling me, "Come with me."

———

MY PHONE WAS HOOKED up to what I'd come to term Levi's *hacking station*. Well, it alternated between that and *command center*.

"Yes," he exclaimed, as his fingers flew over his keyboard, reminding me so much of Cat when she was at work and deep in the hacking zone.

"What?" I asked.

"Unlike the other devices you guys retrieved the night of the takedowns, the one Angelo just used to send these messages wasn't encrypted. It's not Erebus tech or protected by their know-how. He's using his own phone, independent of their supply. Perhaps he didn't want them to know about his intention to reach out to you like this. It suggests that his obsession has been festering and is now getting in the way of his good sense."

"Yet again," I gritted out.

"Exactly."

"So you can track him?"

"Let's find out."

"Even though it wasn't an actual call?"

"Even with texts, the phone in question needs to connect to the nearest cell tower to route the communication, which basically registers its location with the network."

"What if it's a burner?"

"It doesn't matter. It's still going to ping to the nearest cell tower. It's gonna connect to a network."

He saw me watching him pulling up this screen and that, moving rapid-fire between all of them before I could even begin to make heads or tails of what exactly was happening. He kept me abreast of the situation, explaining what he was actually doing. "Right now, I'm trying to intercept metadata to find the general location that the messages were sent from. And I'll also compare pings from numerous cell towers to narrow down the location to a precise position—triangulation, essentially."

"Whoa."

He smiled out at me. "Yeah."

As he continued working, he told me over his shoulder. "Sorry, I should have mentioned it before, but I was in a rush to get this done before he ditches the phone, or Erebus gets wind of this security breach, but I have access to everything inside your phone right now."

I waved my hand. "I figured that much. It doesn't bother me. I have nothing to hide."

"No, you really don't, do you?" he said, a smile in his voice.

"What?" I asked, amused.

"Just that you really are an open book. You don't hold things back. What you see is what you get. There's no pretense with you. You're wide open."

"You think it's foolish, right? To put that much of myself out there? Not to wear a metaphorical mask? Especially with all the shit I'm caught up in here in our down and dirty world, the mafia of it all?"

He stared out at me for a moment before returning his resolute gaze to his screens.

But, being the insane multitasker that he was, he continued on with our conversation, telling me, "For most of the time that I was pursuing Lynch, I had to construct elaborate façades to keep my loved ones off the trail, to keep them from even knowing how much what had happened in that hellhole was still impacting my every fucking waking moment. It wasn't just my actions that I had to do that with, it was *me*. The version of me that I showed them was a façade too. I created multifaceted smokescreens. I was as far from an open book as you can possibly get. I was basically in survival mode—and attack mode. It caused a hell of a lot of shit for those who cared about me, and for me as well. Now those smokescreens are no longer necessary, I can be open, I can let go." He reached out and gave my shoulder a squeeze. "So, seeing this from you, it gives me hope that it can be done. Honestly, I think it's courageous, Julian. It's fucking incredible."

I grasped his hand on me. "Thank you."

He smiled, then pulled away to give his full attention back to what he was doing.

A few moments passed, and then he thrust his fists in the air. "Got the motherfucker."

18

~Emilio~

Angelo had been found.

That demented piece of shit had slipped up.

While I was obviously glad that had happened, it was biting at me that it had been because of his twisted obsession with Julian. He was so far gone where that was concerned that he'd actually reached out to him in a risky way, one that Levi had been able to use to our advantage.

Mine and Nico's meeting with Carlo and Remo regarding the ongoing progress of our war, as well as outlining plans for when Nico officially took power, details concerning the alliance between the new Marchetti Syndicate under Nico and the Benzino Family, had been interrupted when Julian had burst on in to inform us that Angelo had been located.

I'd been on the verge of both confirming and announcing all at once that I would be taking on the role of Underboss at Nico's recommendation. At his wish, actually.

There'd be time for that later.

Besides, I guess I was running on the high of the

success of the operations the other night, excitable and impetuous. I hadn't even had a talk with Nico alone to confirm my intention to take on the role, and yet I'd been about to announce it to others?

I was used to treading so carefully, but that had loosened in me with all we'd been through since this had kicked into high gear ever since the marriage directive had been put out there alongside the news of that ridiculous Marchetti-Leone alliance. I'd *had* to loosen up in that respect in order to keep pushing forward when things had gotten out of control because of the demented enemies we'd been dealing with. There had been a lot of pivoting. There'd been no true safe way to approach anything.

And, yeah, all of that might have actually had a knock-on effect that was positive—it had enabled me to loosen up in other areas with our foursome. To enjoy things, to enjoy *us*.

But now, as I stood staring at surveillance footage of Angelo Simone, that protective, unyielding and uncompromising part of me was threatening to rise up like a beast of a thing and take control of all other facets.

The workarounds that Levi had put in place regarding his tracking program to predict their movements had paid off when it came to Angelo.

That demon's mistake had led to Lev not only being able to locate him in real-time, but to also build on that with his program and backtrack a lot of his movements.

Apparently, Angelo hadn't gotten the memo that using his phone even to check his map app was also a risk, not just outright communication like calls and texts.

It was clear that our takedowns had also unsettled him in a major way. So much so that he'd actually even tried to reach out to Victoria Munsen and, being unable to do so because she was in jail now, he'd tried to activate previous

Leone Family connections and influential persons to pull her out. Of course, those people were no longer working for the Family and we'd hidden most of them away, too. Well, forced them into hiding was closer to the truth.

Angelo was learning that he didn't have the power he'd believed, that the throne he'd thought he'd simply be able to take when he returned was fucking gone.

Although, there was still Leo Marchetti and Erebus, so until they were also dealt with, there was still a chance that Angelo could use them and their resources to resurrect the Leone Family and forge it in his own design, to his own liking.

He was the only enemy left to take power from a Leone perspective. Erebus, given their ghost status, wouldn't want to take such a public position, one that would garner them attention.

Unless their goal was to permanently settle and come out of the shadows. Because we couldn't access their communications network, or even pull up anything substantial concerning them, we weren't certain. We didn't have the full picture.

But what we did know, right here and now, was that there was now a viable way to get to Angelo himself.

Albeit, a highly dangerous way that would put Julian right at the center of it.

A way that would also have him facing off with his torturer.

I looked out at him as Levi impressed upon Nico that this intel was time-sensitive, that we couldn't sit on it for long and deliberate, or we'd lose this shot.

Julian wasn't showing an ounce of hesitancy. All I was getting from him was resolute determination. He was ready to do this. More worryingly, he needed to. He believed that the key to liberating himself from the burden that Angelo's sickening actions had put upon him was to rewire the power balance between him and Angelo, and to then have the motherfucker put down and erased from the world.

Nico snatched up Julian's phone and read over the text exchange again.

Once had been more than enough for me. I'd barely been able to stand it even then.

"You told him you'd meet him tomorrow night at a location he intended to withhold until the last moment," Nico uttered aloud.

"Yeah. I didn't want to pass up an opportunity to get at him, even if it wasn't ideal. I figured I'd come to you guys, and we'd figure out a plan to mitigate the risk," Julian told him.

"What if it's a trap?" I put to them.

"Well, it clearly is a trap to draw Julian to him," Nico said.

"No, I don't mean his texts with Julian. I mean him using his personal phone that's outside Erebus' protection, so we were finally able to track him. So he can draw Julian to him *and* also have us murdered at the same time, because Erebus could be in on this. They could've struck a deal with him where he gets Julian and they get to take us out. No more Marchetti Syndicate under Nico, no more obstacle to whatever their overarching goal is within the city."

"It's a possibility," Levi admitted. "And that's always going to be the case until we are able to pull intel about Erebus and their intentions. There's a massive gap that leaves us vulnerable. I need Rina back here to work with me on this, *and* we also need Stover. Remember, he was able to see them coming before they showed up at the hospital. How? He clearly has deeper and more comprehensive intel on them."

"We wait for them to return and we could miss our shot against Angelo," Julian said. "Like Levi said, he has eyes on Angelo for now. He has his location. But that could shift if we delay."

"Through being able to backtrack Angelo's movements, Levi also has the location of several safehouses that Erebus has used to keep Angelo safe. Yet, we can't move on all of those at this point, not without leaving our foothold in the city vulnerable. I can't send my soldiers hundreds of miles outside the city to take that on," Nico told us. "Ripping the safehouses out from under them here was one thing, this is another."

"You need to protect your territory first and foremost," I agreed. "Especially if this is a trap, not just to take us out, but to compromise our power here and use it to rise above the blows we've just dealt them all. They know there's an emotional component to the Angelo of it all for us. It would be strategically sound for them to try to exploit that to their advantage."

"Then we use the *emotional component* against Angelo," Julian proposed.

"How?" I asked.

"I take the chip to the place he held me captive, lead him there, and bring him back to the city by extension, the heart of *our* power now. The only issue is, despite this slipup, he's not a total fool, he'll know if I'm not alone. At least at first until I'm able to distract him and hold his undivided attention."

"Yes, I doubt he'd move in and emerge from the shadows until he lays eyes on you," Nico said.

"It also stands to reason that he could have picked up

some of Erebus' evasion tactics. The thing with the phone notwithstanding," Levi pointed out.

"Sunshine," I said, walking to him and drawing him away from Lev and Nico by the monitors. "That would leave you within his reach all alone without immediate backup. For us not to be seen, we're talking about us being several minutes away."

"I know." He laid his hand on my shoulder. "I can handle it. I can handle *him.*"

"It might not even work," Nico told us. "According to Levi's intel, Erebus soldiers aren't with Angelo at this very moment in time. It's him in an apartment block in a small town only seventy miles outside the city. But that could only be temporary. They could be busy elsewhere, deployed elsewhere and set to return at any time. Also, they could be tracking his movements as a means of protection—or to protect themselves from possible betrayal from him—which would mean even if he did follow the chip when he saw it moving toward that emotionally relevant location to him, they could follow *him.*"

"Then have your soldiers at the ready," Julian said.

"J—"

"Nico, we at least need to try this. And *I'm* honestly prepared to. I'm in a good headspace. I'm strong." He looked out at both of us. "I just need the two of you to trust in that, trust in *me.*"

Goddammit.

I had seen him handle that Victoria Munsen situation extremely well.

He'd done so well entering the field again.

He'd even handled the whole thing of Angelo's messages tonight well.

And I'd also seen the changes in him lately in many other ways.

I'd seen him recovering.

Nico flipped his Zippo on and off as he absorbed and analyzed everything.

As he looked out at me in question as to where I stood on it all, I gave him a discreet chin lift.

He pocketed his lighter and stepped up to Julian. "I told you before that you being used as bait to draw out Angelo was off the table."

"I know, but—"

"*But* things have changed."

Julian started in surprise. "You're saying—"

"I'm saying it's a go."

"Thank you. I won't screw this up. It won't be like last time."

"I know it won't. I know you've got this." He laid his hand on his shoulder. "Now go get suited up. Heavy-duty tactical gear, Julian. I'll get the chip. It's in Caterina's room."

That was it then.

It was happening.

As much as it fucking worried me, I also understood how badly Julian believed he needed to do this.

As Julian headed out, Nico told Levi, "Get him set up on COMMs for this. I don't want him out of contact for even a second."

"Got it," Levi said, pushing out of his chair and setting about getting the tech ready.

"You all right?" Nico asked, coming to me.

"He needs to do this. And he's earned our trust back. I just hope he's right, and that this *is* the closure he needs to move on further."

"I hope so, too."

The truth was, we couldn't be sure. Even Julian couldn't.

As much as I hated to admit it, some things couldn't be anticipated. They just had to happen.

But no matter how it played out, we'd be here.

We wouldn't fucking let him fall.

More than could be said for Angelo.

He wouldn't make it out alive.

This would be the last night he drew breath.

19

~Julian~

It had worked.

Nico had sent a couple of his soldiers to the house where I'd been kept, and they'd planted the tracking chip and also set up some specialist tech that Lev had been able to get his hands on really quickly from his father's company, Knightsridge Engineering, which prevented a signal jammer or any sort of signal interference from being activated. One of the conditions of me doing this was that the boys had contact with me throughout, and they weren't going to take the chance of Angelo screwing with that.

Not ten minutes after the chip had been left here, Angelo had been on the move.

He hadn't texted me. Maybe it was because he thought he'd give away the fact that he'd tagged me with that fucking tracking chip, and he didn't want to give up what he believed was his ace in the hole when it came to me— his way to always find me whenever he wanted. Or maybe it was the pull of this fucking place and what it meant to him in his warped mind.

Either way, at least I hadn't needed to deal with putting

on a pretense by responding favorably or even entertaining any more of his sickening messages at all.

As I took in the house that was in renovation mode, some walls torn down, debris over the decrepit floors, there was no recollection for me whatsoever. I didn't remember coming in here because I'd been unconscious, both on the way in and on the way out.

The only part of the place I remembered was that room.

The room he'd kept me bound in the entire time.

His prison.

I didn't like referring to it as a BDSM dungeon, because it was an insult to the entire fucking concept, everything that the lifestyle stood for. He had absolutely no understanding of it. To say it was warped for him didn't begin to cover it.

It was a sexual torture chamber created by an unhinged psychopath's demented fantasies.

"How are you doing, Sunshine?"

His voice in my ear had me jolting from my thoughts.

"Fine. All good."

"You don't need to go anywhere near that room. Just being in this house is enough."

"Yeah, okay. No worries."

I peered down the corridor past the living room, seeing a staircase in the distance. I remembered them telling me that the *room* had been upstairs at the far end of a corridor.

"We're almost in position now. We'll be just minutes out."

"Understood. Good. And Angelo?"

"Levi's tracking him. Fifteen minutes away."

"All right."

The communication ended as I figured he was getting into position with Nico and their soldiers nearby.

I started tapping my foot as I stood in what I assumed

was passing for a living room, despite it being in no state currently to support any sort of *living* going on.

The more I just waited in the same place for that madman to show up, the more anxious I became.

I couldn't.

I couldn't just stand still.

Before I knew it, I found myself venturing down that corridor.

Even that wasn't enough, and then I was climbing the stairs as well.

As I reached the landing and stared at the door in the distance, the one with the keypad door lock that I'd heard the others describe when they'd talked about my rescue mission when they'd thought I hadn't been within hearing range, I realized me starting to walk through the house was about more than trying to allay my building anxiety.

I was being drawn there, specifically to that room.

I needed to step inside again, to be there.

I needed to face it.

I had to confront what haunted me.

And now I was right here, I realized that wasn't just Angelo.

It was the torture chamber itself, too.

A part of me was urging me to turn back around, warning that it was a bad idea. And not just psychologically either.

I mean, I was technically supposed to stay near the exits, so that shortly after Angelo saw me and was drawn inside, I would be able to keep a distance between us until Nico, Milo, and their soldiers moved in and swarmed him.

Before he was able to get too close.

Before he was able to lay a hand on me.

Before he was able to do a fucking thing.

Jesus.

I made my way down the corridor.

I still had time to get back to one of the exits downstairs.

Reaching the door, I found it ajar, so the lock wasn't an issue.

I sucked in a breath and pushed it the rest of the way open, then stepped across the threshold.

The place had definitely been sanitized. There was no trace of anyone ever being here. No blood or... other things staining the floor or the furniture. No bullet holes in the dark red walls even. Anything that might have been damaged during my rescue had been restored as though it had never been.

I guess I hadn't expected all the furniture and devices to still be here, for it to look exactly as I'd remembered it in my nightmares and waking memories alike.

Marco and Leo's soldiers had been sent in to do the cleanup, their goal to make it look like Nico hadn't interfered with Angelo at all, because it had been a Leone matter as far as both families had been concerned. They'd been afraid of stepping on Santino's toes, so they'd made everything look exactly as it had beforehand, leaving no trace of the rescue and the damage done during it at all.

It was fucking eerie.

Why hadn't Santino gotten rid of this place when the truth had come out, when Angelo had disappeared into the ozone?

It was insulting and fucked-up that they'd not only kept the room, but the building itself, instead of tearing it down. It was like a creepy fucking shrine to Angelo *and* his sickening activities, like support for it all.

The chains hanging down from the ceiling near the center of the room, the ones that had held me, were still there, along with another set of chains on one wall, the St. Andrew's Cross opposite, the spanking bench and stocks.

And then my attention was drawn to the bed in the corner.

I shuddered at the sight of it.

"It's okay. It's over now. I'm gonna get you out of here."

"Cat…. Go. Run."

"No, I'm not leaving you."

I ran my hand over the black cabinet by the door. The tools that had been on it before were gone, likely inside the drawers themselves. Not something I relished finding out.

Then I walked over to the chains and touched the metal.

"It will prove impossible for you to resist soon enough. Mmm, yes, you'll break for me so beautifully."

I stepped back from them and took in the rest of the space and the memories associated with it all. I tried to deal with one aspect at a time, but it all came slamming into me at once.

"Argh! Argh! Argh!"

"Jesus," I choked, taking a staggering step back.

No. I wouldn't let it rule me.

And I wouldn't let Angelo's take on it control the narrative.

He'd twisted it, reframed things, and he'd tried to etch that into my mind, skewing my memories.

Now I was here again and remembering, with it being all the more vivid, I was actually able to see it for what it really had been, and not his version of things that he'd managed to make me believe. I wasn't in a weakened physical state anymore. I wasn't on the verge of delirium like I had been then.

My mind and body were strong.

I was steady.

"You'll never survive this. I promise you that."

"I'll kill you."

He hadn't succeeded.

He'd pushed and pushed in a truly demented and unyielding way when I'd been severely compromised.

"You were playing me? After all we've done together?"

And still he hadn't gotten from me what he'd wanted, what he'd been downright obsessive about.

He'd failed.

And *I* hadn't fucking broken.

I really hadn't.

"Julian? Julian, do you copy?"

"The op is compromised. Do you hear me? Julian? Get out now!"

I jolted at Nico's voice coming down the line this time, the sheer urgency in it sending a flood of adrenaline through me.

I must have been spacing out and too deeply immersed.

I tapped my earpiece. *"I'm here, Nico. Sorry. What's happening? You said the op is compromised?"*

As he went to respond, I heard yelling, thuds, crashing, and hell knew what else in the background.

"The fucking ghosts came out of nowhere. We're under attack. Get out of there. We won't make it in time to back you up. They're blocking our way. It could be a diversion to back up Angelo too or to take him out. Their motives are unconfirmed at this time. You have two minutes before Angelo arrives. Get out now."

Before I could get a word out in response, he added, *"Connect with Levi. He'll guide you out of the area unnoticed by Angelo. But that motherfucker is close. You need to leave right fucking now. Do you hear me, J?"*

I swallowed hard. *"I hear you, yeah."*

I heard more yelling in the background, screams and

automatic fire, and then he was gone, cut off, or—*no, don't go there.*

It was Nico Marchetti we were talking about. In battle, the guy was a fucking machine, a dark and twisted warrior. And he was also with Milo. An unstoppable combination. They were fine. They had this.

They *would* be absolutely fine.

They had to be.

It couldn't be any other way.

Focus up, Carver!

I didn't even get the chance to make the connection to Levi, before he found his own way in, his voice sounding in my ear in the next second. *"I'm gonna talk you through escaping in a covert way that will make you undetectable to them."*

I went to start for the door, but then I pulled up short. *"Is that what you think I should do?"*

"What?"

"Would you leave right now if you were me?"

"He's inbound, Julian. Erebus struck without warning. It's not a stretch to assume that they'll follow Angelo to the house, too. The timing can't be coincidental. The attack Nico and Milo are facing has to be connected to Angelo returning to the city. Whether that's to protect him or to kill him for his reckless decision to do this and us disposing of his Leone Family support and soldiers here remains to be seen. Either way, though, it puts you in the line of fire, unless you leave now."

"If I do, all of this will be for nothing. Nico, Milo, and their soldiers will be fighting out there for nothing. The mission to take out Angelo will be a failure. We might not get another shot."

"There's always another chance."

"I can't," I said, staring at the door. *"I can't walk away from this."*

"I understand."

"Yeah?"

"You know that I do. But you need to know that if you stay, you need to put him down. You have to take his life."

"It won't be my first time going to those extremes."

"That won't make it any easier. Not for somebody like you who feels deeply, who still very much exists in the light, despite everything you've faced."

I sucked in a breath. *"I can handle this one."*

"All right, then first thing's first, get out of that room. There's only one way in and out. That door is reinforced steel and it can be locked from the inside and the outside. He could trap you within. I can't open it from my end. It's not connected to the main system."

"That won't matter if I kill him."

"There are no guarantees in combat. If you take some hefty hits, you'll need distance to take a beat, to recover. Head back to the living room and—wait. It's too late. He's there."

"What?"

"He's there, approaching through the backdoor now. Change of plans. Move across the corridor and enter the second room to your left. Go through the window on the far side. Below, there's a garage roof that will break your fall. Exit through there, then make a sharp right, and I'll guide you the rest of the way from there into a better space for the takedown."

"Yeah, okay. I'll take the fight outside."

I pushed out into the corridor, heading for the door that Levi had identified.

But as I went to turn the doorknob, then throw open the thing, something pulled me up short.

That eerily familiar voice.

"Julian, I'm here! I know you are as well. I tracked you. My method isn't pinpoint accurate, so I don't know where precisely you are inside my house. Call out to me, babe."

I hated it.

I hated that it sent a chill down my spine.

181

I hated that it impacted me at all, especially in such a striking way.

I couldn't allow it.

I couldn't fucking live with it.

"Move. Move now," Levi urged me through my earpiece. *"He's seconds out. Coming up the stairs."*

I opened the door and pushed on through.

"Playing hide and seek, my pretty little bitch? Hmm... are you in our special place?"

A shudder went through me, and I clenched my fists.

I stilled on making my way toward the window that was over on the other side of the room, just like Levi had said.

"Move. You're letting him get inside your head and impact your actions," Levi warned me.

"Jesus," I grunted, before snapping back to it and rushing over to the window.

It was one of those single hung windows, so I opened the little locks, then went to slide it up, only to find resistance.

I rapidly took it in. *"It's sealed shut,"* I reported to Levi.

"With what?"

"What?"

"What's it sealed shut with? Glue? Epoxy?"

"Don't know. Either way, I'm gonna use my blade to try to pry it open," I said, as I pulled my tactical knife.

"Depending on what it is, it could be easier to break the glass," Levi warned.

"That would alert Angelo to my precise location before we're ready."

"If you move fast enough, it will also have him following you, and chasing you to right where you want him."

He was good. Always finding solutions to insane situations and problems.

"Angelo is already alerted," a voice came from behind me, sending a full body shudder through me.

Before I could even spin around, hands were on me, digging into my shoulders, my tactical gear thankfully absorbing any damage. But then I was hissing as he ripped my earpiece out.

He hauled me across the room and then shoved me across the corridor.

A kick to my back had me stumbling through the door of the torture chamber.

I staggered around.

And there he was, leaning against the door frame with a creepy nonchalance.

His Ivy League haircut was barely intact, his blond hair in disarray. He was in his usual gray leather jacket and black jeans combo. There was a three-inch red-raw scar across his left cheek and I remembered Cat inflicting it with a whip during my rescue. His right hand was bandaged with gauze due to another injury she'd inflicted, this one being impaling his hand with a knife. He had a Beretta holstered at either hip as usual, but he made no move to reach for them. His goatee was joined by a whole lot of stubble. He looked tired and beyond just that of the dark circles under his eyes, the result of living on the run for the last while.

He opened his hand, and I saw my earpiece there. "Before you're ready? What did that mean? Is this a setup?" he asked, his creepy casualness maintaining as he asked the questions. "Because if it is, I have to warn you that your backup is being kept busy. And also, it would definitely sour our reunion to know you tried to set me up." He tapped the earpiece and brought it to his mouth, communicating, *"Stay the fuck out of this."* In the next second, he tossed it on the floor, then ground it to shit with the heel of his boot.

"Just us now, Julian." His eyes shone with disturbing lust. "The way I've been craving it for too long now."

He pushed off the doorframe and looked me over curiously. "Was that just your backup because you were afraid I'd hurt you? Is that why you're in all that heavy duty gear?" He waved his hand dismissively. "That's not why I came. It's not why I asked you to come to me either during our text conversation earlier."

"Then why?"

"Things are dicey for me right now. Your friends' recent actions have put me in a difficult position. There are no more Leone Family soldiers because of them, no force to command for me, and even the empire itself has been dismantled. There's nothing for me to take power over. I arranged our meeting for tomorrow night because I was planning to come back into the city tonight anyway to meet with Leo and strike a deal for me to temporarily share Marchetti Syndicate assets—the ones that Nico hasn't already taken possession of. Leo owes me for hooking him up with Erebus backup that's keeping him safe from the wrath of Nico because the smart fucker can't risk a massacre."

"Even if you could achieve that, if Leo agreed to that, you don't have an army. The Leone Family is gone. It's over."

"Nah, not yet. And you heading down to this house caught my attention, as you can obviously see. So now I can accomplish both my goals at once. Meeting with Leo and sorting this shit before Erebus gets to me."

"Before Erebus gets to you? They're not blocking the way to you to protect you?"

"Thanks to Nico and all of you, they've turned on me.

I'm no longer useful to them and they already weren't happy about the hit I put out on Caterina after she took Santino from me. They were willing to assist then because I was useful to them, a major in here in the city. But all that's shifted now. As they were hunting me tonight, they must've registered Nico and the rest of your *backup* in the area and looked at it as an opportunity to take that shit-head out before he can take power and then they lose Leo and their last chance to get a proper foothold here with at least one family."

"You said Leo is one of your goals. What's the other?"

The corner of his mouth turned up. "You, of course. I've come to take you with me."

"I'm not going anywhere."

He pulled his guns from his holsters and laid them down on the floor, then kicked them away over to the other side of the room. "I told you that I'm not here to hurt you. There will be no more punishment, either. I'm done with that. I made my point. I made my mark on you. Now I just want to be with you. I want you to be mine."

"That's never going to happen."

"You're wrong."

I pulled my gun, cocked it, and took aim at his fucking skull. "Am I making myself clearer *now?*"

He didn't even flinch as he stood staring down the barrel of my gun. "You're not the type of person to shoot an unarmed man, to kill in cold blood."

"You don't know enough about me to make that assumption."

"Yeah? So, this is how you want this to end? Imperson-ally? A simple bullet to the brain, and it's all done with?"

Son of a fucking bitch.

"Say I buy your denial bullshit even for a moment, Julian. Say you drew me here out of some apparent revenge. Would that be satisfied by just pulling the trigger right now? There's nothing you want to get out of your system first?"

All the intensity and the frustration and sheer rage at being in his presence again, the shit he was spouting... it finally got the best of me.

And then, I was tossing my gun away too, and lunging at him.

He didn't fight back as I grabbed hold of him and slammed him into the wall right beside the St. Andrew's Cross, the force I was using rattling his fucking bones and making him choke.

"Your words are fucking poison!" I roared in his face.

"That's it. Give me your passion," he said, moving to grasp my bicep.

I batted his hand away before he could, then grabbed his throat in a brutal grip that had him gagging, his eyes shooting wide as I severely restricted his airflow.

"It's not passion, you fucking psychopath! There's nothing on my end but hatred and disgust for what you did to me! What you *forced* on me! Our baby died because of you! Cat and Nico almost followed! You put a hit out on the woman we love!"

"Baby?" he rasped. "Caterina... was pregnant?"

"Yes, you fuck!"

"You were... the father?"

"I don't know. It doesn't fucking matter! It was our child regardless! All of ours! Our *foursome!* We're a unit, we're one. And there's nothing outside of that, no others. No one can touch that. Especially not you. All of this is a delusion! A fucking delusion! Do you hear me?"

His eyes narrowed, that nasty side of him coming out to play. "She... didn't deserve...a happy ending. She... murdered her... own father. She's a... fucking cunt. Not

186

worth… your time. Definitely not… your fucking… love."

I roared and hauled him into the stocks.

He smacked against them, and only just managed to prevent himself from crashing to the floor by digging his nails into them.

Sputtering, he turned around to face me. "You were building a family? After what you and I shared?" He gestured angrily around the room. "Right fucking here, Julian! You were with me, I know it!"

"We didn't share anything! You tortured me! You forced yourself, and a whole lot of other things, on me!"

"*No!*" he screamed. "That's not all it was!"

"You're so far gone that you can't even recognize the reality of it."

"You saw into me! When I told you about Santino, you got it! You understood! You saw beneath all the rest! You're the only one!"

"And maybe I could have helped you. *If* you hadn't abused me. If you hadn't subjected me to that sickening shit. That's the fucking sad part of this whole thing. I warned you. I told you to back off, to let it go, to fucking *stop!* But you didn't. You fucking didn't."

"I didn't mean—"

"You did. And now you're trying to reframe it as something beyond that, trying to transcend what you did, trying to twist it into an act of want. Love, even. It wasn't that. If you really care for someone, you couldn't do that to them. Not under any circumstances." I stepped closer. "But you, Angelo, aren't capable of loving anyone or anything."

"Don't do this."

"Do what? Call it like it is? Put the shame you left me reeling from back on you where it actually belongs?"

I pulled my spare knife from my tactical pants. "I led

you here to end this. The only way it *can* end with some-body like you. You're too far gone. Too twisted. Incapable of seeing reason or remorse. You're dangerous to everyone I love. You've taken too much from us already. I won't let you take another fucking thing."

I sucked in a steadying breath, because my whole body was shaking with putting all of that out there, of finally confronting him with it.

"What Santino did to you… he made you into a monster. I won't allow the same thing to befall me. I didn't with what my father did to me, and I won't with what you did either. I won't let what was done to me change who I've worked so hard to become. That's *power* that I have. And nobody is gonna take that away from me. I decide who I am, not what was done to me."

He choked at my words.

Nothing came from him for several moments.

And then he blinked rapidly, squeezed his eyes shut for a moment, then looked out at me, as he uttered in broken words, "You really didn't want it, did you?"

"No."

"You didn't want me?"

"No."

"And I didn't actually manage to break you, did I?"

"No."

"It was just torment to you?"

"Correct."

"And it haunts you now?"

"What do you think?"

"I *think* it's too late," he said, staring out at me intensely. Emotion welled in his eyes. "For me. There's nothing left now. The Leone Family is gone. Santino is dead. You really see me as nothing but your abuser and tormentor. Your fucking rapist. I thought… I didn't see it that way. I thought you just needed convincing, to be pulled from a whole lot of denial. But… it wasn't… it wasn't that." His gaze darted back and forth from my blade to me. "I'm sorry. I'm *sorry*, Julian."

Commotion sounded downstairs, jolting me from his startling words.

"They're here already. I won't make it to Leo." He wiped his eyes with the back of his hand. "You're right, it *is* over now."

With the distraction of the commotion, heavy footsteps rushing through the house, yells sounding out, I was caught off guard when he suddenly grasped my knife-wielding hand.

Then, stunning me more, he held onto it as he lowered himself to his knees.

"I was right about one thing. It's not in you to kill a man in cold blood. I can see the look in your eyes. I can feel it from you." His fingers tightened around me, sending a shudder through me. "You'll still be haunted, though. You won't be free of it. It has to be this way."

Before I could even process what he was saying, he wrenched my hand forward, forcing the knife through his chest, driving the blade deep right into his fucking heart.

His eyes shot wide, and he grunted. "They're… coming. *Run.*"

In the next second, he twisted it for good measure.

With a roar, he yanked it out, then released it, and me, by extension.

He collapsed onto his back, struggling for breath.

Dying.

And I stood there watching him fade away.

Watching my tormentor leave this world until the last of the light in his eyes snuffed out.

I took a staggering step back.

Seconds was all I had to process it before I heard heavy footsteps reaching the corridor and coming in hot.

I managed to get a grip, and I leapt toward my gun, snatching it off the floor and cocking it, just as two guys wearing red and black hockey masks made it to the threshold.

I fired off two rapid shots, driving through their masks, shattering those and their skulls beneath in the process, and they dropped hard right there.

But there was no relief to be had, because as I carefully peered down the corridor, I saw another six rushing down.

I fired, managing to drop another with a chest shot, but no others as they opened fire.

Automatic fucking fire.

It had me jerking back into the room for cover, just as bullets bit into the doorframe.

Fuck.

As I rapidly tried to strategize an escape that didn't involve me locking myself in the torture chamber with Angelo's dead body, considering causing some sort of commotion to dart across the corridor and make it to the window I'd originally meant to, the sound of glass shattering mixed with the automatic fire.

All of a sudden, the door of the room I'd been in earlier opened just a couple of inches, a second before something was tossed through the small space and down the corridor toward the hostiles.

I jerked back as I caught sight of them.

Flashbangs.

I was just out of range within the room when I heard them go off.

The automatic fire abruptly stopped, replaced by roars and sounds of chaos.

"Fuck!"

"It's him!"

"Ah! No!"

Ear-piercing screams rang out.

I looked out, able to see a little now, just as the door opposite flew open, and I got one hell of a shock when familiar wavy hair filled my vision.

"Cat," I breathed.

She must've really been in the zone, or she'd somehow felt me, because she swung her head toward me quickly and winked, before firing down the corridor at the hostiles.

Mere seconds passed before everything went eerily still.

I stepped out to see Cat and a man I recognized as Joseph Stover standing over all the dropped bodies.

They were both clad in tactical gear, like me.

I watched Stover rub her shoulder, and she smiled up at him.

"Cat!" I called, unable to help myself, or the intensity that came out with that one word.

She jolted and turned around.

And then she was running toward me.

I bolted forward too, and we met halfway, throwing our arms around each other.

"Jesus, darlin', I've missed you. We've fucking missed you so much," I uttered, emotion bleeding from me as I held her to me tightly.

"I've missed you, too," she responded, as emotionally as me, burying her face in my chest and clutching me to her.

I couldn't believe it.

She was here.

She was actually here!

Our reunion was interrupted by Stover's voice, all-business, as he said, "Nico and Milo are fine. Unharmed. I saw to it. A few of their soldiers suffered minor injuries."

I looked out at him in question.

Cat assured me, "They're good. He sniped down the remaining hostiles."

"*They're* well. *You're* here. Angelo's gone," I murmured, trying to take it all in.

But I couldn't in that moment.

All I could do was hold her to me and keep holding her.

20

~Nico~

It had taken too long.

Every second that had elapsed since Julian had called to notify us that Caterina had returned had been too fucking long.

But I hadn't been able to leave my men.

Five of them had been injured in that clash with the Erebus operatives who'd ambushed us out of nowhere like the interloping ghosts that they were.

My soldiers were my responsibility to see to.

To ensure they received medical treatment, that they were well, that their families were informed and comforted when anything befell them like it had tonight, and that they were also compensated while they were recovering and unable to work.

No one else could fulfill that duty for me. It had to be the Boss.

At least, that was the way I saw it, and the way I would ensure it would always be under my rule.

With that all in play, it had taken me three hours to pull back into Charon Manor.

It would have taken even longer if I'd had to coordinate the cleanup in that hell house of Angelo's, but Stover had taken care of that. It was something I needed to confirm with Levi, though. I certainly wasn't going to trust Stover's word. He was an outsider, as far as I was concerned. An outsider who had taken Caterina from us. Yes, the circumstances had been complicated and multifaceted, but I wasn't fool enough to not notice that he'd manipulated her in part to achieve that.

I'd sent Milo home right after the battle, while I'd dealt with everything else.

I knew he'd been incredibly on edge about Julian facing off with Angelo, and he'd wanted to be there as soon as possible, basically as soon as Angelo had arrived. With that being unable to happen because of the ambush we'd faced, it had only exacerbated everything for Milo. Then the news of Caterina showing up had intensified everything.

As I finally pushed through the doors and back into the house, I didn't feel any of that intensity. Things were quiet. A calm ease.

At first glance, anyway.

I ventured further into the house, beyond the entryway, and voices reached me.

It sounded like they were coming from the patio just beyond the kitchen.

As I drew closer, the pain of the wait and every other fucking thing was powerfully transcended by the sound of her voice.

More specifically, her beautiful laugh.

Fuck me. That sound from her did things to me.

I stepped out onto the patio and even though I knew she was back, and I'd just heard her voice, seeing really was believing, and I just stood there staring for several moments, taking in the beautiful reality of her being here with us again.

Right where she belongs.

Caterina was in between Julian and Milo, the three of them turned sideways on one lounger, their arms around one another, while Levi leaned forward on another as they all conversed spiritedly and animatedly at that.

She was dressed down in her black Balenciaga yoga pants and a strappy white tank.

She hadn't been back long, and already she was relaxed here again.

Like she'd never left.

But that wasn't all. She was wearing one of my black hoodies against the chill of the night air.

I smiled to myself.

It wasn't just a coincidence.

She could have put anything on to warm her. But she knew me well. Knew what a possessive shit I could be, especially when something came between us, or threatened what the four of us had.

And a *lot* of that had been happening lately.

Too fucking much.

It looked like a small gesture. I mean, it was just a hoodie. But to me and from her, it was a whole lot deeper than that.

It was her reassuring me.

It was her showing me that she was mine; she was ours, that nothing had changed with the physical distance between us lately.

"It sounds like *you* broke *him*," Milo was telling Julian.

Julian looked deeply pensive. Rarely a good thing with him.

Tonight had been a lot for him, no doubt. What he'd

done, facing that the way he had, it had been a hell of a thing. A major feat. A triumph. He hadn't only shown great courage, he'd maintained control. He'd been smart about it. He'd held his own exceedingly well, too.

"He was already in broken pieces after being under Santino's rule for so many years. He just finally realized that, instead of living in the delusion he'd concocted," Julian said.

I saw Milo taking his words in.

Caterina reached out and stroked Julian's hair. "It's over. He's gone. He's finally gone."

"Yeah," Julian said, smiling out at her. He eyed Levi. "Thanks for being there. You know, in my ear, and all that?"

"No problem."

"I know I didn't make it easy."

Levi lifted a shoulder. "You did what you needed to. And it all worked out." He eyed Caterina. "Your timing was killer, sweetheart."

"Yeah," Julian said. "When those fuckers showed up… if it hadn't been for those flashbangs… Jesus."

"Hey," Caterina exclaimed. "You dropped two of them in mere moments. You were handling it well. Amazingly well."

"Still. You coming in when you did, *and* how you did, was perfect." His eyes hooded. "And it was also hot as hell, darlin'."

"*Hot as hell,*" Milo chuckled to himself.

"Is that so?" Caterina teased him back.

Levi chuckled and rose from his lounger. "And I'm out. It's clear where this is heading, and I've got my own video call fuck session to get to." As he passed by, he laid his hand on Caterina's shoulder, and told her earnestly, "I'm glad you're back. See you in the morning."

She grasped his hand on her and smiled up at him. "Thank you for everything you've done here while I've been gone. For saving my life too, Levi. I don't know how to repay—"

"There's no repayment between true friends, Rina."

With that, he grinned, gave a chin lift to Milo and Julian, then turned on his heel.

As he headed off the patio, he caught sight of me.

"Don't worry about the cleanup. I checked, and it *was* completed by Joe and done well. You don't need to concern yourself with it. Just enjoy your night, and Rina being back with you."

"Thank you. Truly."

"Of course."

"Enjoy your night, too."

"I'll try to keep the noise down."

"You're on the other side of the house to where we'll be, so be as loud as you want."

"It's not me I'm worried about." He smirked to himself, then took off back into the house.

And then I was across the patio in the next few seconds.

No more waiting.

I was just a couple of feet out when Caterina noticed me.

And then she was basically leaping from the lounger at me.

I caught her and hoisted her up against me as she wrapped her thighs around my waist.

Our mouths clashed, hot and heavy.

I could barely fucking breathe through the intensity of it.

But I didn't care. Not for a moment.

All that mattered was her being here, having her

wrapped around me again, breathing in her familiar scent, feeling that connection again.

My hands were all over her in seconds, touching every fucking inch of her as our lips and teeth clashed, our tongues dueling like it was the first and last time all at once.

It took me near superhuman strength just to pull back and break our kiss. "Are you—I mean, have you recovered enough to—"

"Am I good to go for a hard and dirty fucking?" she asked, as she dropped down from me and took a step back, shoving a hand through her now mussed-up hair a couple of times. She clearly needed the distance to be able to think and summon any semblance of rational thought, too. And I fucking loved it.

She looked out at the three of us. "I'm good. Healed up. You don't need to worry where that's concerned. I promise."

I went to reach for her, to put an end to the disconnect again after she'd stepped back like that.

But she took another step away and even held up her hand.

"What's wrong?" I asked.

"Nothing. It's just… we need to talk about—"

"No talking. Not about anything. Not tonight."

"I hear you. And, believe me, I know where you're coming from. But there *is* something we need to—"

I snarled and grasped her hips, shoving her onto the patio table.

I smacked her thighs apart and a cute little gasp of undeniable excitement escaped her.

I stepped between them as I loomed over her, breathing her in. "*Principessa*, there's no rational thought for me right now. You're here within our reach after far too long. You're ours and the need to reestablish that, to lay claim all fucking over you, is all I can see, all I can think about, all that's currently driving me. It's only through sheer force of will—and a little decency too—that I haven't already pulled my knife, shredded your clothes to pieces, shoved you down on the hard stone floor on your hands and knees and slammed deep inside your sweet cunt, then fucked you like an animal."

A little tremble of need went through her.

Yeah, she was on the same page.

In my peripheral vision, I saw Julian with his eyes hooded looking out at us, and Milo digging his fingers into the lounger to prevent himself from losing his shit, too.

"Do. You. Understand. Me?" I ground out, growling each word with how on edge I was.

I trailed my fingers over the tops of her breasts in her sexy little tank.

But then she snatched my hand and stopped me.

A loud, exaggerated throat clearing behind me drew my attention.

I swung my head to see Joseph Stover standing there.

As if that wasn't enough of a surprise, there was the fact that he wasn't still decked out in his go-to tactical gear and armed to the hilt, the way we'd known him this entire time.

He was dressed down in just a pair of blue jeans and a teal T-shirt. In casual and relaxed attire. In *our* home.

Before I could get a word out to demand what the shit he was still doing here, considering it was my understanding that he'd disappear back into the ozone after finishing his cleanup and facilitating Caterina's return to the city, he glared out at the sight of me looming over Caterina, and bit at me, "*Fuck her like an animal?* Do you believe that's any way to treat the woman you supposedly love? Especially after everything she's endured of late?"

What the ever-loving fuck?

What was this interference? In *our* lives, our personal lives?

"That's not your concern," I ground out.

Julian rose from the lounger, blatant hostility coming off him. He'd developed a dislike of Stover ever since their interaction during the Shawn Price takedown. "And you clearly have no comprehension of the dynamic between the four of us." His eyes narrowed dangerously. "Nor should you. Nor will you ever."

I eyed Milo. "Why is he still here? And why wasn't I informed?"

Milo pushed off the lounger and held up his hand. "Let's just take a moment to allow cooler heads to prevail."

"That's not answering my questions."

"I didn't tell you *yet* because you had other priorities. You were dealing with a lot. It wasn't the right time. As for why he's still here, he has knowledge of Erebus that we need."

"That's far from being the only reason that I'm here," Stover spoke. "Nor the only reason that I will remain here for the foreseeable future."

The guy had some balls.

"*Vaffanculo,*" I muttered under my breath.

"Nico, it's okay," Caterina said, hearing me.

She pressed her hands to my chest, but eased me back in the process so she could get down from the table and remove me from between her thighs.

As if that was going to help the situation.

Why was she allowing this unwanted interloper to have any power here? Over us?

I grasped her hand tightly, as I seethed at Stover, "You

took her away from us for long enough. That won't be happening again."

"Took her?" he scoffed. "Do you really think anyone can make Caterina do something she doesn't want to do?"

"In the state she was in when you showed up, yes. And you fucking well knew it. You manipulated the situation to your advantage. You manipulated her."

"I did what was needed to keep her safe. Something *you* couldn't accomplish."

Son of a bitch!

I pulled from Caterina and burst toward the motherfucker.

"Nico, stop!" I heard her calling out to me.

The fuck I would.

Blood was roaring in my ears as I went at him.

The arrogant shit moved forward, too.

I was just two feet from him when the mass of muscle that was Milo blocked my path.

But then Julian was there, right there with me, wanting to put the piece of shit down as well.

Milo shoved a hand to both of our chests, holding us back.

That wasn't going to last.

"Move," I bit out. "Fucking now, Milo."

"God, stop! Stop it! All of you!" Caterina cried.

The distress coming from her cut into me, and it actually managed to jar me.

She rushed over to us, and then rounded us to get to Joe.

"This isn't what you agreed to," she told him, standing right in front of him while he was primed for a fight. "You promised me, Joe. You promised me you'd respect my wishes when it comes to my men. This is the fucking opposite of doing that."

"What I heard when I walked out here——"

"It was private. You came out here like a ghost and overheard *and* witnessed an intimate moment between me and Nico." She grasped his arm. "What you heard was Nico expressing how much he'd missed me. It just wasn't done to your liking. But, for the record, it was to mine. They don't treat me like I'm weak or fragile. They treat me like the equal and the warrior that I am. There's no pretense between the four of us. It's raw and open. And sometimes that comes out in explicitly erotic ways, animalistic ways. And that part of my relationship with them isn't your concern. For your own peace of mind, you need to stay away from that entirely."

What was happening?

Why was she taking the time to explain all of this to him?

I could see that she wasn't the shadow of herself anymore, that she had been the night she'd left, the night he'd spirited her away from the chaotic hell that had been bearing down on her at the time. She was a little off, but nothing like she had been. So she had to have recognized his manipulation too by now. So why was she seemingly giving him a pass?

"I just... hearing that... it unsettled me. Concerned me," he uttered, his voice now calm. He even relaxed his stance and took a step back.

"There's no concern necessary. The three of them are with me. They love and adore me. I promise. There's just been a lot of buildup with me being away. It's been hard for all of them."

The surprises kept on coming when Stover looked out at me and said, "I apologize. It was also no fault of your own that she couldn't be kept safe here at the time. There were a lot of factors at play."

I stepped back from Milo. Julian did the same.

"What's going on, Caterina?" I pressed.

She turned from Stover, so she was looking out at all of us at once. Sucking in a breath, she revealed a hell of a thing. "Joe is my biological father."

What. The. Fuck?

21

~Emilio~

Well, this explained a lot.

Certainly Stover's actions regarding Caterina and definitely his *re*actions outside a few moments ago.

I mean, no father wanted to overhear his daughter being talked dirty to. Especially not being told she was going to be fucked like an animal by Nico. *Damn.*

I wasn't sure that was the way to go anyway, so I was glad, in a way, that the whole thing had been interrupted. I'd rather it have been interrupted by Levi, and not the antagonistic dickhead that was Joseph Stover, but it was what it was.

I knew Nico was on edge and extremely worked up, especially sexually. He hadn't had any relief in that respect since she'd been gone, either. And I also happened to know that he didn't take matters into his own hands, so it was even worse for him. While he did let Julian handle him once in a while, like when the four of us were in the throes of some epic fucking, and he had enjoyed playing voyeur where Julian and I were concerned before, that was about as far as it went with him. He wouldn't let it go all the way. It just wasn't his thing. It didn't do it for him.

In fact, no one had really *done it for him* in all the years that I'd known him.

Until Caterina Leone had come along.

She'd changed everything.

Finally having that, then having it taken away, essentially ripped from him lately, had been a hell of a thing to take.

And now she was suddenly back here, I could see Nico struggling with his intense possessiveness when it came to her, see him needing desperately to re-claim her as ours. It was why he'd come on so strong the moment he'd seen her. He could barely keep it in check.

No wonder he'd been knocking back the Johnny Walker Black since we'd ventured in here from the patio.

Well, trying to. Julian had already snatched the bottle from him after he'd already downed two glasses. Taking the edge off was one thing, but anything more and he wouldn't be in any state to have that much-needed *reunion* with Caterina that we were all craving.

A reunion that I really didn't think should be rough, hard, and dirty.

Not this time with her.

Yes, she'd assured us that she was physically fine, but that was only part of it. She'd been through a lot. There was also a shitload we needed to discuss that Nico and Caterina both clearly weren't willing to tonight.

I understood wanting to bypass all the complications and just be together again. So long as that was the extent of it and they didn't try to go beyond tonight with it. But anything more and we'd have some major problems on our hands with our relationship. None of it could be simply brushed under the carpet.

As for tonight itself, I would approach Julian at the first opportunity about going the more gentle route with Caterina tonight, easing her back into being with us physically. He and Nico fed off each other when we got carnal, so if he was on that track, it could work to mellow Nico, too. Also, Julian was the best person to bring this up to Nico. The two of them operated from a dominant headspace and saw things in a very similar way sexually.

I really believed, based off what I'd observed of Caterina tonight as Julian and I had been relaxing with her on the patio, that she needed to feel loved and safe tonight, not like she was our sexual prey to be devoured and overwhelmed by us.

While Julian was merely sipping at the half-full glass of vodka he'd poured himself when the five of us had convened in the kitchen, I was doing the same with my glass of brandy as I listened to both Stover and Caterina conveying all the details concerning the former being her real father, including them showing us incontrovertible proof.

"This is why you took her away," Nico grunted, still with the hostility.

I didn't really blame him with the way Stover had come off earlier.

Not to mention the manipulative shit he'd been involved in regarding the whole marriage situation.

Stover had basically challenged Nico and tried to lay down the law in his own house.

Yeah, that wasn't something Nico would ever stand for.

Not to mention, he'd had enough of that to last a lifetime from Marco and Leo.

"Wanting to get to know Caterina as my daughter was *one* of the reasons, yes," Stover admitted. "Away from other influences."

I grimaced. There it was again from him.

"Joe," Caterina admonished.

He held up a hand in apology.

But it clearly wasn't going to be the end of it.

He didn't like us with her.

Whether it was personal, or perhaps because it was a foursome situation, or he was simply pissed at having to compete for her attention at this dicey stage of him finally revealing the truth to her, I didn't know. But it was detrimental, regardless. Especially with him staying here under the same roof as us.

Which he would absolutely be doing now. I had no doubt in my mind there.

Because I knew Nico.

He wouldn't kick him out now.

Knowing that Stover was Caterina's true father with that slamming up against her awful relationship with Santino, he'd want her to find some peace with it all. He wouldn't push Stover away from her. He wouldn't do anything to deny her this.

"Other influences, hmm?" Nico said. "You mean, those in us who've been there with her, all the while *you* were busy living up to the Absentee Father of the Last Quarter Century mantle?"

Stover's eyes narrowed. "Things were more complicated than you can possibly imagine. I did what was best for Caterina."

"Yes. Leaving her to suffer under a madman sure sounds like *what was best* for her. And now, here you are playing hero."

"How dare you?" Stover bit back.

Nico stepped up to him. "You see? So keep that in mind before you come at us, before you judge us. *And* before you dare to lay down the law in *our* home."

Good. He wasn't actually intending to escalate things, as it had initially seemed. He was just making a point and putting him in his place, something that needed to happen in order for this new living arrangement to have any chance of working out. Even temporarily.

Stover studied him curiously. "Is it close?"

"Is what close?"

"Your *feral* state, as Caterina terms it?"

Nico eyed her. "You told him about that?"

Before she could answer, Stover said, "No. I've been watching you for a long while. Ever since you started playing with my daughter."

Nico folded his arms across his chest. "It's nowhere close at the moment. And if you're asking because you're worried for Caterina's safety—"

"I'm not."

"It sure sounded like it," Julian piped up. "And to be clear, it's a part of him that's not going away. So you're gonna have to make peace with it. He'd never hurt Cat. Never. Not in that state or any other. She's everything to him. She's everything to all three of us."

Stover eyed him. "Living my life the way I have, I tend to come across aggressively. I'm difficult to deal with at the best of times. I also give very little ground in any situation." He looked at Caterina for a moment, his eyes softening, before he addressed the three of us again. "As I'm sure you can all imagine, this life isn't what I want for my daughter. This brutal existence, the world of the mob and so many other dangerous elements. When I took Caterina with me, I'll admit that I did hope that I could pull her away from it, to offer her a better life. But, as she's made clear to me in no uncertain terms, it was what *I* deemed a better life, not her. And she's hellbent on staying with the three of you, that you're it for her, here to remain in her life." He sighed heavily, actually showing some sentiment too, as he went on, "My chance to give Caterina a different life died a long time ago, through decisions that me and her mother made. All I can do now is support what she's built here for herself." He rubbed his jaw. "Coming from that op earlier, then walking in on what I did out on the patio, it set me off. And I'm sorry. I'll work on it, on toning down my harsher… edges."

While Caterina smiled out at him, clearly proud he'd been able to put that out there, me, Nico, and Julian eyed one another, more than a little taken aback.

"Then why ask about my *feral* state?"

"Caterina informed me that she experiences a similar thing. It's something I believe I can help her with. Having you there sharing that could assist and possibly even help you to better control it too."

Nico looked out at Caterina. "Is that what you want, *principessa?*"

"I'm going to try to work on it, but I don't want you pushed into anything."

"Would it make you feel better?"

She nodded.

He turned back to Stover. "We'll talk then."

"Good."

"But not tonight. No more of anything tonight. The four of us need some time together as I'm sure you can imagine given that we've been apart from the woman we love for weeks. I have no doubt that you need to get some rest, too."

"I set him up in the room a few doors down from Milo's," Caterina spoke. "I hope that's okay that I—"

"It's absolutely fine," Nico told her.

Now he'd calmed down quite a bit, it was clear he'd recognized what I had when it came to Caterina. What she needed right now, that she was a little off, a little over-whelmed, that there was a lot that was unspoken that she hadn't yet voiced. That she needed care, understanding, and love, not a fucking ravaging.

"I'm just going to help him to get settled, show him where some key things are around this massive place," she told us.

"No problem," I said.

"No rush, Cat."

"We'll be upstairs making sure you have everything you need in your room, make sure everything's good now you're back," Nico told her.

"Thanks," she said, although she looked a little confused.

No wonder. There wasn't anything to do other than change the sheets, seeing as though the same set had been on the bed since she'd been gone.

As we watched her leave the kitchen and lead Joe out, Nico waited until she was out of earshot, then told us, "What should we do about the nursery?"

"You mean, either lock it up, or leave it be so she can venture inside?" I asked.

He nodded, then admitted with a rare vulnerability that I'd only ever seen with him when it came to a dicey Caterina matter, "I don't know the best way to approach it, what will be the best way for *her.*"

"We shouldn't hide it," Julian stated. *"If she does try to cut you out, it's not through lack of care or love on her part. It's pain. A lot of fucking pain."* He eyed Nico. "You told us that's what Lev said to you, right?"

"Part of it, yes."

"That she might try to shut down," I mused. "Part of her agreeing to go with Stover was her doing that."

"Exactly. We need to try to prevent her from slipping

back into that now she's here with us again," Julian said. "We're obviously direct reminders of the baby, what's been lost."

"Maybe fucking tonight isn't the way to go either," Nico uttered, the strain of him even voicing that possibility obvious.

"She needs to decide that," Julian told us. "Let her guide it. But we shouldn't hide the room. It could actually be a place that helps her to process her grief, that helps all four of us to do it together."

"If it does happen tonight, we need to take it easy," I pointed out.

"He's right," Julian said, looking at Nico.

"Take the lead."

Julian cocked an eyebrow. "What?"

"I'm too worked up. And being loving and easygoing when it comes to fucking isn't exactly my strong suit, is it?"

Julian and I grinned at each other.

"What?" Nico asked.

"You're serious, N?"

Nico frowned. "Of course."

I shook my head at him. "Nico, we've never seen you as *loving and easygoing* as you have been since Caterina came into our lives."

He shoved a hand through his hair. "All I want to do right now is unleash all fucking over her, fuck her for hours on end, be balls deep inside her as she breaks apart in ecstasy for us, to fuck her until I can't fucking move anymore."

"And you can do that," Julian told him. "Just as worshipping her, instead of as a predatory claiming, which was obviously your original go-to."

I laid my hand on his shoulder. "You underestimate yourself when it comes to the softer moments needed at times in our relationship with her. But you're definitely capable of it. You've shown it before several times. You're just second-guessing yourself because of what's happened lately, then her being taken away, then Stover coming at you."

"Stover... fuck," he grunted.

"You handled that well," Julian told him.

"I didn't want to."

"But you did it for her," I said. "See?"

The corner of his mouth turned up. "I do."

Julian grasped our shoulders, essentially forming a huddle of sorts. "She's back. She's actually back here with us."

We stared out at one another as we finally had a few moments to take in the weight of it.

"There's no fucking way we're letting her go again. Not for any amount of time," Nico ground out.

"Never," Julian agreed. "Things don't feel right anymore without her."

They sure as fuck didn't. "She's ours. Here to damn well stay."

22

~Caterina~

Things had been intense.

I'd been so focused on getting back here, on being surrounded by my men again, that I hadn't looked beyond that. I had only seen our reunion through rose-colored glasses. I hadn't entertained any of the rest when I'd imagined it. None of the complications, the pain, nothing.

I hadn't exactly left in the best way, or on the best of terms.

I'd basically taken off against what the three of them had wanted.

Had it been the right decision at the time?

Yes.

Yes, it had been.

I'd needed to get away. I'd needed to clear my head, and that wouldn't have been able to be achieved while still in the middle of all the madness that had been bearing down on me at the time. I'd also needed to heal physically, and that also wouldn't have been possible while trying to evade a fucking hit. And it had been safer for my men for

Joe and I to lead those pursuing motherfuckers away from them.

But doing that hadn't come without consequences.

To us, to our relationship.

I knew it had taken a hit and as much as they'd been playing it off and basically tiptoeing around me and being *so* careful, I knew them well now, and I could feel it from them, feel the strain.

I'd worried that bringing Joe back here with me would be trying for the guys, given the way I knew him to be when he interacted with other people, something he was only used to doing in combat or through fieldwork, not as an actual feeling human being. But I hadn't been able to bring myself to say goodbye to him, or even to send him somewhere else in the city to be nearby while we were still immersed in this war.

At least he was getting a grip now where his aggression and disapproval toward the guys was concerned. It had taken some of the weight off.

Some of it.

As I approached my room, my pulse picked up, and I started to drag my feet.

I was nervous.

We'd agreed just to be together tonight, not to get into everything. Just to relish being with each other after all that time apart.

But what if all the unspoken shit between us caused an awful awkwardness?

And what if I couldn't handle the physicality? What if it triggered my grief over the miscarriage? What if I fucked up everything? More than I already had by leaving in the first place?

Shit. I'd never felt so unsure of myself before.

It just felt like a lot was on the line when it came to our

relationship. I needed this to go well in spite of everything. It mattered *so* much to me that it did.

I reached the door and stopped outside.

And then I heard their voices.

"Waking up with her wrapped up in us tomorrow."

"Wow, N. That's the sweetest shit you've ever said."

"Nah, all bets are off when it comes to Caterina, Sunshine. He's said a lot of sweet shit about her, and to her."

I heard all of them chuckling.

"What about you, J?"

"Sitting down together and working on our partnership. Maybe her reading me a bedtime story, too."

"You're still hoping for the bedtime story thing again, huh?"

"Fuck off, big boy, you would be as well, if you knew how great it was with her. She tucked me in and stroked my hair until I fell asleep, too."

More chuckling sounded, which had me smiling, the sound warming me *and* serving to do a lot to calm me down.

"Milo? What about you? What's the thing you're most looking forward to about her being back?" I heard Nico ask.

That was what they were discussing? Wow, it was… it was amazing.

"Getting that stunned, yet excitable look from her when I make her one of her favorite foods or meals. Ah, there's also seeing her kick ass when it comes to the hacking, her and Levi going head-to-head. That's gonna be extreme."

"Yeah, it is. Our monstrous and feral sides going head-to-head should be one for the ages too."

"Or a cataclysmic event, N."

More laughing broke out.

And it was absolutely wonderful.

The next thing I knew, I was pushing open the door and stepping inside.

I closed the door behind me, and all eyes were on me in the next second.

There the three of them were, just chilling on my bed.

Julian was sprawled across one side of it, his head propped up with his elbow, his sexy chiseled chest and those nipple hoops on display, with him only wearing a pair of his cobalt-blue boxers.

Milo perched on the edge in his usual ramrod straight position in his crimson boxers and one of his go-to white tanks that really highlighted all that beautiful ink and his powerhouse muscle.

And Nico was leaning back against the headboard, his knees pulled up a little with his feet planted flat on the sheets in a pair of his black lounge pants, his tattoos and those mouthwatering abs on display.

It was quite the sight.

Highly eroticizing.

It had a hot thrill running through me.

"Sorry I took so long," I blurted out, my uneasiness as they stared at me rising up again and threatening to get the best of me.

What was happening? This wasn't me. *Get a grip.*

"You were barely ten minutes," Milo told me.

"And even if you were longer, we didn't put a time constraint on it," Julian added. "On you settling your *dad* in for the night. That's a big deal, Cat."

"Especially for you, *principessa.*"

Yeah, it was. And I was still processing it.

I smiled and walked over to the bed. "Something we can spend hours discussing in the coming days, if you all like." I winced. "Or don't like, given how it went tonight. I'm sorry he was aggressive and—"

"Don't apologize," Milo said.

"Especially not for somebody else's actions," Julian told me.

"We'll figure it all out. It won't be a problem," Nico assured me.

I stared between them. "You're all being so incredible about this, about all of it."

"Aren't we usually?" Julian jested.

"You know what I mean."

A chin lift and some sort of silent communication between Nico and Julian had the latter pushing off the bed and coming to me, while Nico looked on, scooting to the side of the bed and Milo went to sit beside him.

"We've had enough negativity lately," Julian said, reaching me and taking my hands gently. He stroked his fingers over mine, sending little sparks of need through me, just from that. It just went to show how much tension had been building up for me since I'd been away from them, from their touch. "Don't you think so, darlin'?"

"I do," I uttered, my voice unsteady, overcome by their understanding, by the intensity I could feel coming off them all, the care, the sheer level of *love*.

It was a lot to take in.

It was amazing, awe-inspiring.

And it was also heartbreaking that I'd been away from it.

Worse. That me leaving could have done something to hurt that.

To hurt *them* and what we had.

Emotion at the thought of that overtook me, and then Julian was stepping into me and wiping away some stray tears that spilled down my cheeks. "Shh. It's all right. You're all right. You're here with us now. We're with you. Let all the rest go, because we're not going anywhere."

I smiled out at him. He was always so perceptive, so

gifted at reading people, especially those close to him. He could see down really deep.

"And neither are you," Nico rumbled, pushing to his feet. "Ever again."

It was a promise and a threat all at once.

His possessive side was showing.

And I was actually right here for it with how I was feeling at the moment.

"I don't ever want to," I told them all. "That means you're all stuck with me, I'm afraid."

Julian grinned and leaned in, brushing his lips over mine. "Sounds perfect," he whispered against my lips, a moment before he swept his tongue over them, then took me in a sensual kiss that had me weak at the knees within seconds.

I ran my fingers over his chest, giving teasing tugs to his sexy nipple hoops, and it had him groaning into my mouth, his hands delving into my hair and ramping up the sensuality of it all.

Nico was there in the next moment and Julian broke our kiss so he could slide his hoodie off my body, then pull my strappy tank up over my head. A single flick to the back of my bra had it popping open.

I looked out at him in a heady daze as he surprised me by carefully easing it off me, then tossing it aside.

His striking sapphire eyes burned into mine as he pressed his big hands to my breasts and kneaded them softly, in a mind-whirling erotic way that had me panting within moments.

I caught sight of Milo grabbing three condom packets from one of the nightstands. "It's okay," I uttered, just about able to summon rational thought. "I'm still on birth control." And no complicated other medications inter-fering with it this time.

"Okay, sweetheart."

The three of them stilled for a moment, as the unspoken nature of that rolled over them.

But, fortunately, they managed to move past it, and then Julian shifted and trailed his tongue along the column of my throat, over my lips, dipping into my mouth, then teasing my lips again.

Fingers hooked into the waistband of my pants, and I turned slightly to see Milo there, his eyes hooded, as he then drew both my pants and panties down my legs, until I was stepping out of them, then standing surrounded by my men completely bared to them.

"Ready for us, baby?" Nico asked me, his voice strained, like he was struggling to keep himself in check.

But he didn't need to. I wanted it. I wanted them so badly.

I grasped one of his hands on my breasts. "Yes. Beyond ready."

In the next second, Milo trailed his hands down my stomach, then over my pussy, his fingers dragging slowly through my folds. A rush of pleasurable intensity rolled through me that had my body arching and pushing back against him. I smiled when I felt him naked behind me now, his hard dick against my ass cheeks. It had me pushing my breasts harder into Nico's hands too and turning my head to give Julian better access as he continued teasing my mouth and neck, sending trembles of bliss through me.

Nico dropped to his knees, then kissed all over my pussy, startling me yet again with his tenderness. "Fucking missed you," he uttered between kisses.

My response caught in my throat when I felt my ass cheeks being spread open, then Milo's tongue circling my asshole.

"Oh God," I choked.

At the same time, Julian trailed his tongue down to my breasts, then started biting at my nipples, sucking and teasing the hell out of them.

When Nico dragged his tongue through my folds, a cry escaped me, the three of them driving me higher and higher as I succumbed to their attentions and the pleasurable reverie they were creating for me.

It wasn't long before I was shuddering around them, and as Milo thrust his tongue inside me at the same time that Nico nibbled at my clit, ecstasy crashed into me and I writhed against them as I came screaming out into the room.

As I was still in the throes of it, Milo gathered me into his arms, and then he was laying me down in the middle of the bed. He covered my body with his, then took me in a deep kiss that had my head spinning and me clutching at his big biceps.

"Damn... missed your hot little kisses, *bellezza.*"

"I've missed yours," I said, grinning up at him and chasing his lips as he went to ease back.

I stopped him from doing that, linking my arms around his neck and holding him to me, then deepening the kiss that had a sexy rumble emanating from him.

He ground his cock against my thigh, and I bucked my hips in need.

All too soon, his cock was gone as he moved to the side, still kissing me, but no longer fully on me.

I realized why in the next second, when I felt the familiar sensation of lube being spread over my asshole.

I looked out through the kiss to see Julian there.

Then I was moaning as he added more and pushed two fingers inside, getting it nice and slick. A thrill ran through me from his toe-curling movements and the thought of where it was obviously leading.

"Keep her cunt nice and wet," I heard him say a moment before I was jolting when Nico was there again, slicking his tongue all over my pussy.

Like a whirlwind this time, making me buck on the bed and moan into Milo's mouth as our tongues tangled.

The burn in my ass became heated pleasure as Julian worked his magic with the lube, and then I was thrusting my hips and pushing harder against his fingers. "Yeah, that's right. Show us how much you want it, darlin'."

Milo broke our kiss and then I watched as he turned toward Julian on his knees and then Julian squirted lube all over Milo's cock and slicked it all over his shaft with his free hand, while his other was still pumping into my ass, teasing and pinching Milo's crown as he went until Milo was panting from it.

Nico pushing two fingers inside me had me swinging my head toward him.

He smirked devilishly as he curled them, then flicked my clit with his tongue, making me arch off the bed.

I almost came right there when Julian also jerked his fingers out of my ass, the sensation intense in the best way.

"Fuck!" I cried. "More. Please, more."

He chuckled darkly, then eased back to watch as Milo grasped my waist and hoisted me up, then slid beneath me.

A gasp of excitement escaped me as I felt his slick cock pushing at my asshole in the next moment.

He stroked my hair and my breasts as he rocked into me, filling my ass with more and more of his cock, until he was fully seated inside me.

I threw my head back against his chest, and then I was whimpering when he didn't move and just stayed still inside me letting me adjust. He was being so gentle, so careful.

They all were.

That was made even more apparent when Nico settled between my spread open thighs, grasping his rock-hard cock, and then eased inside my pussy, an inch at a time. My eyes rolled back in my head as the slow and easy of it had me feeling every moment of the fullness consuming me.

"Fucking, yes," Nico growled. "Too long. Too fucking long."

I bucked my hips, my desperation growing to unbearable heights.

I saw Nico give a nod to Milo a moment before they both started to move, alternating their thrusts.

Their deep and long thrusts, the unhurried pace ramping up the intensity several notches.

I realized then.

They weren't just being careful.

They were taking everything in, relishing being with me again.

And they were loving me.

It wasn't rough, hard, and dirty as it usually was when all four of us came together.

It was all-consuming in a whole different way. One that took my breath away and warmed me down to my bones at the same time.

My whole body trembled as pleasure engulfed me, and through the haze of it, I looked out to see Julian climbing onto the bed, now naked.

He grasped the base of his cock, and then he was rubbing his crown over my folds, titillating my clit with his piercings in a way that had me whimpering with sparks of bliss adding to all the rest.

Shit. They had me so completely.

I could barely see straight, let alone think.

It was just this. Just us in this moment together.

Just sensation. Just the utter peace of being with the three of them like this.

Julian's movements faltered, which was highly unlike him, and I turned my head to see the reason for it. Milo had reached out behind him and he was fingering his ass, stabbing rough and deep.

"Motherfucker," Julian choked, slamming his hips back and forth in a call for more, which also had his crown and piercings bumping against my clit rapid-fire.

Over and over and over.

"Shit!" I cried.

Nico and Milo's thrusts came faster and harder then, Nico fisting his hands in Julian's hair for something to ground him, while Milo fisted *my* hair with his free hand while slamming into me and Julian at the same time.

Pre-cum leaked all over my pussy and the warm, sticky sensation was another level.

In the next second, I was losing it and ramming back and forth against Nico and Milo, fighting to meet their thrusts, taking and succumbing to everything they were giving me.

"Fuck, fuck, *fuck!*" I screamed, as it all collided and pleasure wracked my body, and I came in a shuddering mess all over them.

"Goddammit," Milo grunted a moment before I felt him spurt inside my ass.

In the throes of it, he twisted his fingers inside Julian, which set him off, and then he was coming all over my pussy.

"Fuck," Nico growled, his thrusts becoming deeper and jerkier, before he then pulled out of me at the last second, then rose up and sprayed his cum all over my breasts.

Marking me like Julian and Milo.

Reclaiming me.

Just what tonight had been about for all of us.

What we'd all needed it to be about.

23

~Julian~

"I'm sorry. I'm so sorry, Julian."

I opened my eyes and for the first time in a long time, a residual feeling of pain, shame, and dread didn't follow, didn't seep into my conscious state.

"They're… coming. Run."

Things last night hadn't gone as I'd expected.

In more ways that one.

But specifically when it came to Angelo.

I'd actually managed to get through to him. He'd actually fucking heard me.

And it had broken him into pieces.

For a moment in time, he'd come out of that delusional state, or perhaps what he'd purposely convinced himself that reality was, and he'd seen the truth. It had reconnected him with his own pain and I knew he'd recognized that he'd levied that pain on to me. It hadn't just been for domination purposes, or to teach me a lesson, or whatever the fuck he'd been spouting. A lot of it had been in a bid to pass that agony of the abuse he'd suffered onto somebody else, to cast it out. In a really fucked-up way.

Passing down pain to others in order to make yourself feel better… that was a weak person's way of handling things. It was obviously the wrong way to handle it. And that was coming from somebody who'd tried many different things in the beginning after what had happened with my father, many different ways to cast all of that poison out. Many of which my therapist had classed as *unhealthy* ways.

It had taken time—and mistakes—to figure out the way that was right for me *and* also healthy.

But Angelo hadn't explored anything beyond causing damage.

Seeing him that way, seeing what had happened to him, how twisted he'd become because he wouldn't deal with it, because he'd buried it and even reformed it entirely in his mind… it had hit me deeply.

I'd been so close to burying it, too.

I wouldn't.

I wouldn't make that mistake.

I'd also thought that putting him down, watching the despicable bastard die right in front of me and by *my* hands, would give me some solace when it came to all of this.

But that wasn't what had done it.

That wasn't where the peace had come from.

In fact, I hadn't technically even taken his life. *He* had.

There *had* been peace in knowing that a threat like him was gone now, that after what he'd done to Cat and Nico, after causing the loss of our child, he'd suffered that fate.

But in the context of the kidnapping and what he'd subjected me to, that peace had come from him acknowledging what he'd done, to essentially retracting all his claims that I'd been into it, to cutting through the shame he'd left me with and then taking it on himself as it originally should have been. As it should be for anyone who subjected someone to what he had.

It was definitely a weight off. I did feel lighter.

But there was more work to be done.

And, for me, for how I now recognized I needed to go about my way of recovering, that involved returning to therapy properly. To giving my full participation.

I went to lift my arm, only to find that it was tangled up in Milo's.

I smiled as I looked across the bed where I was on one end, Milo beside me, half over me and half over Cat with Nico doing his usual spooning thing to her that had become common practice for him whenever the four of us fell asleep together. I also had my thigh draped over her leg that was across Milo's abs.

Last night had meant a lot to all of us. Having her back with us, taking our time to worship her like that, rather than going the usual dirty and animalistic route. Even Nico had managed it. Hell, he'd needed it that way too, as I'd seen him recognize halfway into it.

There was definitely more to work through, something that was no doubt going to be trying with the war we were still immersed in.

I carefully eased myself free, then slipped out of the bed.

As I did, I caught sight of the alarm clock and realized that I'd woken up incredibly early. It was barely five in the morning.

And yet I was starving. My stomach was even growling in protest.

I guess going into combat last night combined with the fucking had worked up an appetite. We'd skipped dinner with the arrival of Cat *and* Stover throwing a wrench into things in that respect.

227

Time to remedy those hunger pangs now.

I snatched up my boxers and pulled them on, then I headed out of the room.

After making my way down the staircase and nearing the kitchen, I heard grunts of frustration coming from within.

It didn't sound like Lev. I'd learned that when he was frustrated, it went hand-in-hand with a whole lot of *mother-fuckers*, not merely grunts.

I entered the kitchen and, sure enough, it definitely wasn't Lev.

In fact, the sight of Joseph Stover instead had me tensing up.

He had his back to the door, and he was sitting up at the kitchen table with a first-aid kit open before him, the contents spilled all over the place. He was just in a pair of jeans and shirtless, blood dripping down his right arm from what appeared to be a nasty stab wound, while he tried to stitch it up. Clearly, he wasn't having much luck.

"Morning," he spoke, jolting me.

He'd obviously sensed me, because I hadn't even made a sound as I walked in.

The guy was good, no doubt. Then again, living in the shadows for years and doing the work that he had, that was to be expected. Kind of a given for survival.

"You're not gonna be able to stitch that yourself. The angle is too awkward," I told him, walking over there, and gritting my teeth at the need building in me to help him. As much of an asshole as he was, he also happened to be Cat's dad.

He turned on the chair, angling himself toward me. Arching an eyebrow, he asked, "What do you know about it?"

"More than I'd like. Milo is the most skilled in this

area, but I can hold my own." I held out my hand for the needle. "Here."

He frowned and hesitated for a moment before giving it to me.

I examined the wound. It looked like it had been caused by a blade with a serrated edge. And it was deep. So deep that stitches were an absolute necessity. He'd cleaned out any dirt or debris, at least. But we'd need to get him on a course of antibiotics, too.

"This obviously happened last night, so why didn't you have it seen to?"

"There were other priorities."

"Like your daughter?"

He nodded. "Like getting her settled here again."

"So you just bled all over the place last night?"

"I'll clean it up. It's just on the sheets in the guest room."

Lovely. "That's not what I meant."

He stared at me, clueless. *Wow.* "You could have bled out. It was dangerous to your health. That sort of thing?"

He lifted his other shoulder. "I'm fine. The blood loss wasn't severe. Compression worked for most of the night."

I shifted my weight, then got down to stitching him up.

"The last person I did this for was Cat's mom."

"Bianca? Really?"

"Yeah."

"Injuries inflicted by Santino?"

I nodded. "He had her beaten. He was gonna have her killed too, if we hadn't gotten her out in time."

"Piece of shit," he growled.

"He really was."

"*Was,*" he mused. "That's going to take some getting used to."

"For all of us. Especially Cat." I looked out at him.

"Although, with you now being in the picture as her dad, that should help."

"Perhaps."

I cocked an eyebrow. "What does that mean? Are you not planning on sticking around?"

The harshness in my tone was blatant, as a surge of protectiveness toward Cat rolled through me at the idea of him leaving, of fucking abandoning her after dropping this major bomb on her.

As if she hadn't already had enough to deal with.

There was no way she was going to suffer through more.

"That wasn't what *I* meant." He scrubbed his free hand over his face. "Having me around on a more regular basis may not be beneficial to Caterina."

"You're her dad."

"And you know better than most that it can be the absolute worst thing."

He'd looked into me. No surprise there with how he'd been with us regarding Cat.

"This is different."

"I understand that it would be nice to think that, but there's a lot about me that you don't know, the way living how I have has made me. I'm not a positive influence or—"

"She doesn't need a positive influence. She's not a child. She's a grown woman who's developed her own values and direction. Caterina Leone can't be influenced. Many have tried, and all have failed." I finished the stitching and snatched up some gauze, starting to wrap the wound to protect it. "But what you *can* do is give her what you denied her long ago." Off his raised eyebrow, I spelled it out, "A choice. Let her decide what's best for herself in regard to you remaining close by or not once all this is over."

I watched him taking my words in as I saw to the gauze.

And then he smiled.

In the next second, Levi walked in, rubbing his eyes, before his gaze strayed to us, and he did a double take. "Huh," he said, as he walked to the coffeemaker and set about making some coffee. As he waited for the machine to get to work, he turned and leaned against the counter, eyeing us. "It's a good thing you didn't have Rina see to that. She's not exactly gentle where that's concerned."

"Don't I know it," Stover said.

"Really?" I asked.

"Definitely not," Levi confirmed. "She stitched me up once and it was almost worse than suffering the damage from the injury itself. Fucking shit."

"She sees it as a task that needs accomplishing ASAP," Stover explained. "She disconnects from all the rest when she's in that frame of mind."

"Well, that may have altered now. She used to be like that with Camlann Corporation too, but she's let a lot more into her life now. Her and I are even partnering."

"I have seen changes in her," Stover admitted. "The one regarding this *monstrous* side of hers is concerning, though." He looked out at Levi. "Speaking of that, is that why you haven't been in the field through all of this?"

"Partly. I need to reel things in now that I've dealt with those I needed to. And engaging in an all-out combat situation isn't really conducive to that. Street fighting is one thing, that's another. Plus, I made a deal with my loved ones that in coming here and being away from them, I wouldn't put myself in direct, outright danger."

Stover smiled. "How times have changed. I'm happy for you, Knight."

"Thanks. I'm happy, too."

"Told you it was possible, didn't I?"

Levi grinned. "Well, I thought you were just talking big."

The two of them chuckled at that. Something a little too dark to laugh about, but then again, considering both of their backgrounds, it made sense.

I finished with Stover's injury, then stepped back, telling him, "We'll get you on a round of antibiotics, along with some painkillers, to take the edge off. But in the meantime, take it easy where that injury's concerned."

"Understood," he said, easily. *Easily?* I guess we were making progress then.

I walked over to where Levi was, as he started pouring a coffee. "Want one?" he asked me.

"I'm all about the food right now, thanks," I said, heading for the cupboard and pulling out a packet of Maltesers. After taking time to deal with Stover's injury, I was now well beyond being able to take the time to actually make something proper for breakfast. I needed to take the edge off my hunger pangs first.

As I went to dive into the packet, I pulled up short as something hit me in the gut.

Nico pressed his hand to her belly. "This little baby needs taking care of, Caterina."

"And we're making another doctor's appointment too," Milo said.

"All right," she conceded. "Yes, to both those things. But first, I need to eat something really bad." She looked out at me, pouting her lips.

"Yes, you can finish off my Maltesers," I told her.

"You need something much more substantial than that," Milo spoke.

"I will. In the morning. Just a snack for now."

Milo eyed Nico for support.

"Let her have her snack. It's clearly some sort of craving."

"Julian?"

I blinked out of that memory to find Levi eyeing me worriedly. Stover was looking on as well with a similar expression.

"Fine. I'm fine. I just… when she was pregnant, Cat had a craving for one of my favored snacks—these."

Levi laid his hand on my shoulder. "I'm sorry, Julian. Have the four of you talked about the miscarriage yet?"

"It's only been a few hours."

Levi exchanged a knowing look with Stover.

"What?" I asked, looking between them.

"Don't let it go on too long, is all," Levi told me.

"She'll likely try to push it into the background to focus on the war," Stover said. With a grimace, he added, "I taught her how to bury things when necessary, when rational thought needs to prevail."

"She might also see the grief as a weakness," Levi pointed out.

"It's a normal human emotion."

"Agreed, but it's—"

"Caterina. It's Caterina protocol," Stover interjected.

I shook my head. No. She'd come a long way from those days.

I mean, sure, there had been a setback with that after the trauma of the miscarriage when she'd agreed to take off with Stover and be apart from us. But that had been complicated by a whole slew of things, including believing she was keeping us safe by drawing those fuckers away.

"It'll be fine. She'll express it," I told them.

Levi looked away, obviously not wanting to directly

interfere or go any deeper into it beyond a warning and trying to help us in the right direction.

"Let's hope," Stover said, with an ominous tone that I didn't like. More so, a tone that said he didn't really have that hope.

No. She was back here with us now and we'd figure everything out.

24

~Nico~

I'd woken up to coldness.

All three of them had left the bed by the time I'd come to.

Where Julian and Milo were concerned, I'd figured they'd wanted me to get as much sleep in as I could, while that was still possible. Before we were diving back into the thick of it all once again.

But Caterina had been another story.

Because, as I'd started waking up, I'd felt her respond when she'd registered me shifting against her, obviously realizing I was awakening. And then she'd hurried off the bed like her sexy little ass had been on fire.

My sleep-infused call to her had been cut off by the bathroom door closing, then even locking.

And since then, I'd put my pajama pants back on and settled at the foot of the bed, watching the door and waiting for her to emerge.

For a good ten minutes of that wait, the shower had been running.

But another ten had elapsed since that had stopped.

I rubbed my thumb over the ring I'd taken out of my nightstand drawer several minutes ago.

Her ring.

The ring that she'd been without since she'd been away after Stover had made her leave it behind, so she couldn't be tracked.

"This ring represents what the four of us now share together."

It wasn't what it had been framed as to our enemies, not an engagement ring. It was far beyond that. It was about the four of us, our relationship. And, more than even that, it had been intended as something for *her*, to give her hope through the nightmare we'd endured.

"In those moments when you're alone, or feel alone, you'll need something to hold on to. Something more immediate than the promise of winning this war. And that's what the special ring we're currently having made for you is intended as… something to hold on to."

And she'd had to leave it behind.

At a time when she would've needed it most.

And, honestly, at a time when *we'd* needed her to have it with her most, a symbol of our foursome still being intact across the distance and the obstacles between us. To know that things were still *intact* on her end.

Because, as much as I understood the need for her to leave and why she'd made that decision, particularly at a time when she'd been shaken and not thinking clearly, at its heart it still felt like she'd walked away when she should've stayed and fought for our relationship.

I hated even thinking that, even acknowledging that it was how I felt, but I hadn't been able to shake it. The disappointment and resentment that I felt toward her for doing that. Maybe it was irrational, but either way, I needed to put it out there to her in order to take away its power and the way I knew it would fester if it wasn't addressed, the way it could poison our relationship going forward.

As ridiculous as it sounded, her leaving the bed this morning had triggered all of that for me, the act of leaving us in the cold. It felt like a small version of that happening again.

"This is what you do, Caterina. You run and shut down. And you know what? There's always going to be a reason to. With anything."

Those were the words I'd levied upon her months ago.

She'd come a long way since then.

But now there was this.

Her leaving, then her hightailing it into the bathroom in what I was interpreting as her trying to avoid not only the intimacy of it, but to avoid dealing with everything unspoken that we'd put on hold last night.

Just for last night.

I couldn't allow it to go on longer than that.

I pushed off the bed, intending to end this wait with her, to see to this thing right here and now.

But then the door opened and Milo and Julian strode on in.

Milo was carrying a tray of food. Caterina's favorite egg white omelet and bowl of berries combo.

And Julian was radiating a whole lot of urgency.

"Dammit, I thought the two of you would still be asleep," Milo said, walking over to the nearest nightstand and putting the tray of food down. "I'd planned to bring this in for Caterina and have her wake up to breakfast in bed with all of us here in the bed together. I would've brought you something, too, but you don't like to eat in the morning, especially not until after your smoke and espresso." He thumbed Julian. "And this one couldn't wait. I found him in the kitchen scarfing down some chocolates, while Levi was making him a breakfast sandwich."

"I took longer than expected because Stover needed my help with his arm," Julian explained.

"His arm?" I queried.

"It needed stitches. He suffered a nasty stab wound last night. Didn't tell anyone because he didn't want the focus on his shit, just on Cat settling back in here."

"Speaking of that," I said, holding up the ring. "I'm going to—"

"*Don't,*" Julian told me. "Fucking don't, Nico."

"Don't what? Sort all this out between the four of us, so it doesn't fester and worsen?"

"Don't push her to give you the answers and relief that *you* want."

"You can't tell me you don't want the same."

"Of course I do." He gestured at Milo. "So does he. We all do."

"Then what's the issue? Why are you asking me to let it go?"

"It's not about letting it go." He shifted his weight and folded his arms across his bare chest. "I got into the Caterina of it all with Stover and Lev a little bit down in the kitchen. They were worried about her shutting down, advising that we don't let it play out like that. But then it hit me. They're both on the periphery these days when it comes to her. They haven't been in the thick of it like we have with her. They haven't seen her change and evolve with us. They don't really know that version of her. Especially not to the depth that we do. The four of us have all grown together. *Because* of each other, because of our four-some relationship. Cat leaving was a setback, of course. But there was a lot bearing down on her at the time."

"You're saying we should wait for her to come to us?"

"I'm saying that if we don't, we won't know what's actually real, what's actually coming from her, rather than from the pressure that we'd be putting on her."

"This is Caterina, J."

"This is her after being shaken really badly, Nico."

"Even before losing the baby, there were cracks," Milo piped up.

"So, you want me to tiptoe around this? Or worse, actually, simply ignore it altogether and just hope she comes to us and addresses everything?"

"Just give it a little time. She only got back last night," Julian said.

I pushed off the bed. "You're acting like I haven't already made allowances. Last night with that fucker, Stover? Then the whole Levi of it all."

"And the Levi thing worked out incredibly well," Julian pointed out. "He's become an indispensable ally *and* a friend to all of us, not just Cat anymore."

"I agree, but the rest... I don't fucking know about that. Stover being her actual father... Caterina distanced from us, yet physically here now... all the unsaid shit..." I scrubbed my hand over the coarse stubble plaguing my jawline.

"Nico—" Milo started.

But I'd heard enough.

I'd stayed on my fucking *leash* enough.

I tossed her ring to him. "Enjoy your breakfast in bed. I need to video conference with Carlo concurring where we're at after the ambush the other night. When you're done, shore up security at the Manor now she's back. Even with Angelo dead, the hit could still be active. She could still be a target so no one can know she's here outside of our most trusted own."

"Nico, wait—"

I held up my hand.

Julian tried to stop me from leaving too, but I dodged him, and then stormed out.

25

~Emilio~

Rocco and I had finished up bolstering physical security around Charon Manor.

Everything was in place.

Security had been tighter than it had ever been.

And yet I was still concerned.

We weren't just dealing with mafioso soldiers this time around.

Erebus was another level altogether, unlike anything we'd come up against before.

It meant that no matter how strong security was, how intense our protection protocols were, there was no true safety. Not while they remained active.

And as much as I was glad that Caterina was back with us, the stress of worrying about her being so with her still a target was very fucking real.

They'd already gotten too close the last couple of times.

Hell, beyond that. They'd killed our child and nearly killed her and Nico, too.

I really couldn't stand the thought of another situation like that playing out.

She'd been through too much as it was. And the three of us had also, right along with her. It was something that had finally really gotten to Nico.

But it was being compounded by his fear of losing her.

Something that was being further complicated by Stover being in the picture now as her true biological father.

Sipping at my coffee with a few drops of brandy in it, I stepped out onto the patio to take a beat. Julian and Levi were sparring again and Nico was making calls from his office, strategizing his rule once the final leg of this war was over. Basically, he was doing everything he could, using any excuse he could in order to avoid all three of us—and Stover. The only one he'd allowed close had been Levi. Talk about things shifting, big time.

The morning that Nico had taken off while Caterina had been in the bathroom, Julian and I had spent time with her when she'd finally emerged. Some good, quality time. But it hadn't felt right without Nico also being there, something Caterina had been upset about. We'd told her he was busy and run off his feet with everything going on, but it had been clear that she'd only bought that to an extent. She knew Nico. She could see through one of his smokescreens.

The problem was, him doing that had actually seemed to put Caterina off voicing what remained unspoken between the four of us. Like it had been a setback.

Now was the time to see to all of this because we had to wait on tracking Erebus with Levi and Caterina working together until certain parts and devices came in. Caterina had run a complicated idea by Levi and they'd both determined that they'd needed more power to pull off what they intended. I didn't understand the specifics, because their skill level and know-how were way beyond mine. What I did know was that it would take several days for the parts, devices, and whatever the fuck, to be delivered. Acquiring them at all was apparently extremely difficult, and it was something that Stover was assisting with via his black ops contacts.

As I ventured further onto the patio, I caught sight of him and Caterina in the distance, over by the trees of the surrounding gardens.

They were training.

No. More than that, I realized, as I zeroed in on them.

Caterina's movements were too wild and powerful to be merely sparring.

She was in her *monstrous* state. Unleashed.

Dammit, this was something Nico had promised her that he'd be a part of.

Honestly, it was something he needed to be a part of. Especially because he'd finally found a way to control it and pull back during the takedown of Elia. Caterina didn't even know that yet, and neither did Stover. Nico could really help her with this. Even better than Stover.

Not to mention, Stover should be resting his fucking injured arm.

His care for this daughter was clearly outweighing his commonsense.

Well, we were all guilty of that when it came to those we loved.

I put my mug down on one of the patio tables, and drew closer as I saw Stover wince when he had to use his injured arm to block her attack, when they became more vicious and rapid-fire, as she obviously reached the height of her animalistic state.

Their voices gravitated toward me as I got closer.

"I was protecting you, Caterina."

"You took me from my men! And now look at everything! It's a mess! Our relationship is fractured! I can feel it! I shouldn't.... I shouldn't have let you! I shouldn't have left! I just... I couldn't handle it! I couldn't handle the guilt of it, the failure! Being around them... it would've made it worse! That's what I thought, what the grief had me believing! But I should have trusted in them! In us!"

"It can be resolved. They love you very deeply. You just need to—"

"Argh! Argh!"

He narrowly missed her blow, dodging just in time, and her fist plunged into the trunk of a tree instead.

The miss only enraged her more and fueled her state.

"Try to regain control now. Re-anchor yourself."

"No! It's better like this! Get away. Get away from me! I'm gonna hurt you!"

"I'm not leaving you like this."

"Go!"

I went to step in when movement coming from around the house caught my attention and pulled me up short.

And then Nico came into view, sprinting into the fray.

"Caterina!" he called out when he was about twenty feet away.

She stilled at the sound of his voice, then spun toward him.

As he kept coming, she pulled from Stover, who then slumped against a nearby tree for support, and watched like me as Caterina ran at Nico.

Definitely not in a lovey-dovey romance movie sort of way.

No. She came in hot, screaming in animalistic fury and pain.

An unmistakable snarl escaped Nico as he hit, indicating he was in his *feral* state, too.

Both of them at the same time… *fuck me.*

He snagged her around the waist and used her momentum against her to toss her onto the grass.

She landed on her back, but only for a moment, before she literally rolled with it and came up in a primed crouch.

"Say it!" she yelled.

He started.

"Say it!"

He shook his head and took an unsteady step back, clearly fighting himself.

And then she was launching herself at him, slamming her hands into his chest and knocking him back.

Her hits came hard and fast, snarling and growling sounding from them both as they met blow for blow.

Nico managed to snag her around the waist.

He took her hits as he drove her into a tree, a grunt escaping her as it winded the hell out of her.

"You left us!" he roared down at her. "You fucking left us!"

"No!"

"You gave up on us!"

"No!"

"Then why?"

"To keep you safe!"

"We could've done that together! Could've kept *you* safe together, too! There was another way. There's always an alternative! But you couldn't even wait for us to find it, could you? You didn't give us a fucking moment to breathe after losing the baby, after almost losing you for good as well! You fucking left us there in the dust!"

She slammed her hands up and out, dislodging his grip, then kicked him back so brutally that it had him stumbling a couple of feet, before he managed to regain his footing.

"You fucking ran, Caterina! Like you used to!"

"That's not it!" she screamed at him, completely irate.

As she ran at him in her animalistic state, and he hauled her around and away from him, wherein she hit the grass on her hands and knees this time, I caught sight of Julian coming out of the kitchen and onto the patio, zeroing in on what was going on. The two of them going head-to-head in their dangerous states.

Although, it was clear to me that Nico was severely holding back in a way I'd never seen from him before when he was like this. He'd only pushed her away from him. He hadn't hit her—and he never fucking would.

Julian cursed at the state of Caterina and shook his head in utter dismay for her, hurting for her.

Meanwhile, Stover hovered nearby, keeping an eye on the situation carefully.

"All I do is cause you pain!" she cried suddenly, more than rage breaking through this time.

"What?" Nico barked at her.

She grimaced and clenched her fists, clearly trying to fight the emotion that was setting in and starting to impact her, starting to pull her from her state.

"No! Stop!" she yelled aloud to herself. "No one and nothing can hurt me when I'm like this!"

I saw him suck in a couple of breaths and squeeze his eyes shut for a moment.

When he opened them, he was back to his regular self, and he told her calmly, "For me, it was about having power over my own life. At least that was how it made me feel, while I was far from in control because of those around me keeping me beneath their boots, forcing me and manipulating me. But for you, it's self-preservation. And fear too, it seems."

She held up her hand, not wanting to hear his words, to have them impact her.

But he persevered and stepped closer to her.

"I can control it now. You see? After all this time fighting my humanity, that was always the key, Caterina. Holding onto what makes me feel the most human. I thought it was a weakness, especially in battle. To care, to love. To think about any of that in battle, I thought it would compromise me. But it doesn't. *And* it's what enables me to walk that line now, to control *it* rather than it being the other way around."

It happened then.

It fucking worked.

She slumped to her knees.

"You did it," Nico breathed, crouching down beside her.

She reached out and grasped his biceps, urgency spilling from her as she told him in a broken, unsteady tone, "We lost the baby because of me. Because I was too stubborn to agree to be sent to a safehouse. You almost died because it was my idea to venture out to Stonewell. Your home was broken into because of me, because they wanted me. With me not around, I just… I guess I thought it would be a reprieve from all the shit I bring, all the pain. But I hated it. I hated being away from you all. There was a hole. There always is when I'm not around the three of you constantly. But… all of this… all that I bring to you… I can't… I can't have the three of you hurting. I love you. I love you all so much. And now it's ruined. It's all fucking ripped to shreds."

I walked over there, watching as with shaking hands she pulled out her ring from her pants pocket and held it on her palm. "I missed this. I… I found it on the night-stand. But the three of you just left it there. You didn't give it back to me, and I thought… I thought it was because you knew it, too. That now with me back here, you could see it as clear as day. That all I bring the three of you is pain, despair, and a whole lot of insanity."

Nico clasped his hand over hers, sealing the ring between them, and drawing her gaze to his. "I'm upset because we *can't* bear to lose you, Caterina. Because the idea of you pulling away is what's fucking painful. The idea of you feeling better off and happier by being away is absolute torture."

"I wanted to tell you how that's so far from the truth, how much I missed all of you and regretted that it'd needed to be that way in the moment at the hospital. But then I hesitated when I felt you waking up next to me, because I was scared that putting all that out there would just sweep everything away with a whole lot of fucking poison. I could feel the strain between all of us, and I was afraid with it so fragile, that unloading things would shatter everything completely. *That's* why I avoided it that morning."

"The *poison* set in when you *didn't* talk about any of it," Nico told her.

"I'm sorry. That was the opposite of my intention and—"

"You don't bring us pain, *principessa.*"

Julian jogged over just as I reached the two of them.

"Far from it," he added.

"Not pain, but we do all bring our fair share of shit to the table," I said. "It's part of being together, bolstering and loving one another—accepting that and incorporating it into our foursome."

"It's what real family does, Cat."

Nico nodded, watching as she looked between all of us, trying to take our words in. "And none of what happened is your fault. External forces, our enemies, were responsible for that. They have been since this started. We *all* agreed on you staying instead of heading out to a safehouse. It was a collective decision. But that wasn't what caused the accident. Angelo and Erebus did. End of story. There was nothing we could have done. We didn't see them coming and we couldn't have. Not at that stage of things, especially. It just happened, Caterina. It was brutal and tragic and fucking agonizing, but it was something that was done to us, not something we're responsible for. And what's more is that we can't alter any of that. All we can do is move forward."

"And when you feel like this, feel overwhelmed and in such deep pain, share it with us. We want you to, we need you to, and you need to as well," Julian told her, coming to crouch down on her other side. "Believe me, I've learned my own lesson there."

I leaned down and laid my hands on her shoulders from behind, and she craned her neck to look up at me. "When you first came into our life, I thought it was going to be hell. I saw you as a threat, as a massive headache, in all honesty. But I was wrong. About you, about all of it. You've changed things for us. You've filled a hole for the three of us in a way we'd never imagined possible. You've brought a peace to us that we've never experienced before. You're one of us and you always will be. Nothing and no one can change that."

"You've changed everything for the better," Julian said.

Nico lifted his palm and took hold of the ring. "No more unilateral decisions from any of us in the name of the supposed good of us all. Let's make that agreement here and now. We fight together, we hurt together, we're together on everything. I know it's hard for you because you've never had the support of a familial unit like you do in us now. But can you do that for us going forward, *principessa?* Can you make us that promise?"

She nodded, emotion taking her over. "I promise. I'm sorry. I'm so sorry."

"No apologies," Julian said, stroking her hair. "You'd been through a severe trauma, and you dealt with it how you believed was best."

"I love you all so much," she uttered.

We smiled out at her as Nico slid our ring back on her finger, the symbolic nature of it not lost on any of us.

As we all rose back to our feet with her in the middle, us surrounding her, I looked out to see that Stover had gone. He was nowhere to be found. He must've headed back into the house while we'd been in the thick of it all, realizing he'd no longer been needed to assist, that *we* had it, that we had *her.*

She moved in a slow circle, looking out at each of us. "I'm never leaving again," she vowed. "And while we're putting things out there, you don't need to tread so carefully around me. My first night back with you all, it was a good call, an easy way to sink back into things. But I'm good in that respect now."

"Are you saying—" Julian started.

His words caught in his throat as her demeanor shifted and her eyes hooded, as they darted up and down our bodies. She was almost salivating over the sight of us.

"I want your marks all over me this time." Darkening emerald eyes locked on ours. "Fuck me up, boys."

God-fucking-dammit. She had us.

All the fucking way.

The three of us exchanged a nod of agreement.

And then I snagged her around the waist and hauled her off her feet.

I carried her deeper into the forest; the guys following.

When we were secluded enough, I pushed her up against a tree and ripped open her jeans. I dropped her down to her feet, and then I was yanking them and her boots off her in the next moment. Nico was there, too, pulling off her jacket with a sexual ferocity that bled into all of us, turning the intensity up several notches.

As he managed that, Julian moved in and sucked on her neck, making her moan out and sink her fingers into his hair.

When he pulled back, there was one hell of a hickey left in his wake.

Nico pulled a flip knife from his pocket and then he was stepping up to her and cutting through the straps of her tank and bra, then yanking both down roughly to expose her breasts.

She panted with erotic excitement as he cut the rest away, then crouched down between her thighs.

I slapped at them and she spread wider for us, just as Julian scraped his nails over her breasts, circling around and around, before dragging them down her stomach, then raking them up and down, making more blood-red marks over her soft skin.

"Shit," she cried, throwing her arms out above her and digging her nails into the bark of the tree to brace herself.

Her whole body shuddered as Nico cut through one side of her the silky black panties and purposely nicked her a little.

He moved to the other side and did the same thing until pearls of blood formed.

He brushed the ruined fabric away, and then I spread her cunt open, and he smeared the blood through her folds, paying extra attention to her clit that had her crying out and bucking her hips.

I wanted a taste of her there this time.

I signaled Nico, and he stepped aside, pocketing the knife.

Taking in the highly arousing sight of her completely naked while we were still fully clothed and surrounding her as she sank against the tree for us like some sort of exquisite offering, I kept her cunt spread open and vulnerable for me as I crouched down and licked the length of her.

The taste of her dripping cunt mixed with the blood Nico had drawn had my cock reacting almost violently, straining against the zipper of my jeans.

I teased her with slow and long tantalizing licks that had her rolling her hips with sensuous movements while she slicked her tongue over her lips.

"Milo," she uttered, her calling my name in such a needy, raspy tone doing things to me.

So much so that it had me diving into her sweet cunt and becoming fucking ravenous, sucking, licking, biting, and savoring every moment of her taste.

She grasped my hair and started grinding against my face, taking her pleasure in that hot-as-sin way we all loved from her.

"Yeah, there it is. Ride that tongue, darlin'," Julian uttered, turned on as fuck. In my peripheral vision, I saw him open his pants and shove them down, pulling out his cock and fisting it roughly.

"Ah! Shit!" Caterina cried, her whole body shuddering as she came all over my face.

As I pulled back, she sank against the tree, boneless.

But then Nico was there, yanking her off it.

At the same time, Julian shoved me onto my back.

In the next second, Nico carried her over to me, making her straddle me. Then, with his hold on her hips, he rammed her down onto my cock, making the both of us roar out into the surrounding forest.

He released her, then started slapping her ass cheeks in turn, rapid-fire with hard, jolting slaps that had her crying out, and getting the message to ride me wildly.

She dug her nails into my pecs and slammed up and down, her breasts bouncing in my face as she worked her sexy little hips.

Julian worked with Nico. As he continued slapping her ass, Julian smacked at her breasts, making her grunt and hiss, but fuck me ever harder, as the rough treatment got her off as usual.

Nico stopped, then spread her ass cheeks open, and spat inside. "No lube. This will have to do." He spat again, a groan coming from her as she felt it dripping inside her. "Are you gonna be our filthy little princess and take a big, thick cock up your tight ass, baby?"

"Oh fuck," she gasped, trembling with need at his dirty words. "Yes… *God*."

He signaled me, and I grasped her hips, holding her still on my cock.

Little whimpers escaped her at the friction being cut off.

Nico chuckled darkly, then gestured at Julian, who came over, stroking his cock madly.

Julian reached around where Caterina and I were joined and gathered her wetness that was dripping all over both of us, then spread it over his cock.

Then he stepped behind her.

Nico held her ass spread open as Julian sank inside. With her angled a little, I was able to enjoy the erotic sight of his cock pushing into her spread hole. It had me groaning and straining not to move to it, especially when he drove deeper and I felt him rubbing against me.

"Ungh... yeah," Caterina choked. "Those fucking piercings."

"I know, darlin'. Feel them teasing the fuck out of your tight little ass, huh?"

"Yes," she gasped. "Shit."

Nico released her and stepped back, opening his jeans and pulling his cock out, stroking himself off as he walked around to Caterina's side.

"Almost there," Julian told her. "You're welcoming my cock like our filthy little whore. Ungh... fuck, Cat... yeah, that's it."

The moment he was fully seated inside her, Nico fisted her hair and twisted her head toward his cock. He slapped it against her cheek and she opened, then he thrust in deep, making her splutter around her mouthful of him.

Julian and I started to move.

I rammed up into her rapid-fire and Julian pressed his hand to her back, keeping her steady as he alternated his own deep, stabbing thrusts with mine, giving her the fucking of her life, while Nico plundered her throat.

She gave as good as she got, slamming back and forth against us, lost to it all, wanting more, more and fucking more.

Nico released his hold on her hair and she took control, fucking her own throat with his cock like a wild thing.

Our wild thing.

As Julian reached around and clawed at her breasts, she did the same to me, scraping her nails over my pecs and down my abs, drawing deep-red grazes all the way along that heightened every fucking thing for me.

Pleasure, pain, and a whole lot of intensity engulfed us all.

Our groans and curses collided with Caterina's muffled

screams, echoing through the dark night like a twisted sexual symphony.

I reached out and brushed my thumb over her clit.

I'd barely touched her there when she came, so much other stimulation already overwhelming her.

"Damn," I grunted as she clenched down around my cock.

It was so fucking intense and that, combined with all the buildup... I just couldn't hold it, and I came deep in her sweet cunt.

I cursed and threw my head back as she kept riding me through it, working her hips with a mad pace that had Julian squeezing her breasts, then roaring out into the night as he came, too.

"Fuck," he rasped against her cheek, her mouth still full of Nico. "What you do to us... damn, darlin'."

Nico pulled out of her mouth and she sputtered as she drew in a couple of ragged breaths. "You're gonna come again and I want to hear your screams, *principessa.*"

He slid his cock between her breasts and Julian leaned in and squeezed them around him, holding them steady and making her gasp at the sensation, the two of them taking control of her at once.

Nico started thrusting roughly and like a fucking beast, and she dipped her head and swirled her tongue around his crown, whenever he thrust near her lips, while she continued milking every last drop out of me and Julian still buried inside her.

Nico took hold of her breasts, while Julian and I played with her cunt together, dragging our fingers through her folds, teasing her clit.

"Fuck! Fuck me!" she cried, rolling her hips and grinding against our wandering fingers. "Oh my God!"

Her thrusting faltered just as Nico cursed and came all over her neck and lips with a bellow.

She drenched my cock and our fingers, then collapsed back against Julian's chest.

"Holy shit," she breathed, looking out at us as she coyly licked Nico's cum off her lips.

She looking sexy as hell.

Covered in cum, in our marks, her eyes shining with carnal satisfaction, her bare body slick with sweat and her own juices.

Hot fucking damn, she was really something.

Our special something.

Now and forever.

26

~Caterina~

"This is truly amazing. Thank you," I uttered, completely taken aback as I sat beside Julian up at the kitchen island, while he debriefed me on everything that had transpired with Camlann Corporation since I'd been gone, getting me back up to speed on it all.

He'd done a phenomenal job with it.

Especially considering he'd also been running his own company alongside mine.

He truly was another level.

It was incredibly impressive.

"No worries," he said, lifting a shoulder.

"*No worries?*" I asked, incredulous. "It's a huge deal what you've done for me, how you've kept Camlann on track while I've been gone." I wrapped my arms around him and held him to me. "This means so much to me. *Thank* you, Julian."

He chuckled at my enthusiasm and wholehearted appreciation. "It was seriously my pleasure," he said, as I eased from him. "And with all the systems you have in place, the sleek setup, it was easy to sink into it. I'm highly impressed."

I smiled out at him. "Thank you." I shifted my weight. "And Hazel?"

"She's doing well. She's already back at work, despite me offering her some time off for her mental health with full pay *and* compensation. She didn't want it. She wanted to get back to work as soon as possible."

"Yeah, that's her."

"A workaholic like you, hmm?"

"I'm striking more of a balance now."

"Well, you kind of had to. Not being able to be there physically during the forced marriage and having to operate your empire remotely. Then the whole safehouse thing."

"Ah, so you think it's forced work-life balance, only able to exist under similar circumstances to these?"

Before he could answer, an alert flashed on his laptop screen.

My alert.

One I'd set up months ago.

It had finally happened.

And I couldn't quite believe it.

"Jesus, here it fucking is, Cat," Julian said, eyeing me excitedly.

I sucked in a breath. "The Brimbank Waterfront Development has finally been announced and put out there."

"It's time. You already have everything prepped."

"It's not finalized from a partnership perspective. Between you and me, I mean."

He frowned at me. "You already put so much work into it as a solo effort. Our partnership got derailed by everything that's been happening. Don't wait for me. You can't afford to miss out on this opportunity. This is what you've been waiting on for a long time. It will skyrocket Camlann Corporation into the big leagues, as I've said before."

"Julian—"

"*No.* I want this for you. I already have a massive piece of the pie here in Tolhurst and beyond. This is your chance now to do the same without being dragged down by Santino's efforts to derail your every move, and succeed beyond what you already have."

"But I—"

"We'll partner on our original idea of the *mega-hub.*"

"You're sure?"

"I am, darlin'."

"But this would be a major coup for Carver Group, too. Just turning away from that—"

"How about we make a deal, then?"

I settled in, eyeing him curiously. "I'm listening."

He turned on his chair to face me head-on. "Those skilled workers—the innocents—displaced with the fall of Leone Realty… you incorporate a large percentage of that workforce into your expansion efforts, specifically on the Brimbank Waterfront job. The rest I'll absorb into Carver Group. We can iron out the specifics, draw up contracts, all of that."

I couldn't believe it.

"Wow. First declining to accept the *Social Good Award* in person at the Business Forum so that *I* wouldn't be overshadowed, and now being so benevolent and caring when it comes to all these employees that aren't even yours to really worry about."

"We do what we can, right? And I'm in a better position than a lot of people to be able to do quite a lot. To give back and to protect those whose livelihoods would be devastated without me doing this."

"Without us doing this."

"Really? You'd be on board with this? I mean, I've already put things in place hoping that you would be, but I left the way open for you to back out. Nico thought you'd go for this and told me not to worry about waiting on your go-ahead because you'd trust me to make that sort of executive decision on Camlann Corporation's behalf, but I found a loophole anyway, just in case."

"I appreciate you doing that and finding an out for me. It means a lot. More than you can imagine, actually." I laid my hand on his bicep. "But I agree with your plan and I *am* on board."

"Perfect." He pulled up my proposals that I'd prepared for the Brimbank Waterfront development. "Now, because you're not supposed to be here in Tolhurst and Stover managed to bring you in under the radar, we can't have you submitting these directly. But I can do that for you on behalf of Camlann Corporation, if you're good with that?"

Yeah, it was the same reason why I hadn't been able to go to Hazel and see that she was well in person after what Marco had done, scaring the life out of her like that.

"I'll reach out to Nova Henderson and notify her too," he added.

"Thank you, Julian."

"Of course, darlin'. We work as one, right? We're a team. Through everything."

I smiled. "Yeah. Yeah, we really are."

As he started preparing the submission right there and then, I watched for a while, excitement rolling through me at the prospect of it all.

But there was even more beyond that now.

And I wanted him to know that.

I wanted all my men to know.

"I'm going to work on it, you know?"

"What's that?" he asked, distractedly, focusing on the submission.

"Developing a healthy work-life balance."

"You and Nico both have that issue."

"But you don't. You work hard *and* play hard."

He eyed me as he continued typing. "You're asking me to teach you a thing or two where that's concerned?"

I grinned. "I am. Do you think you can handle that? I can be a bit stubborn."

"Just a bit?" he asked, chuckling.

"Hey."

He shook his head. "I'm fucking with you. Nah, it's not stubbornness. Anyone calling it that is an ignorant shit and clearly doesn't know you. It's determination and a shit-ton of perseverance. Maybe a little tunnel vision, too. And, Christ, darlin', I really fucking admire that about you."

"Aww, *amore mio,*" I crooned, nuzzling against his arm.

He turned to me slightly, nuzzling back, while he continued with the submission.

And it was really nice just being with each other in that way, taking one another in, and savoring the closeness of it all.

I'd felt that way with all of us having every meal together for the last few days. All six of us had sat down together and just shot the shit, talking about casual things, business aspirations, random things. Anything that didn't concern this war. Just sinking into a sense of normalcy while we could, while we had a brief reprieve.

The guys had been right when they'd first encouraged me to let go of the burden once in a while and focus on enjoying each other, focusing on the good, when things were hard, when all hell was breaking loose externally.

And now those moments were everything to me.

I'd even been able to catch up on Levi's life in great detail. His relationship with Brianna, Mason, and Colton. It had been great to reconnect with him like that. We'd been at too much of a distance for too long. As bad as things had been to have called Levi in, at least a positive component had come along with it, and that was being able to strengthen our friendship, something that meant a great deal to me, but something that had faced some strain with the craziness going on in both our lives.

"Done," Julian announced, pulling me from my thoughts. He pulled from the laptop and turned to me, giving me a double high-five. "Congratulations, darlin'. It's begun."

"What's begun?" Nico's voice came from the kitchen doorway, and we looked to see him and Milo standing there eyeing us curiously.

They'd just gotten out of a video call meeting with Carlo, discussing their alliance, as well as providing each other updates on the current situation within the city.

"Cat's just submitted her proposals for the Brimbank Waterfront development. All that shit's out now and she's in."

"Damn, that's worthy of some major celebration," Milo said, walking into the room, with Nico doing the same. Milo told me, "He'd been in the process of planning a *Welcome Home* celebration for you, but you came back here without any warning, so it couldn't be put into effect. But we could do it for this instead?"

I eyed Julian. "You were planning a whole celebration for me?"

"Yeah."

I stoked his hair. "You're truly unbelievable, you know that?"

"That's our Sunshine," Milo chuckled.

"We *should* celebrate," Nico said. "On the quiet, though, given the situation," he added, giving Julian a look, because he was known well for going big with everything.

I shook my head at the three of them. "It's just a submission. I didn't get it yet."

"We've all seen your proposals. You're a shoo-in, *bellezza.*"

"Absolutely," Nico uttered.

I chuckled. "I appreciate your faith in me, but let's just wait. Never celebrate until a deal is done."

"It's not always about the destination, Caterina," Nico told her. "The journey is also worth recognizing along the way."

"Like this journey of ours? This intense, crazy, and amazing journey that is our relationship?" I smiled out at them all. "Huh?"

"It certainly has been intense," Nico said, coming over and planting a kiss on the top of my head.

"Intensely amazing," Julian added, tickling me and making me giggle.

It had all the guys chuckling. Apparently, they loved that sound from me.

Milo came behind me and stroked my hair on his way to the kitchen counters. "So, are the two of you going to take a break for lunch, or what? Lev's going to be down in a minute. He's taking a break from working on a couple of college assignments and then video calling his loves."

"What about Joe?" I asked.

"Outside *training* with himself again," Milo told me.

I frowned. "Has he said anything to any of you?"

"About what?" Milo asked.

"I mean, do you think he's keeping his distance intentionally?"

"I think he's observing the situation," Nico spoke up.

"To what end?" Milo questioned.

"Isn't it impossible to know with him?" Julian cut in. "Besides, he shouldn't even be training at all. I told him to take it easy where that stab wound is concerned."

"There's no way that's happening," I told him. "He's used to working through much worse conditions."

"Given what you told us about the content of your conversation with him while you were stitching him up, Julian, it stands to reason that Stover is likely figuring out where he fits into Caterina's life. Right now and also going forward. He was dropped into our dynamic, so it's a lot to figure out from that outside perspective, especially when he's missed a lot of the changes in his own daughter," Nico spoke.

A silence fell over the room as I absorbed his words and what he was suggesting.

It was a strong possibility.

But with Joe, there was usually more than just one thing going on at a time.

For now and for the sake of keeping the peace, I'd let it be.

If it went on much longer, though, we'd need to have words.

I hadn't come back here with him and insisted on him staying right here, only for him to back away. If it was just him trying to get his bearings and do right by the situation, I got that, but anything else… no, that wouldn't sit well with me.

Like him maybe planning to leave and disappear into the ozone again.

Now I knew he was my biological father, I couldn't just let that go. It meant something to me. It had definitely impacted me. I couldn't have him simply taking off again.

Was that what he was doing, why he was keeping a

distance? He'd already decided to do that after we were done with this Erebus situation? Was this his way of preparing me, to make the break easier, by keeping away now all the while that he was here?

Had he decided that after he'd been unable to help me with my *monstrous* side and Nico had needed to step up instead?

"Caterina?" Nico called.

I looked out to see all of them eyeing me with concern. Julian was stroking my arm.

"Fine," I told them. "I'm fine. Just thinking about it. Him, I mean."

"Of course. It's still a lot to take in. It hasn't been that long since you found out the truth about him," Nico said.

"Or if he's just here until the war is over and Erebus is gone," I uttered.

"I really don't think that's it," Julian told me.

I arched an eyebrow. "You don't?"

He shook his head. "He wouldn't have said all that stuff when I was fixing him up. He certainly wouldn't have cared about treading carefully here."

Milo added, "And he could've escalated things with Nico instead of backing down."

I nodded, absorbing what they were each saying. "Valid points. You're right. Yeah."

Julian wrapped his arm around me. "You know," he told Nico and Milo, "Cat was talking about wanting to strike a work-life balance once all of this is over."

"Really?" Nico asked.

"I'm liking that," Milo said. "For you, too, Nico. Well, once everything is in place and you've established your rule. Should take a few months for things to settle, just like Carlo predicted during our meeting just now."

Nico nodded. "I agree on both counts. Especially the

balance aspect." He looked out at me. "What were you thinking of doing with more downtime from work?"

"The three of you," I rebutted with a sly wink.

"Damn," Milo exclaimed.

Julian whistled.

And Nico smirked.

"And taking up some hobbies. Exploring things I've yet to because my whole focus, until you guys came along, was on work."

"Maybe building upon our family, yes?" Nico filled in for me, where I hadn't been able to finish my sentence and actually put the words out there.

"Down the road a little, once everything there... settles... yeah."

A charged silence descended, one wrought with heavy emotion.

Sadness.

The weight of loss.

I couldn't stand it, and in the next second, I was shooting to my feet, to startled looks from all three of them.

"This is no longer working for me," I announced. As their expressions moved from startled to perplexity, I told them, "The separate rooms situation. Only crashing in the same room after we fuck." I grinned out at Nico. "I'm going to sell my apartment, because I want to move in here officially and not as part of some sort of ruse as it originally started out as. Because I want to be with the three of you always. *Here* with the three of you." I turned to Julian. "What do you think?"

"I *think* it's time for me to get rid of my penthouse, too."

I smiled. "Perfect."

Then, before they could demonstrate the full breadth

of their reactions, I stayed in the excitement of the moment and strode to the kitchen door. "Come on. There's something I want to show you—and run by you all."

Clearly curious as hell, they all followed me out as I led the way down the corridor and then up the staircase to the second floor.

I stopped outside Nico's bedroom. "I'm thinking renovation."

"Oh, damn," Milo exclaimed.

"A woman after my own heart," Julian breathed.

I looked between them.

Milo explained, "Julian's been pushing for Nico to renovate this and that inside the Manor for years."

"And yet he always resists and denies my every request," Julian told me.

"Your extremely *out there* requests," Nico retorted.

"Debatable. Highly debatable."

Nico rolled his eyes at him. "What were you thinking, *principessa?*"

I gestured at his bedroom and the room to its left, right at the edge of the corridor. "We make a more functional space, big enough for the four of us by combining your room and this one here, knocking a couple of walls down, opening it up, that sort of thing. Or we could combine yours and the one I'm staying in. If not here, then some-where over on the other side of the Manor near Julian and Milo's, if that works better. I just picked here because this is where we sleep together most. But instead of it being separate rooms going forward, it's just one for all of us to cohabitate together."

"With a massive heart-shaped bed!" Julian exclaimed. "Zebra-print sheets with a matching shag rug that—"

"See?" Nico cut in. "This is why I've shut him down in the past."

"Hey, it's gonna be a shared space. We need to include everyone's styles, N."

Nico pinched the bridge of his nose. "Fuck me."

Julian laughed. "And you'll also have to deal with Milo's messiness right up close."

"I'll work on that," Milo vowed. "It won't be an issue."

"That's something," Nico agreed.

As they got into it, I tried the knob for the room beside Nico's that I'd never been in before, speaking aloud to myself, "I really think this will be the best bet to—"

"Caterina, wait!" Nico called out.

But it was too late. I'd already opened the door.

My breath caught in my throat as I stood there frozen, my brain trying to make sense of what I found inside.

I'd expected it to be empty, given that it was one of the few rooms in the mansion that was never used.

But that had clearly altered.

Or it had at least begun to.

I stepped inside in what felt much like a trance, the surrealism of the moment taking me hostage, as I took in the huge bookcase in the shape of a tree, the cozy-looking turquoise couch, and, most prominent of all, the golden crib against the right wall.

"Oh my God," I choked, walking to it.

Hesitantly, and with trembling hands, I reached out and ran my fingers over the spectacular crib. The extremely *out there* crib. "Julian," I rasped. "You did all this?" I asked over my shoulder.

"Yeah. I was putting this nursery together as a surprise for you. I'm so sorry, Cat."

I frowned and turned around, finding them all looking on with a great deal of worry.

And pain.

So much pain.

"It's beautiful. Extraordinary." I smiled out at him. "And over the top in the best way. Just like you."

"Thank you, darlin'." He wrung his hands. "We discussed getting rid of this stuff, or closing the room off, but then we figured this could actually be a place that could help us all process our grief over losing our baby."

"But if it's hurting you, we can get rid of it immediately," Milo told me.

I looked out at Nico, who seemed at a loss, just observing quietly, clearly not sure how to approach this situation.

None of us were.

There wasn't exactly a set of instructions for how to deal with this sort of thing. Everyone processed loss and trauma differently, and what worked for one person didn't always work for another.

"I think it's a really nice idea," I told them.

I ran my hands over the crib again, taking it in, thinking about what it could have been, picturing how we could have used this room, what it would have been like to have actually had our baby with us here.

"Caterina?" Nico called carefully.

I looked out at them. "I just… I'd never imagined being a mother before, having a child, none of that. Not even getting married. It just wasn't on my radar as something *I* wanted. Because of the overarching fear that was connected to all of that because of my father, that sort of thing—especially marriage—intended as a means of control, the mark of taking my choices away. But things changed when the four of us drew closer together. And when I was pregnant, I finally started thinking about what it would actually be like to build our own little family on *our* own terms, what it would be like to be a mom, and all the little things we would do together with our child. And then…" I shoved my hand through my hair. "And then the accident happened and in a single moment, I woke up to find all those plans I'd made in my mind, all the hope of building that little family with you all… it had all just gone away."

"I know, Cat," Julian uttered, emotion bleeding from him as he came to me and wrapped an arm around me.

"We all wanted this baby so badly," Nico said. "And losing it… it hurt… it hurt a fuck of a lot."

"Our little miracle," Milo murmured.

It was what he'd said when I'd first revealed the pregnancy.

"She really was," I said, smiling sadly. As I nuzzled against Julian and took that comfort from him, I realized as I looked around the room, that it really was proving to be another source of comfort. The shock of it was being replaced by a safe place to think about it all, to think about *her*, to start on the path of making some sort of peace with it. *Peace* was a bit of a stretch. But maybe *acceptance*. There was so much love here, so much hope, put into the place and having my men in here with me, it only served to add to that in a really soothing way. "I like being in here," I told them.

"I'm glad," Julian said. He pulled back a little to look at me. "You know, after what happened with my takedown of Angelo the other night, it *did* help me. I'd needed to do it, to face him again. It's just the way I'm wired, I guess. But it wasn't a miracle cure to the trauma and all the shit what he burdened me with. So, I'm going to restart my therapy sessions with Roslynn and go all in this time, not cut myself off like I had been doing. I can set you up with her, if you like. For this grief over the miscarriage, but also a lot of other trauma that Santino caused, which you haven't dealt with over the years. It could help you feel a lot lighter."

"Yeah, I'd like that. I think it's a great idea."

"Good. I'll set it up then."

I saw Nico looking on with a whole lot of relief.

"You're not going to lose me," I told him, figuring that was where it was rooted. "Not to this grief, not to Joe, not to anything or anyone. I'm here for the long haul, I swear it. Hence, me wanting to figure out the room situation."

"I know," he said, coming to me and sliding his hand to my cheek, stroking softly. "It couldn't be any other way now. You belong with us."

"No fucking doubt there," Milo said, joining us.

And then the three of them wrapped themselves around me, holding me tightly.

Supporting me.

Cherishing me.

Loving me.

I couldn't believe how far things had come.

Despite the pain along the way, the trials we'd faced, the obstacles we'd come up against, there was *this* through it all.

Our found family.

I finally belonged somewhere.

I was no longer wandering alone.

And I never would be again.

Because of them.

Fuck, I was never letting go.

27

~Caterina~

I made my way toward Levi's room.

The equipment we'd been waiting on had arrived, so it was time to get down to working together to root out Erebus. Fortunately, the time it had taken to get what we'd needed had come right as Erebus had been reeling from our victories. Many of which my men had accomplished while I'd been sequestered away at the safehouse and recovering.

This last leg, though, we'd do together.

I'd bring everything I had to the table once again and destroy those motherfuckers. We'd remove Leo and bring that bastard down, with Milo getting the justice he'd so long been denied. And then Nico could officially take power.

As I approached the room that Levi was staying in, music reached me. Someone singing an edgy, hard-rock song.

"Dangerous, feral, ruthless/ Far from toothless/ Dark horses to the rotten core/ We collided with a ball of sunshine/ Pink bubblegum, cotton candy/ Vicious things tangling in the night."

"Wow, Colt. That sounds incredible," I heard Levi speaking.

A voice via speakerphone returned, *"Yeah? Did you notice how I made the drums heavier and emphasized the bass a bit more?"*

"It's definitely got a harder edge. You also altered the melody a little, yeah?"

"I did. Shit, I can't wait to play it live. It's gonna kill. You're gonna be there, right?"

"I wouldn't miss it."

"Even if you're still with Rina and her guys helping out?"

"We're at the tail end now."

"Yeah? Because we fucking miss you. Big time, brother."

"I know, cupcake. I've been down here longer than I anticipated."

"Because of that black ops group that's complicated everything. Bree told me."

"That's right. But now Rina's back, we'll crack it."

"All right. I'll let you get back to it. I've gotta put some finishing touches to a couple of other songs. Group video call later tonight?"

"You've got it."

"Love you, Lev."

"Love you, brother."

I heard Levi blow out a heavy breath as their call ended.

He was clearly feeling the weight of things, of being away from his family.

I had to make sure that wouldn't last for much longer.

He'd already done so much for me and my men as it was.

I gave him a few moments, then I rapped on the door.

"Come on in," he called out.

I turned the knob and stepped inside to find him sitting on his made bed with his phone beside him and his laptop out. He slapped the lid closed, then rose to his feet.

"Hey," I greeted.

He smiled out at me. "Hey there." He folded his arms across his chest. "What's up, sweetheart?"

"The equipment is here."

His eyes lit up. "Excellent."

"Ready to get started?"

He looked back at his laptop, hesitating.

"What's wrong?"

Unfolding his arms, he blew out a breath, then told me, "When you got back here and we were waiting for Nico to arrive, you mentioned that the boss of Erebus is apparently Nathan Donahue. So I put out feelers—very carefully—across the Dark Web like we discussed, monitoring forums, darknet marketplaces, and accessing encrypted chatrooms."

"And I warned you that it likely wouldn't yield any results."

"Right. Because he's so elusive and also because of the fear that he inspires through Erebus' activities, their influence, so nobody would come forward, not even through these more *covert* avenues."

"Was I proven wrong?" I grinned. "Because this is one instance where I'd be happy to."

He cocked an eyebrow. "Wow. That's really something, Rina."

"Shut it," I said, chuckling.

"Right. You can't help it if you're the shit, and so damn good, huh?"

"Exactly."

Unfortunately, the jesting died away all too quickly, as concern took its place for him.

"I've had a darknet crawler running and searching for specific keywords related to Erebus and Nathan Donahue, through the onion network for the last few hours. I was hoping to pick up chatter related to them, but I found a direct post from Joe instead."

"What? You're serious?"

He nodded solemnly, then opened up his laptop again.

He accessed the post, then turned the screen toward me so I could take it in.

It was an encrypted message that matched Joe's old encryption key, making it clear that it was definitely him who'd sent it out.

"Red Bishop. Things have shifted due to resistance. Current mission is mutually assured destruction. Abort and I'll step into the light. This ends with me. Contact me via our old protocol."

"Shit," I choked. "Red Bishop is one of Donahue's aliases. Did he respond?"

"Yes, but it had a TTL expiration, so I have no idea what was said. By the time I got to it, it was already deleted."

"What the hell is he playing at?"

"Trying to end things here and now, it seems."

I shook my head to myself. "We're *going* to end things. We're on track. And now the equipment is here, we'll get it done. He's being a fucking martyr."

"For you. It sounds like he's intending to sacrifice himself to protect you and those you love."

"No. It's because it's easier in his mind to martyr himself than to actually fucking live. To come out of the shadows. To face what he's been hiding from all this time —a relationship with his long-abandoned daughter, my mom, everything he left behind when he became a ghost."

"With Santino gone and us taking down Erebus, he'd have no reason to continue to live like that, off the grid and cut off from everyone. I wish we'd known about his connection to Donahue a hell of a lot earlier. There's a lot we could have done. He spent years barely living, just existing and on the run."

"He's stubborn, and he doesn't like other people being pulled into his problems. I'd like to think it was about protecting us, but a lot of it is also driven by ego. You know how he is."

"I do, yeah."

"This isn't happening," I seethed. "No fucking way."

"I hear you, Rina, but this is Joe we're talking about. He's always several steps ahead of everyone."

"Not Nathan Donahue."

"I disagree."

I cocked an eyebrow. "I'm not following. He hasn't been able to eliminate the threat that Donahue and Erebus are."

"The opportunity has presented itself, but he hasn't taken it. I'd say that's the first time ever that he hasn't jumped at the chance to take out an enemy. And he hasn't for *you.*"

The realization of what he was saying sank in. "The moment Erebus started getting its claws into the city, he could've made his move."

"Exactly. But it would have ruined you and those you love. Fuck, it would have ruined my father, too, and me by extension."

"Because he's never avoided going the extreme route to destroying a threat before. And, in this case, that would have basically meant leveling an entire city, so there was nothing for Erebus to take, and also taking out Donahue's people at the same time."

"Yes. We've both looked into him. Hell, a few years ago we looked into him together. We found out that he's committed acts likening to mass fucking genocide in the name of decimating an enemy before. He won't shy away from it as a rule. But he does appear to have a line that we didn't think he had before. And that's those he loves."

"So, for him, the only viable option left is self-sacrifice? Fucking shit... it's from one extreme to the other with him."

"It's how he's lived his life for so long. He doesn't operate anywhere close to *normal.*"

I shook my head to myself. "I know how to stop him from doing this, but I need something from you first. Or, more specifically, access to a certain something."

Intrigue shone in his eyes.

Before I got into it, I laid my hand on his and told him resolutely, "Once we've tracked these assholes, I want you gone, Levi."

"What?"

"You've done enough. And I'm sorry that I need you to do more, that what I'm up against can't be done solo."

"Rina, it's no problem. You know I live for this stuff."

"Now you have a lot more to live for, Levi. Things are different for you now. And I want it to stay that way for you. You've fought too hard and come too far for it not to be. So, once we're done, the moment we access the intel that we need, you head home to your loves. Okay? Promise me."

He took a moment, then gave a nod. "All right, sweetheart. You have my word."

"Thank you."

"Now, what is it that you need access to?"

"Something that will ensure *I'm* the one a step ahead if he actually does this, if I can't talk him down."

AS I MADE my way down the corridor intending to have a little talk with Joe about what the fuck he thought he was playing at, I was pulled up short by the sight of Nico and Milo carrying in some of the equipment that had just arrived.

I couldn't help but marvel at the sight of the quantum processor that Milo was hefting in. It looked like some sort of next-gen, futuristic chandelier, with gold wiring visible on the inside, along with coiled fiber-optic cables that connected to the cooling system. It was contained in a sleek glass panel that was reinforced. Once it was all set up and connected to our systems, it would be lit with glowing LED indicators with pulsing blue lights of the circuits, signaling that the processor was ready to get to work.

Through our separate research into Erebus via their hacks, and Levi looking into the devices that had been retrieved from the *safe zone* takedowns, it had become apparent that Erebus used military-grade cyber defenses that would take some major equipment to crack, the encryption so fucking advanced. This portable quantum processor was slated to help with that. Erebus was using post-quantum encryption, meaning mine and Levi's regular hacking approaches weren't enough and wouldn't get the job done. Hence this.

For starters.

There was also the real-time intrusion spoofer we'd managed to acquire thanks to one of Roman Knight's contacts, something that Nico was carrying in. As I'd looked into the hack when Erebus had infiltrated my system, I'd discovered that one of the things they were also doing was employing AI-based counter-hacking. So we needed to fight fire with fire by using this spoofer to create thousands of fake hacker profiles to overwhelm that aspect of their security. While employing that smokescreen, with the aid of the quantum processor, Levi and I would carry out the real hack.

Milo caught sight of me and grinned. "It's really something, isn't it?"

"It sure is."

"Having one of these is a dream come true, hmm?" Nico said.

"Definitely something I can cross off my bucket list," I admitted.

"I'll take some photos once we get it set up," Nico told me.

"Thank you!"

"We'll make a scrapbook," Milo joked.

Scrapbook. That jolted me right back to my immediate task concerning Joe.

But before I could get back to it, Milo told me, "I'm gonna set up a redundant generator to guard against a blackout. I'll also rig some emergency shut-offs so we can kill the power in case Erebus tries to fry the system. No way in hell are we letting that happen."

"Perfect," I said, smiling out at him. "We'll also need to set up some Faraday shielding. With these guys having military-grade tech, we can't rule out them sending out an EMP if they detect our hack."

He nodded. "I'll take care of it."

This was where his tech-savvy skills were really going to come in handy. And, judging by the enthusiasm all over him, he was happy to get down to it, to put those skills to good use like he had with reinforcing and updating the security system in and around Charon Manor.

As the two of them brought the equipment into the largest living room where Levi had already set up his stuff while I'd been away, I stopped at the threshold.

"What's wrong?" Nico asked, putting down his piece of equipment while Milo was settling the processor into place.

I shoved a hand through my hair. "It's Joe. He's—"

"He's what?" the voice belonging to the man himself sounded.

I spun to see him now just a few feet from me, his ghost-like movements meaning his entire approach had gone undetected. Despite him training me to do the same, I still couldn't pick up when he was doing it.

He was dressed in one of the many teal shirts he had on hand, along with a pair of worn blue jeans. He was sipping from a tall glass, the brown smoothie-thick liquid with an orange tint looking a whole lot like Nico's protein shakes that he used to skip breakfast when he was in a rush or preoccupied with this matter or that. There'd been a lot of that lately with all his meetings.

"Thanks for this suggestion," Joe told Nico. "Definitely hits the spot. This is your own recipe?"

"It is, yeah. Created through a whole lot of trial and error."

"I might have to steal it, use it on a more permanent basis."

"Have at it," Nico said.

I reached out and stroked his arm. He was really giving it his all, trying so hard when it came to Joe.

And what was Joe doing in return? Merely just *playing* nice, while secretly looking to get himself fucking killed!

"Permanent basis, huh?" I snapped. "How will that be possible with you dead?"

That actually got a reaction out of him. He jolted, the glass shaking in his hand. Fortunately, he'd already consumed half of it, so it didn't spill all over him. Although, that was a fraction of what he deserved for this bullshit he was trying to pull.

"What's going on?" Nico asked, looking between us with a whole lot of concern. And suspicion when it came to Joe.

Joe's gaze flicked to him briefly before it settled on me. He at least had the decency to look regretful. "You saw my message to Nathan."

"What message?" Nico cut in.

"The message where he offered to give himself up to end this nightmare," I ground out, my eyes drilling into Joe.

"That wasn't part of the plan," Nico ground out. "It certainly wasn't authorized."

"There wouldn't have needed to be a *plan* at all if he'd accepted my offer," Joe bit back at us in that almighty know-it-all way of his. This time, he was wrong, though. It *wasn't* the right way. He was making a bad call. A really bad call.

He looked at me. "You clearly didn't see Nathan's response."

"The message had a TTL expiration." I eyed Nico, explaining without the jargon, "Time-to-Live expiration, which meant it deleted itself after a certain specified timeframe."

"Well, he denied my offer."

"Your offer to *step into the light* and basically get yourself killed, offer yourself up to him in exchange for him aborting his current mission and pulling his troops out of Tolhurst."

He gestured at the equipment in the living room. "It would have nullified the need for all of this. For another battle, too. For more fucking risk to all your lives."

"*If* Donahue could be trusted to keep his word. And that's a major *if*. Let's not forget that your history with him involved him betraying your entire unit when you were overseas. He was dishonorably discharged and even up for prosecution until he disappeared into the ozone. Your strategy was beyond reckless. It was insane. It was the work of a man with a fucking death wish!"

"That's not—I was trying to do what was best for you, to protect you!"

"You're no longer in a position to decide what's best for me. *I* decide that."

"Caterina—"

"No! You don't get to come out and reveal that you're my true father, then try to fucking sacrifice yourself like this! You don't get to make that emotional connection with me, then rip it all away by getting yourself killed!"

Julian came out of the kitchen down the way, shoving a spoonful of Nesquik cereal into his mouth from the bowl in his hand. He must've been in there with Joe having a second breakfast to the healthy one we'd all shared earlier.

"This is also the direct opposite of the advice I gave you concerning Cat," he told Joe as he reached us and stood off to the side of Joe. "Giving *her* the choice? Remember?"

He'd actually said that? I beamed out at him. Of course he had.

"Things are more complicated than that and they go far beyond personal sentiment," Joe argued. "Do you understand me?"

"We're well aware of the complications," Nico told him. "We've been in the thick of it. For a long time, we were even operating without vital intel because you actively withheld it. Yet, we've not only survived under this onslaught, we've thrived. There's a way to do this, to end it, without losing your life, or any of ours in the process. You need to trust in that." He stepped up to Joe, breaching his personal space and looming over him. "You need to fall in line here or you need to fucking walk. And *that's* where things get really fucking simple. Make your choice, because I won't tolerate any more unilateral moves and action that could put those I love, all my soldiers, and my allies at risk." A growl escaped him as he uttered, "Do. *You*. Understand. *Me?*"

They locked glares.

The intensity ramped up, and I saw Julian still with his spoon in his bowl, and Milo stop his setup in the living room to watch the interaction on tenterhooks, clearly prepared to step in at any moment to bolster Nico.

I readied myself, too, knowing how Joe could be.

His ruthlessness was beyond Nico's.

Although he often thought otherwise and was hard on himself when it came to this sort of thing, Nico Marchetti *did* have a line. When it came down to the bedrock of it, he was a good man.

Honorable.

Loyal.

And loving.

All three of my men were.

Despite the world we'd lived in for so long turning us into monsters, that wasn't all that we were.

We'd still somehow managed to maintain some semblance of our humanity.

Of goodness.

Of fucking decency.

Our *ourselves*.

Those parts that we'd had to bury deep down in order to survive against the brutality that had bombarded us for so long.

"I understand," Joe said, surprising me. Surprising all of us.

He stepped back from Nico.

And then he followed his agreement up with a caveat. Much more like him.

"However, if things go south, I *will* do whatever it takes to end this. If your plan doesn't work, I'll put mine into effect."

"Joe——" I started.

"No," he said, holding up his hand. "I won't fail again."

"What are you——"

"When you were a child. Leaving you here. Thinking you'd be better off here. But now… knowing all the pain it caused you… everything you've suffered through… I clearly made the wrong call. I failed to protect you once. I won't fail again. You're my daughter."

With that, he turned and disappeared back down the corridor.

Julian shoveled in a mouthful of his cereal. "Intense bastard," he muttered between bites.

Nico wrapped his arm around me. "It won't come to what he's suggesting. We're close, so close. We're ending this. Mark my words."

28

~Nico~

"The goal is to crack Erebus' system and access their communications network, as well as to locate their chief operational center," I spoke as Caterina and Levi settled down to get to work on their end of things. The vital end of things at this juncture. "The place where Donahue is rooted, as verified by the research of Joe's that I've reviewed."

"It's going to take time," Caterina told me.

Levi nodded. "We're dealing with multi-point security."

"A brute-force hack isn't a viable option," Caterina added.

"Not an option, not possible, unless you're down with waiting years," Levi said, a glint in his eye.

"And you're going to hit multiple servers at once, yes?" Milo asked them over his shoulder as he checked some of the cable connections.

He'd really been in the zone when it came to setting all of this up, ensuring there were backup protocols in place for every eventuality, shoring up everything.

"Correct," Caterina confirmed.

"Cat, while you're focused on this, I've got Camlann and I'm keeping an eye on any developments regarding your submission for the Brimbank Waterfront development," Julian told her, munching on his favored Maltesers.

He'd been doing a lot of stress-eating over the last few days.

Part of it was him being on edge like we all were, because we were so close to the finish line, and we needed everything to line up now in our favor. But the other part was him trying to reconcile the Angelo of it all, that bastard finally being gone, him having confronted him. Right now, because of the tense state that everything was in, the Manor was locked down, so that was causing a delay to him resuming therapy.

Just a little longer.

"Thank you, baby," Caterina told him.

Stover swept on into the room, pocketing his phone. "I have good news," he reported.

"You did as I suggested and reached out to those contacts of yours?" I asked. Well, it hadn't exactly been a suggestion.

"Yes. The threat of it getting out that a group like Erebus had been operating all this time worked to get their asses in gear and move them from their apathetic states. Especially when I was able to use the evidence that you and your people obtained from your recent takedowns proving that Erebus existed. The photographic evidence of their personnel, surveillance footage you gathered from around the city of their activities that had been caught on camera because they'd believed they were untouchable thanks to Leo and Angelo's influence. They severely underestimated your power over them. Basically, once you locate the communications network, you'll need to mine the data then send it along to said contacts. They'll use it to expose Erebus to the world and every single member will be hunted to the ends of the earth. It won't be put on you to track down and annihilate all operatives. I'll lead the teams that they'll be assigning to that task. As for locating Nathan at the chief operational hub, he's fair game. He can be taken out. When it comes to the hundred or so Marchetti soldiers still following Leo, you'll have to employ the same methods that you did with the Leones to get rid of them, as they're not Erebus operatives. As for Leo himself, annihilate the bastard, and I'll take care of the cleanup myself so it won't come back on you, despite the personal connection he has to the lot of you, especially you, obviously, Nico."

"Good," I said, taking in his report. "Exactly what we need."

"As you know, storming the Marchetti mansion to take out Leo, while he's bolstered by his hundred Marchetti soldiers and a couple hundred of Erebus' operatives isn't feasible without mass casualties on your end, or without blowing the place off the map, which would land you all in hot water with arrests on the horizon."

"Once we locate these key areas of Erebus' and take action, it should draw them from the mansion. As you explained, it would be protocol for them to retreat to these chief locations under threat immediately," I said.

"Correct. Their chief communications hub is the brain and the nerve center of their entire operation. Take that out and they're floundering. Combine that with killing the big boss himself and they're done for."

"Then let's get to work." I laid my hand on Caterina's shoulders from behind. "Anything you need as you go along, let us know, all right?"

She turned and brushed her lips over my cheek. "Will

do." She looked out at all three of us in turn. "Love you, my boys."

"We love *you*."

I eased back and turned to Stover. "Carlo and I have teams prepped to move as soon as we get these locations. I'm arranging a call that I need you on to discuss tactical approaches."

"I'll be there."

"All right, let's leave them be," I said, gesturing at Caterina and Levi, who were already getting underway.

As we headed out, Julian pulling out his phone and getting down to the business end of things for Camlann Corporation and Carver Group, Stover headed down to the gym to resume *keeping his skills sharp*, and I went for the patio, craving a smoke.

"Nico, hold up," Milo's voice sounded behind me just as I'd made it out to the patio.

I turned as I fired up a smoke and took my first soothing drag. "Everything okay?"

He shifted his weight uneasily, then sucked in a breath. "I want the role, Nico."

"Yeah?"

He nodded firmly. "I want to become Underboss. Work alongside you in an official capacity finally, do this thing together, be at your side all the fucking way."

I laid my free hand on his shoulder. "You always have been, brother."

"Right back at you. You're the one who got us through all of this all these years, too."

"Let's call it a team effort." I stepped back and took another drag. "You're sure you want this, though? This is your chance to walk away from that side of things. You'll still be here with us, but you have the option of keeping out of the mafioso politics and business of it all."

"Nah. I want to stay in. Besides, things will be different once you take power. We'll have control that was always denied us before. No more compromising. No more oppression. It'll be a new day. I want to be a part of you bringing that about."

I held out my hand, and we shook firmly. "I can't wait."

"Me neither."

My phone buzzed in my pocket, and I stepped back as I pulled it out and eyed the call display.

Rocco.

I took the call. "You've got me. What's going on?"

"Just wanted to let you know that Carlo Benzino and Remo Caruso are here. Figured you'd want us to show them on through right away. He's just parking his sweet-ass Ferrari now. They'll be at the doors any moment."

"Thanks. I'll see to them."

There was no more secrecy needed regarding my alliance with the Benzinos, so them showing up here wasn't a security concern for them.

Although it did concern *me* as to why they were here right now.

Had something happened on their end of things? Had there been an attack?

No. That couldn't be possible. I had eyes everywhere at this stage. There wasn't one single thing that happened in the city concerning our families without me knowing about it.

"Carlo and Remo are here," I told Milo.

He frowned. "What for? Did something happen?"

"We're about to find out."

I STARED out at Carlo and Remo, the two of them sitting in the chairs opposite my large leather one on the other side of my desk in my home office.

Carlo's perfectly tailored pinstripe suit stretched as he rested his arm along the back of Remo's chair and stroked the shoulder of his maroon bomber jacket, then walked his fingers up his neck to his beanie covering his head.

He clearly really had to be touching him right now. In any way possible.

I wasn't surprised, given the news they'd just imparted to us.

I eyed Milo who was standing beside my chair and we exchanged a grin, a whole lot of relief passing between us too that the news they'd come to tell us was actually something positive and uplifting, something to be celebrated, rather than an emergency or a report of hell raining down upon us.

The two of them were getting married.

"Those snakes of the Marchettis and Leones would never hesitate to use what we love against us. Best not to give them ammunition."

That was what Carlo had told Caterina and me when he'd revealed the truth of his relationship with Remo to us.

He'd been right about it.

And, as such, he'd had to live a lie for years on end.

The two of them had needed to hide what they truly meant to one another. They'd been unable to live their lives as they saw fit, to live their truths.

But things were different now.

Soon, that would be solidified.

And that was when they were planning to reveal their relationship in the most definitive and undeniable way. Not by easing into it, but by throwing a big wedding, the likes of which I doubted the city had actually ever seen before.

"Congratulations," I told them both.

"Vi auguriamo tanto amore e felicità," Milo said, earning a smile from them.

"Thank you," Carlo said. He leaned forward in his chair. "Now, I did intend to come here to relay this news in person and to invite you personally. However, I do also have another reason for coming by."

"An ulterior motive already?" Milo said with humor. "I thought this new alliance was above such things?"

"It is," Carlo said, with a whisper of a smile, recognizing the good humor *and* the dig at the ridiculous former Marchetti-Leone alliance between two utter madmen. "I definitely wouldn't refer to it as having an *ulterior motive*, either."

"A dual purpose," Remo offered up.

Carlo's eyes lit up. "Perfect, my love. Well done."

I leaned back against my chair, folding my hands on my lap. "What can I do for you?"

"In the spirit of our alliance, I came to you first. Rumor has it that Julian is intending to put *Nocturne* on the market. We'd like to purchase it and move into businesses of that nature going forward." He linked hands with Remo. "We are fans of such establishments and now we can actually enjoy that in the open without any issues. However, *Nocturne* is on your territory. That's why we've come to you first. I'm also prepared to offer something in exchange. A seventy percent stake in our Zenith Grand Casino."

Interesting.

When Caterina had been looking into Carlo during the time where we'd been unsure of his true motives and if he could be trusted as an ally, she'd gotten a look at his books in the process of that investigation. As a result, I knew exactly how profitable both their casinos were, what a lucrative investment this would actually be. He was being very generous. Largely because of territory concerns, something that had been a very touchy subject under the previous rule of Santino and Marco.

I didn't want that to be the case here.

Whenever there was fear or needing to tread so carefully, issues would arise and people didn't act or respond in the best of ways.

Besides, our alliance was nothing like what had come before.

There was mutual respect, *and* we'd also been fostering a friendship.

"I don't have territory concerns when it comes to the Benzinos," I told him outright. "But I am interested in this proposal. How about we both buy out Julian, split it down the middle, and I take a smaller stake in the casino?"

"You're telling me that you don't need a gesture of good faith?"

"Pretty much."

"Well, I'm happy to hear it."

"Our bond is solid, Carlo. And unlike my *predecessors*, I don't play games with those I respect and admire. There'll be no mask from me. What you see is what you'll get. And so long as we remain transparent with each other, we'll do well down the road."

"I wholeheartedly agree, Nico." He leaned forward in his chair and held out his hand. "And I accept your revised proposal."

"Pending Julian's agreement, of course," Milo cut in.

"Of course," Carlo said.

I was sure Julian would be in agreement.

He'd already mentioned wanted to sell *Nocturne*. With everything that had happened, things had changed for him and that life had been part of that change. He didn't want that anymore.

"Julian will insist on *Nocturne* needing to remain above board if he's to sell to us, though," I warned Carlo.

"I'd already anticipated that after his past experience with being used by your father and Leo."

"This is actually part of our plans to move toward greater legitimacy," Remo informed us. "We're aiming for eighty percent of our business and holdings to be fully legitimate within the next few years."

"Another vision we share," I told them.

"Very good," Carlo uttered heartily.

"While you're here, you'll be the first to hear the good news." I gestured at Milo standing beside my desk, his arms folded across his chest, his big biceps bulging and a whole lot of ink on display with him just wearing his white tank. "Milo has accepted the role of Underboss of the Marchetti Syndicate."

"Perfect," Remo said, eyeing him. "I've got a bunch of tips I'll pass onto you, if you're interested."

"I'm always looking to learn what I can. Anything to assist Nico."

"Amazing answer," Carlo said with a chuckle. "Congratulations, Milo. You've long deserved such a role." He looked to me. "Just like you finally taking up the mantle."

"Just that son of a bitch, Leo, to remove," Remo muttered. "And his foolish remaining few."

"And Erebus. Speaking of, we might as well strategize our tactical assaults while we're all here. I can call in my Capos if you like. Rocco is already here on your end. Is Tony nearby? Cassio?"

"Tony's coming back from transporting our product to Harlow. Cassio is overseeing a Flower Market delivery."

"Ah, yes, of course."

I rose from behind my desk and asked Milo, "Bring Cassio, Rocco, and Tony in. I'll retrieve Stover." I eyed

Carlo. "He knows more about how these bastards operate that all of us combined."

"Agreed. His input will be valuable. But, Nico, although I am grateful to him for helping to bring us together, keep in mind that he is an extreme puppet master. He's been working alone for so long that a team dynamic is very much a foreign concept to him."

"I'm aware. Don't worry, he's being monitored."

More than he realized.

As I headed on out of my office to retrieve Stover, anticipation thrummed through me.

All of this, the equipment arriving earlier, Carlo and Remo showing up here tonight with their news, the business they'd wanted to discuss… it was all emphasizing just how close we were to achieving what had seemed near-impossible only months ago.

We were right on the verge.

And then the time would be ours.

Fucking finally.

29

~Julian~

Days had passed with Cat and Levi going hard at it

We'd gotten to see the both of them in absolute obsessive mode.

They reacted much the same way, only uttering hacker jargon to one another, the occasional high-five when they made some sort of headway, and then forgetting to eat and losing track of time and everything around them completely.

The only way they would eat while they were deep in it was for us to bring them snacks that didn't interfere with their efforts too much, as in things they could quickly pick up with one hand, rather than actual meals.

It had even gotten to the point where Milo had hauled Levi away physically from the command center and dropped him off in his room to sleep for a few hours. The same had gone for Cat, Nico throwing her over his shoulder and carrying her upstairs to bed.

We were in the end stage now and they were obviously feeling the pressure, because we couldn't move forward until we had those locations. Extremely well-hidden and protected locations.

As I walked into the room with some cookies for snacks, just to mix things up from Milo's insistence on only healthy snacks, Cat slammed her fist down on the desktop.

"Fuck. Their AI just locked me out of the reflection loop. We need to reconfigure the intrusion spoofer before we trip their alerts."

"I'm on it. Give me forty seconds," Levi said, rapidly typing away, so fast that his fingers were basically a blur of motion.

"I'm guessing this isn't the best time to bring you these snacks?" I spoke as I came up behind them.

Not even hearing me, Cat told Levi with a whole lot of urgency, "Hurry, or they'll be able to trace the signal back to us."

"I've got it." He shoved his hands through his curly hair. "Motherfucker, that was close." He looked over at her, grinning. "This is our Mount Everest, Rina."

"Seems to be. But there's nothing I haven't been able to crack. These assholes aren't fucking with my record."

He chuckled. "Damn straight."

"The two of you are something else."

They both turned their heads to look at me.

"I'll take that as a compliment mixed with a slice of fear," Levi jested.

"You'd be right on."

"Hey, baby," Cat greeted me, reaching out and stroking my arm.

"Long time, darlin'."

"We're making headway," Levi told me.

Cat turned her attention back to the task at hand, her touch leaving me.

A gasp escaped her. "Screw that, we're in! We're in, Levi!"

He swung his head to her monitor, his eyes lighting up. "Fuck, yes!"

"Which one is that?" I asked.

"Their communications network."

"Start siphoning the data now," she told Levi.

"On it," he said, getting right down to it.

As she started examining what they'd just accessed, she reported, "Excellent news. For once, when it comes to these guys. We can destroy it from here. We don't need to send any teams."

"It's also definitely possible to siphon all their data," Levi assured her.

"As soon as you're done, I'll fry their system and —fuck!"

"What? What's happened?" I asked.

Levi turned to look over at her. "They know what we're doing and they're trying to apply countermeasures." He asked her worriedly, "Can you hold them off while I finish this?"

"Not for long. How close are you?"

"There's a shit-ton of data, Rina."

"You're talking minutes, rather than seconds, then. Shit."

"Yeah. Okay, focus on trying to ascertain their chief operational hub, just in case they interrupt my process here. We can't fucking start all over again."

"Agreed."

With that, she shifted her weight, then went *hacker intense* again. That was what I'd been calling it since this whole thing had started.

"You won't believe this," Levi uttered after several moments of me putting the cookies down near them, then getting caught up in the hypnotic quality of their rapid-fire movements.

"What's that?" Cat asked distractedly.

"I'm running a search through their files and data as it's coming in, and there's some intel about Nathan Donahue. A list of residences, security protocols put in place for his travels, falsified documentation with a whole slew of aliases listed, way beyond the very few that Joe knew that turned out to be burned aliases."

"Put it into your program," Cat told him. "Right now."

"One step ahead of you, sweetheart."

She grinned. "I'd say we're pretty even *steps-wise*, Levi."

"Ah, you and your competitive spirit. Fucking love it."

"Friendship goals, huh?"

"For us, definitely." A few moments passed, and then he was telling us, "Okay, I'm running a script that'll feed all incoming data into my program as it comes."

"Make sure it's protected, in case they try to access it, or they employ counter measures."

"Got it covered." He grimaced at me, letting me know he hadn't actually thought to employ that extra measure until she'd mentioned it. I wasn't surprised. There was *so* much going on all at once.

I winked at him and saw him getting to it right away in the next second. *Phew.*

"I've got it!" Cat cried all of a sudden.

"Seriously?" Levi asked.

"Yeah. I've found their operational hub! This is it. It has to be it. Hold on—"

In the next few moments, I saw her pulling up security footage for a particular venue. She was asking him to cross-reference it with the data he was pulling in.

"It tracks," Levi confirmed. "That's the place. You've fucking done it, Rina!"

They high-fived, then started screaming and crying out excitedly.

And, fuck, I was right there with them.

It didn't take long for the noise to spread through the house, and then Nico and Milo were rushing on in. Probably would have been Stover, too, if he hadn't been outside throwing knives, or whatever the hell it was today.

"What's all the screaming about?" Milo asked, coming in and looking every which way, on high alert. It was amusing for the circumstances and I started laughing, which earned me less-than-impressed looks from him.

"You've done it," Nico realized, taking in Cat.

"Damn fucking straight she has," Levi confirmed.

"*We* have," she told Levi. "There's no way we could have done any of this separately, not with the way their system is set up." She gestured at what he was doing. "As soon as you retrieve all the data, I'll send the command to fry their system and put it out of commission for good. They'll lose all their data and their communications network will be shot to hell. This will absolutely cripple them."

In the next second, she was scribbling down on a notebook beside her that was filled with formulas and insane calculations.

She ripped out the page she'd just scrawled on, then rose from her chair and handed it to Nico. "The coordinates for the physical location of their chief operational hub."

He took the paper and pulled her to him, kissing her deeply.

I could basically feel the strain as he forced himself to break the kiss before he lost control.

She grinned at him. "Wow."

"Yeah," he said, wiggling his eyebrows at her.

"Go," she told him. "Get that to your teams. Prep. All of that."

"Or *I'm* not gonna be able to control myself. One more kiss or touch and it's all systems go over here," I warned them both.

That was what all the intensity of the last few days had done to all of us. Especially with Cat basically being out of commission while she'd been in the zone, where it had been nothing but hacking and brief naps, no time for anything else.

But it had paid off in a major way.

This was it.

We had their location after all of this time.

We had a path through to putting down these fuckers.

It was fucking on!

30

~Caterina~

It was bittersweet.

Levi and I had achieved what had been near impossible.

We'd acquired every byte of data from Erebus' system.

We'd destroyed said system and devastated their communications network.

We also had more than enough *proof* that Joe's contacts would be able to use as well.

And we had a location on Donahue, thanks to the last piece of the puzzle generated from Levi's specialized program.

Not to mention, on a personal note, I'd achieved the greatest hack of my life.

Everything was set to take Erebus and what remained of the Marchetti resistance under Leo down.

We were just one night away from victory.

Everything was slated to go down tomorrow night.

But the bittersweet aspect was that it meant Levi's part was over and done with.

It meant he needed to go home.

He was leaving.

I pulled from my thoughts as Milo wrapped his arm around me while we waited in the foyer as Levi finished packing up.

"You doing okay, *bellezza?*"

"Yeah," I murmured. "I know he needs to get back, but he'll really be missed."

"I know," he said, softly stroking my hair. "We'll make sure the two of you keep in much closer contact than before. You won't be so distanced anymore."

"That's true. Good point." I beamed up at him. "Thank you."

"Anytime."

Footsteps sounded, taking our attention, and we both looked to see Nico and Joe walking down the corridor together and making their way to the foyer, discussing some final details about the upcoming operation.

I zoned out as I caught sight of Levi at the top of the stairs with Julian, the two of them chatting away as Julian helped him with his bags.

They'd developed a friendship when I'd been gone, and I knew that Julian was going to miss him as well.

As they reached the foyer, Levi dropped his bags, then came to me and threw his arms around me.

I chuckled against him as he basically enveloped me in a bear hug.

He pulled back, holding my arms loosely as he beamed down at me. "That super hack was a blast, sweetheart. We should do it again sometime. Although, without such insane stakes."

"I'll do my best to arrange that," I jested.

"Or you could just hang out," Julian suggested. "You know, at least *try* to do the whole normal thing?"

"Hmm. I used to think *normal* was overrated," Levi

mused. "But toning things down can also bring a little peace." He eyed me. "Keep that in mind, yeah?"

"I will." I gave his hands a squeeze. "Thank you, Levi. For everything. It means more than you know."

"I've always got your back. And I know that goes both ways. Just don't be a stranger this time."

"I promise. Things are different now. There's no more need to keep our friendship a secret."

"Or your skills, for that matter."

"That, too."

"It's about time you felt that freedom. You've earned it several times over."

"And you've earned that peace you'd been fighting for over far too long."

He smiled, squeezed me to him, then stepped back.

Then his attention went to Joe.

"Nice seeing you again."

"Right back at you, Knight. Keep doing what you're doing now."

"Will do."

And that no-nonsense goodbye was over as quickly as it had begun.

Nico stepped forward, and a smirk graced Levi's lips as he told him, "It's been interesting and unexpectedly pleasant getting to know the real you. Turns out you're not the asshole I took you for beforehand."

"Damn," Milo uttered.

Amusement danced in Nico's eyes. "The feeling's mutual. You're not just the antagonistic shit I took *you* for."

They shook hands. "In all seriousness, I'm truly grateful for everything you've done. Thank you, Levi. You'll always have an ally in me and mine."

"Anytime, anywhere," Milo added.

"Much appreciated."

They hugged it out, then Levi turned and slap-shook with Milo. "It's been fun."

"*Fun.* You're something else, aren't you?"

Levi grinned. "That I am."

Julian grasped his arm. "Come, let's get you settled in the armored car Nico's insisting on transporting you back to Stonewell in. With armed escorts, too."

"It's just a precaution," Nico said.

"Aww, I'm touched."

I chuckled. "Only the best for you now."

He smiled out at me as he reached the door. "See you soon, Rina."

"That's a promise."

"Good."

With that, I watched as Julian walked him out, the two of them chatting away about sparring.

I turned to see that Joe had gone off somewhere again.

He was restless like that.

Especially here with my guys and under these strained circumstances.

But Nico and Milo were there and coming to me in the next moment as the emotion of saying goodbye to Levi and watching him go slammed into me.

It was what needed to happen.

And, besides, things would be better going forward than they'd ever been when it came to maintaining our friendship.

So much easier.

So much lighter.

It was all good.

I WAS SO WIPED, I could barely make it up the stairs.

Apparently, I didn't have to worry about that because, in the next second, Nico was sweeping me up in his arms and carrying me bridal-style up the stairs as Milo and Julian chuckled.

They followed us up as Nico carried me into my bedroom.

And then all three of them were there, carefully stripping me out of my clothes until I was completely bared to them.

Groans and growls surrounded me.

"Not tonight," Nico spoke, using his firm and uncompromising tone. "She's exhausted."

Julian brushed his lips over mine sweetly. "You're going to get some solid sleep tonight, all right?"

"No arguments here," I agreed.

In the next second, Milo was there with one of my silk night dresses. He slid it on me.

"Aww, I feel so special. Even being dressed."

"You *are* so special," Nico said.

"So fucking special to us," Milo added.

Julian picked me up this time and settled me under the sheets in the middle of the bed.

And then as I got comfortable, my eyes growing heavy, I heard a whole lot of stripping, before they then climbed into bed with me, the three of them wrapping themselves all over me.

"Mmm," I murmured sleepily, sinking into it all. "I wouldn't have it any other way."

"It's going to be just like this every night for the rest of our lives," Nico assured me.

"Perfect," I breathed. "So perfect. Just like our love."

The last thing I heard was them all telling me how much they loved me, before I let their warmth, love, and safety infuse every part of me, as sleep took me.

31

~Emilio~

An infernal beeping jolted me awake.

My eyes snapped open, and I rapidly took in my surroundings.

All four of us were entwined in Caterina's bed, her in a sexy turquoise night dress and the rest of us in our boxers. Julian was almost horizontal, his head on my lap and his legs twisted around Caterina's. Her breasts were pressed up against me, her head half on my pillow and on her own, and Nico was wrapped around her from behind, his face buried in her neck.

And that buzzing continued on through it all.

I managed to reach out and snatch up my phone, seeing a blazing red light coming from the screen.

The moment I took it in, a wave of adrenaline tore through me.

The early-warning system had been tripped.

Just.

I'd woken up right away, thankfully, the second the alert had started going off.

I pushed out of bed and rounded it to Nico's side, shaking him. "Nico, wake up. We have a situation."

He groaned, but opened his eyes right away, then released Caterina and sat up, scrubbing his hand over his face. "What's wrong?"

"The early-warning system has just been tripped."

"What?" he rasped, blinking rapidly to get his bearings. "How long ago?"

"Less than two minutes."

"You're certain it's not a wild animal again?"

"It's been tripped in four places—and counting."

He pushed off the bed and snatched up his pants, pulling them on swiftly. "All right. I need eyes out there ASAP. We need to know what we're dealing with. Pull up the surveillance footage from the cameras you and Rocco planted in the vicinity of the sensors."

"On it," I assured him, rapidly bringing up the app on my phone and accessing the information, analyzing it as quickly as possible.

In the meantime, Nico pulled on his white tee, then tossed my tank to me, which I caught with my free hand. And then he was setting Julian's jeans and gray V-neck tee on the bed beside him, and doing the same with Caterina's yoga pants and tank.

I growl escaped me as I rapidly pieced together the situation.

"What?" Nico asked, as he went to wake up Caterina and Julian.

"It's Leo."

Our eyes locked.

"Here with Erebus operatives or his Marchetti soldiers?"

"These aren't Erebus. They're not moving in the uniform and highly trained way Erebus operatives do.

There are no eerie masks either. Plus, these guys are all decked out in Leo's signature black leather trench coats. Like some kind of *Matrix* reenactment."

"Or Grim Reapers."

"That too. That's obviously their intention. They're armed to the teeth. The system has even identified a couple of RPGs."

"How many soldiers?"

"From what I can make out... all of them." I shoved my hand through my hair. "From the moment the early-warning system is tripped, to the point of impact, is just enough time to evacuate. Us, our soldiers and all personnel, via the several evac paths we've laid out."

"I'm aware. We're not evacuating. We're not letting the Manor fall. They won't take our territory. Worse—our fucking home."

"Understood. We fight."

His eyes darkened. "We *fight.*"

"I'll call in Cassio and his soldiers to back us up. And the Benzinos?"

"No. Inform them, but leave them out of it."

"Nico—"

"I can't risk more soldiers being put at risk than already will be with this attack as it is. The assault on the Erebus operational hub is within hours. Nothing can interfere with that. Leo pulling this tonight sure as fuck won't."

"Can you two keep your strategizing bullshit down?" Julian grumbled, turning over in his sleep and grabbing what had been my pillow and shoving it over the back of his head. "It's the middle of the night. Jesus, guys."

Nico ripped the pillow from his grip, then smacked him over the head with it. "Wake up, J. This *strategizing bullshit* is relevant to right here and now."

"What?" he groaned, pushing himself up into a sitting position. "What are you talking about?" His eyes went to Caterina, and he reached out and stroked her hair as she slept.

"The early-warning system has been tripped. Leo and his soldiers are headed right for us," Nico told him outright.

"Caterina, time to wake up," he said, gently shaking her next, as Julian jumped out of bed and snatched up the clothes that had been tossed on there for him, and rapidly started dressing.

"What's happened?" Caterina asked, her eyes opening, then darting frantically from Nico to around the rest of the room, as she shot upright.

"Leo's coming for us. Right now," Nico informed her. "With his own soldiers."

She frowned. "No Erebus?"

"No."

She snatched up her phone in the next second. "They must have moved very recently. Like, tonight, while we were asleep. With us destroying their communications network, their protocol when things go dark must have been to return to their operational hub for orders and debriefing, all of that. There's no way they'd be on board with Leo doing this. He's the last mafioso leader they have in their pocket to bring about their plan of settling here and taking control via the connections that being patrons to somebody like Leo brings. Not to mention him risking the last of his loyal followers by coming at us. At a fortified fucking location. There's no doubt that they'll sustain casualties."

"Although, it does put us at a disadvantage that we can't go for the kill," I pointed out.

"Agreed. It's much easier to kill than to merely

temporarily incapacitate. It takes a lot more strategy and finesse," she said.

"And it'll slow us down," Nico mused.

"Perhaps that's what Leo is counting on," Julian suggested.

Caterina scrolled on her phone for a few moments, then reported, "Yeah, Erebus is no longer at the Marchetti mansion. They moved out in small units throughout the night, using their usual difficult-to-detect ghost protocol."

"All right," Nico said. "Get dressed." As she started doing that quickly, he snatched up his phone, telling us, "I'll coordinate with Rocco and Tony, get everything in place before they hit." He eyed me. "You've re-calibrated the Manor's countermeasures to deliver non-lethal hits, yes?"

"Yeah. It's good to go."

"Set to activate when hostiles are within twenty yards?"

"Correct."

"Good. We'll—"

The bedroom door flew open and Stover barreled on in, fully suited up in heavy duty tactical gear with a sniper rifle in hand. "I'm gonna need your best snipers. Have them meet me on the roof. We'll fan out, take different angles, covering the entirety of the perimeter and pick off the majority of these shits coming at us."

"Wow, Joe," Caterina uttered, thankfully having just finished dressing before he'd burst on in.

"I have a connection to the security alerts as well," he told us.

Of course he did.

Without authorization.

To his credit, Nico moved past it, the urgency of the immediate situation taking precedence, and he merely told him, "The kill isn't authorized. Just drop them."

"Understood," Joe said.

"Caterina and Julian, you'll work with Tony and his soldiers, focusing on internal security. Milo and I will partner with Rocco and Stover to incapacitate and thin the herd before they're able to hit the Manor directly."

Yeah, this definitely called for both my *wrecking ball* approach and Nico unleashing his *feral* state.

"You're sure you can let go without resorting to murder?" Caterina asked him.

"I've got it. But you're not quite there yet, hence me keeping you out of this aspect. And partnering you with Julian. He brings a different energy to you than I do during the heat of battle."

"Okay," she said, accepting it easily, knowing well where she was at, and working with us, even though I knew she didn't like being pushed onto the sidelines in any way. But she could see beyond that for the bigger picture. Just one of the things that made her perfect for us.

"Leo is mine," I ground out.

"Taking him out ASAP is the best tactical move," Stover spoke. "Whoever can get in a shot——"

"Leo is Milo's," Nico interjected in that non-negotiable tone of his.

"Thank you," I told him.

He grasped my shoulder and smiled.

And then he turned to us all, and ordered, "Let's move."

———

I BARRELED through a half a dozen hostiles who'd just reached the courtyard, roaring out into the night as I took them down in a burst of power and strength.

As soon as they hit the ground with bone-rattling

thuds, Tony was there, backing me up, and pistol whipping two of them into unconsciousness. A boot to the skull to the others from me put them out of the fight.

A familiar snarl caught my attention, and I looked to see Nico hauling a badly beaten opponent into the side of the house, the brutal impact knocking the fucker out.

Nico spun back, covered in blood that wasn't his own.

But he hadn't killed anyone or lost control in his unleashed state. It had been merciless and brutal, sure, but strategic.

He'd come a really long way. With that and so much else, too.

I turned back and Tony came up beside me, the two of us signaling our soldiers nearby to converge as we watched another couple of dozen of Leo's soldiers sprinting into the fray, coming at the front side of the Manor, looking to breach it.

Before we could launch ourselves at them and put the fuckers down, a rumbling thunder sounded, shaking the ground beneath our feet.

I turned to see flames raging in the next moment, climbing into the night sky, debris flying every which way.

"RPG fired!" Nico called over. I saw him tapping his earpiece and communicating with the other team leaders. And then he was rushing over to me, kicking one of the hostiles in the face who was giving one of his soldiers some extra trouble.

He made it to me, telling me in harsh breaths, "It was fired by Leo. Caterina has eyes on him. While they were fighting off the approach through the tree line coming at the patio, he and a few of his soldiers were able to breach the Manor. She spotted him entering from the southwest doors."

His words slammed into me, harder than I'd even expected them to.

This was it.

This was the chance I'd been waiting on for so goddamn long.

I took in the immediate situation, though, weighing it all up.

The roars of battle.

Yet more incoming soldiers about to descend.

The ongoing gunfire coming from the Manor's countermeasures being put into effect.

Sniper fire from up on the massive expanse of the roof.

The Manor being breached.

Now a fucking explosion.

"Nico, I—"

"Go. We'll deal with this."

I hesitated.

Sticking close and protecting him was a massive part of me.

But I really needed to do this.

I needed to end that motherfucker.

My parents deserved their long-denied justice.

And the world needed to be rid of that demented shithead.

"Yeah," I breathed, giving him a chin lift.

And then I was bursting back into the Manor, my gun at the ready as I went.

———

THE CLOSED DOOR to the command center was being defended by six of our soldiers, who were beating back just as many, holding their own well.

I saw the site of the explosion several feet down. It had taken out a good portion of the corridor and blown a hole in Nico's office, the space exposed now, with part of the wall being ripped away. I noticed another battle taking place around there as our soldiers fought against the trench coats.

And then I saw that motherfucker.

He was inside Nico's office, the trench coats there covering him as he rifled through Nico's stuff, then tried futilely to bypass security on Nico's laptop to access his files.

I couldn't get through the corridor while it was jampacked with numerous battles taking place.

I grunted, and made a beeline through the kitchen instead, finding the patio doors shattered, glass all over the tile.

As I pushed out, my boots crunching on the jagged glass, I caught sight of Julian and Caterina working together amongst our soldiers to beat back the trench coats who'd attacked from the tree line. Julian executed one of his fancy kicks that sent one of his opponents flying across the patio, and Caterina was there hauling a chair into the bastard and knocking him out cold. Then they exchanged a signal that had Caterina leaping toward Julian. He grasped the underside of one of her boots as she hit and tossed her into the air, where she then leapt into a spinning kick that downed two of their opponents in one go.

Impressive.

I took out two fuckers who tried to stop my sprint to Nico's office from this roundabout route I'd been forced to take, firing off a bullet to the kneecap of each one. Shrieks filled my ears as they dropped hard.

Time seemed to stretch on painfully as I kept running and downing more on my way.

Rationally, I knew it was only seconds.

But every single one that went on by where I wasn't already there in that piece of shit's space was one too many, an urgency building within me that I'd never quite felt before. It sparked a rage that I wasn't used to bringing into battle.

I was just a few feet out when I caught sight of Stover descending from the roof, then running over to back up Caterina and Julian, firing off non-lethal shots with his rifle as he went.

Part of the rear wall of Nico's office was blown out. The easy access that it afforded in this situation was being made less so by the two trench coats standing guard and protecting their boss.

Not for long.

As they caught sight of me, reading my intention and registering the danger that I posed, they went for me.

I stopped them before they could even begin to do much of anything, snagging the closest one and slamming his back against my chest, trapping him in a bear hold, while I smashed my boot into the other, the force of it knocking him right onto his ass.

I spun with the first guy in my hold, basically dragging him with me, as I reached down and hauled the fallen one up with one hand, then smashed him back down onto the concrete, his head smacking painfully against it, the impact knocking him out.

I wrenched the other guy's head back, speeding things up, as he struggling uselessly against me, his body weakening too quickly for him to really put up much of a fight. He went limp in my arms, and I tossed him away, then stepped over the debris and into Nico's office.

Leo had his back to me.

He still thought he was protected.

The guys over by the door on the other side were

LEIA KING

engaged in a vicious battle in the corridor with our soldiers. Preoccupied to the max.

It was just him and me.

He was muttering to himself, then slamming his fists down on Nico's desk and raging, "Marchetti Holdings was to be mine! Why did he give it to you? A fucking kid! A weak little shit!"

"He's stronger than you can possibly imagine. Stronger than your ego will ever allow you to recognize," I hissed through my teeth.

Leo jolted and spun around.

His gaze darted from me to the felled guys just outside. He'd been so consumed with his clear obsession with trying to regain Marchetti Holdings that he'd completely lost sight of his surroundings.

"What are you doing here? I want to see Nico face-to-face."

"He's done with you. You're nothing to him." I stepped forward. "But you are to me. You're the man who murdered my parents, motherfucker."

His eyes shot wide. "How do you—"

"Oh, it's all come out, Leo. Every twisted little thing and detail."

"It was my right! I had to *take* it!"

I smashed my fist into his face with a roar.

It sent him reeling back against Nico's desk, slapping his hand to it to stop himself from landing on his fucking ass.

"None of it was yours!" I thundered. "But your ego fucked up everything! Your obsession for power that never belonged to you, that was too twisted in your hands! You injected poison into the Marchetti Syndicate and destroyed it in your greed and megalomania! You tore lives apart!

316

You subjugated Nico! You took my parents from me! You fucked all over everything!"

I burst forward and snagged him by the throat, jerking him to me. "That all ends here."

One of his guys broke from the battle over by the door and went to draw his gun.

A flash of movement rushed across my vision a moment before the guy was slammed into, a grunt escaping him as he jarred painfully against one of the still intact walls, his gun clattering to the floor in the process.

And then I saw Nico standing there, breathing heavily, obviously having sprinted over here like a madman.

All to back me up.

All to protect *me* this time.

He dropped the guy with a brutal blow to the side of the head, then spun toward me.

"You little shit!" Leo raged in my hold at Nico. "Think you can take everything from me and live through it?"

"I already have. Sending your soldiers here was your last foolish action, from the mind of a man with no strategic judgment whatsoever, a man obsessed only with power and enforcing said power with ridiculous bursts of violence and brutality. It takes more than that to rule. I warned you. I warned you repeatedly."

"But all you did was discount him," I growled, shoving him against the wall with my hand still to his throat.

"You know no honor. No loyalty. You have no true concept of the meaning of family either," Nico told him. "You're nothing but a danger. Scum who killed a man much greater than you in Enzo Bardi. And now you'll be dealt with as traitors should be." Nico gave me a chin lift, then stepped back, giving me some room as he watched justice about to be delivered.

Movement from Leo caught my attention just a split second before he drew a knife from the pocket of his coat.

I snagged his wrist, stopping him before he was able to drive it into my flesh.

He screamed as I did more than that, wrenching his hand up higher with a brutality that had a definitive snap sounding.

"An underhanded shit right to the end, huh?" I said, of his attempt to stab me like that. "Nothing but a coward hiding behind a whole lot of violence. You make us sick." I yanked his knife free, then spun it in my hand. "Good fucking riddance," I growled.

And then I drove the blade into the side of his throat.

Blood sprayed all over me.

He spluttered and wheezed, clawing at my arms in desperation.

In real fucking fear.

I shoved away from him, and Nico walked to me as we watched Leo sink to the floor and choke to death on his own blood.

As he finally got what he deserved.

THE BATTLE HAD WORN DOWN.

In fact, after Leo being taken out, many of his soldiers had just laid down their arms entirely, realizing they'd been fighting without cause at that point.

Now the massive job of the cleanup was underway.

I'd been drawn away from Leo's dead fucking body by needing to check in with our soldiers. We had a dozen critically injured who'd now been transported to the ER, along with many other minor injuries sustained by others. But there'd actually been zero fatalities, thank fuck. A lot of that had been the way we'd all worked together in concert, having one another's backs, like a true massive unit. It had made a huge difference. Another had been the way Nico had coordinated the response to Leo's ill-fated home invasion.

I made my way back to Nico's office because I needed to see that fucker dragged away. I just needed one last look.

But then I was pulled up short as I encountered Nico, Caterina, and Julian, all now gathered together discussing the cleanup details.

Thankfully, only minor injuries had befallen all of us, too. Except Julian's cheek was concerning me. He'd merely dabbed the nasty gash with a piece of paper towel from the kitchen, but it was still bleeding down his face.

Before I could speak to it, I noticed that Nico looked stressed.

"What's wrong?" I asked as I reached them. "Aside from the obvious of us being woken up by a home invasion, of course."

"It's Stover. He's MIA," he told me as he pulled out his phone and dialed rapidly.

It picked up quickly, as I'd expected, given that we were just coming off an emergency situation. "Rocco, eyes on Joseph Stover? What? No. Don't try to pursue, I've got it."

He hung up, then told us, "Stover took off. Rocco's not sure when, because he and our soldiers were in the thick of it, but he was spotted disappearing into the forest shortly after word of Leo's demise started to spread through the battlefield."

"He's obviously decided to take matters into his own hands, seeing this home invasion as things not going to plan," I surmised.

"Foolish, considering we now know that Leo was acting independent of Erebus," Nico muttered.

Caterina stepped up to him and stroked his bicep. "We prepared for him doing something like this, and going rogue. I have the means to track him. Let me do that."

He nodded.

With that, she headed off to get to work.

I smiled to myself.

There's our woman.

32

~Nico~

"Are you okay?" I asked Milo as he watched a couple of my soldiers dragging Leo's corpse away in a body bag.

He finally turned from staring at the scene and eyed me. "He was *your* uncle."

"By blood only."

"Well, yeah. There was never any love lost between the two of you."

"Especially near the end."

The truth was, it had been from the moment Leo had become Underboss that had shifted everything and worsened our relationship to the point of no return.

Milo knew that, really, but we both also knew why I wasn't speaking to it.

Because the fucker had only become Underboss as a result of murdering Milo's father.

He shoved a hand through his spiky hair, and admitted, "It was a lot. Hearing him spout all the shit that he did, knowing how if your father had just had faith in mine, then things could have gone a whole other way."

"Even if it hadn't been that night, Milo, with Leo in the

picture, and on an obsessive power trip, he would have found another way. The only thing that would have stopped it would have been Marco removing him from power."

"I hear you, yeah." He sighed heavily. "And there's no point imagining things being different or going another way, because it's not our reality, and it can never be. What happened can't be undone. My parents are gone." He brightened a little as he said, "But I have the three of you, our own crafted family. And now, I do feel like justice has been served. Not just because I was able to put that motherfucker down, but because *we're* taking power now and undoing the mistakes they made. We've rooted out the poison that had infected everything."

I laid my hand on his shoulder. "I'm glad you feel that way. I'm so sorry that it took such a long time for the truth to come out and for you to get the justice that you deserved."

"All that matters is that I did."

"I agree."

We turned at the sound of a disgruntled sound to see Julian coming into the living room, the one where we'd had the command center set up. Pretty much the only room on the ground floor that hadn't sustained any damage whatsoever, thanks to us focusing a lot of our defense there to protect the equipment within.

"Told you it needed stitches," Milo said, gesturing at the now treated gash across Julian's left cheek from a hit he'd taken during the battle, wherein he'd had his face smashed through a window.

"Five," Julian muttered.

I walked to him and inspected the work my on-call doctor had done. "This will barely scar at all. She did a phenomenal job. Don't worry, J."

"You think Cat will find it hot?"

"Absolutely. No doubt about it."

"You know how she is," Milo chimed in.

"Yeah. She likes it rough. Down and dirty as fuck."

"She sure does," Caterina spoke, walking in with a tablet in hand, her attention half on us, half on it. "Table that for later, my boys."

"Incredibly difficult to do after just coming out of my *feral* state, *principessa.*"

"I'm right there with you."

"You controlled it really impressively this time. Yet again."

"Thanks to the three of you. You held me steady through it all, even just the thought of you."

"We're glad," Milo said.

"Nicely done, darlin'."

"So, here's the situation. The tracer I planted on Joe is active and he's on the move. Moving dangerously fast, actually." She propped up the tablet on one of the desktops and gestured at the map with the bright-red circle moving in real-time.

"The protein shake obsession he developed really came in handy," Julian commented. "What did you call it? The thing you dropped in one of them?"

"An ingestible micro-RFID tag," she told him. "Something I had Levi procure from Knightsridge Engineering. One of their advanced prototypes. It can't be detected through regular means. It has no beeping GPS signal. Because the tracker transmits data through the body's natural electromagnetic fields, even if Joe goes digitally dark, I'll still be able to track him."

"Talk about next-gen tech," Milo spoke.

She lifted a shoulder. "That's Knightsridge for you."

I took in the tracking dot on the map. "He's not heading to the chief operational hub."

"No," she confirmed. "He must've lied to Levi and me about Donahue not taking him up on his offer to *step into the light*. It looks like they've arranged another meeting location."

"Where he's gonna get himself killed," Julian groused.

Caterina told us, "As you know, from accessing their communications network, I've been able to tag many of their operatives. And right now, at least thirty of them are in Joe's vicinity. It looks like they're converging at this prearranged meeting location."

"Does he really think he can win out against those odds?" Milo asked.

"No. He'll try to take them down with him," Caterina said, pinching the bridge of her nose, her distress clear. "He thinks he's doing right by me, by us."

"Sounds more like a lack of trust to me," I spoke.

"He's overcompensating for not being there for Cat in the past. It's skewing everything for him," Julian said.

"Well, I'm not going to let him do this," Caterina ground out with a whole lot of conviction.

"*We* won't," I stated.

She frowned out at me. "Nico, no. Your soldiers are all geared up to take the operational hub, to finally end this. Carlo's too. Everything is set. So many people are involved in this, so many lives impacted and—"

"*And* Nathan Donahue still needs to be taken out. Something good has come out of Stover going off half-cocked. We now know that Donahue won't be at the operational hub."

"But we can't split their focus. I've shown you how many operatives they'll need to take down in order to render that place ineffective. Everything you and Carlo have at your disposal will be needed."

"Agreed. It should be the four of us."

"What?" she exclaimed. "But the operational hub assault? Don't you need to—"

"Everything is set, strategized down to the last detail, covering every eventuality, thanks to Stover and the operational tactics you and Levi were able to obtain on Erebus from your hack. It doesn't need to be me who leads that assault."

"You're sure?"

"Yes," I said, taking her hands in mine. "But *you* need *us* on this."

"Besides," Julian said, stepping forward with Milo. "It's been a long time since we've gone on a mission, just the four of us."

"One last one for the road, beauty."

She looked out at each of us in turn.

And then she gave my hands a squeeze and nodded. "Let's do it."

33

~Joseph Stover~

"I failed to protect you once. I won't fail again. You're my daughter."

My daughter.

I'd failed my own daughter.

She and her mother both.

They'd endured so much suffering because I'd made the wrong call.

More so, because I hadn't stepped in when I should have.

I'd relinquished control and sat back and let things play out.

And it had *hurt* them.

The two people who I cared about most in the world.

Truthfully, the only two people I'd ever cared about.

This was my chance to rectify that.

To do right by Caterina.

Tonight had been too close. The enemy had come into their home. If it had been Erebus themselves, they wouldn't have survived it.

The takedown of the operational center was fast approaching, but I hadn't been able to leave it in their hands, knowing how skilled and fucking brutal Erebus was. I couldn't risk Caterina falling. I couldn't risk those she loved falling either. It would surely break her.

She'd been through far too much as it was. I couldn't let her suffer anything more.

I stared at the entrance to the storage facility, one that Erebus had used in the past, but that had been abandoned when I'd been on a mission a few years back that had exposed this as one of their arms storage facilities.

It had come as no surprise to me that Nathan had chosen this location for our meet. It had marked the time that I'd first directly crossed him as the leader of Erebus.

The time before had been me exposing his illicit activities when we'd served together.

The storage facility was a former aircraft hangar, the airport it had belonged to no longer in service. It hadn't been for years.

As my boots crunched on the tarmac, making my presence known intentionally, the air shifted.

I already knew they were here.

I hadn't come this far surviving in this fucked-up world of ours not to be able to pick up on a threat in my vicinity.

They were hiding for no reason.

Or, perhaps, knowing Nathan, to emerge dramatically.

He was a big fan of that and the intimidation factor.

He should know better than to believe that would work on me.

Then again, he had grown far too bold of late.

Trying to take the City of Tolhurst, working to settle there and inject the poison that was Erebus into the infrastructure and sources of power there… it had been beyond brazen.

The fact he'd chosen Tolhurst at all had been foolish, doing it to take a dig at me, to get under my skin, while severely underestimating what I would do once word had reached me.

I strode to the entrance and pushed open the heavy steel doors.

As I walked further into the space, the rumble of footsteps sounded.

And then they were there like ghosts in the night, bursting in from the several entrances to the space, stepping out of the shadows, thirty of them surrounding me, a sea of tactical gear and those eerie masks.

One of them stepped forward and pulled his mask up, resting it on his gray buzz cut.

"It's been a while," he spoke, that familiar sadistic smirk of his settling on his face.

He had a few more age lines since I'd last seen him, but he wore them well. He was still a roided-out monster of a man. The bulk of the tactical gear he was decked out in only served to emphasize that. And those eerie pale-blue eyes fixed on me with that usual menacing edge.

"Nathan," I ground out, resisting the instinctual urge to pull my gun and shoot him dead right here and now.

That wasn't the plan.

Not yet.

"I didn't think you'd have the balls to finally come out of the dark and face me."

"I didn't think you'd be stupid enough to try to take Tolhurst alongside that sadistic shit, Santino."

"It was a mutually beneficial arrangement. The tide has turned for Erebus. We no longer want to operate from the shadows. We want to be front and center."

"An impossibility. Erebus has always been a shadowed group. It's the foundation of its entire makeup. Getting greedy, even beyond what you already are, and trying to alter that was a mistake, as I'm sure you've realized with the resistance that you've come up against."

"Resistance. Yes, those who are fighting your battles for you. Carlo Benzino and the Marchetti boy."

"That ends here today. You pull your men out and go elsewhere. You've already lost too much to maintain a foothold there as it is. You know you need to cut your losses. And that was our agreement for me coming to you."

"In exchange for you preventing their attack on my operational center."

"There will be no need for the attack when you make it clear that you're retreating and turning your attention elsewhere. I'm certain you already have another place in mind anyway—or several."

"That I do." He stepped closer until he was just shy of my personal space. "But first, let's discuss your part in all of this."

"My part was clear."

"Yes, yes. You'd give yourself over to me. Take your punishment and then allow me to *reconfigure* you to my liking without any resistance."

"I'm a formidable asset."

"You were, certainly. What you can do, very few can match. Even the best of my operatives. Even me. Where fieldwork is concerned. Your ability to move undetected, to eliminate a threat."

"Exactly. And in return, you'll pull out of Tolhurst."

"I knew you wouldn't be thrilled with the likes of me infiltrating your former home. But that's what it is to you, Joseph. A *former* home. You haven't resided there for years. Decades, even. You did have a personal connection to it, but we both know that Bianca Leone is no longer in said city." He started striding up and down in front of me, making a show of thinking on it, as he rubbed his clean-shaven jaw. "So it got me thinking. Why such resistance? Why go to such lengths to try to spare it from me? Why *risk* yourself by intervening directly, too?" He stopped right in front of me, his eyes darkening. "Because of Caterina Leone. Your *daughter.*"

A chill rolled down my spine.

"What are you talking about?"

"Please. Spare me your futile attempts at denial. We were inside her system. To gain intel on *her* specifically. It didn't take much from there. Not with the reach I possess."

"It makes no difference either way. The deal still holds."

"With the decimation of our communications network, my priority is not to bring in somebody like you anymore. I need *her.*"

"The hell you do."

"At first, I considered Levi Knight. He was a part of it, as we've discovered. But I don't want to destabilize Knightsridge Engineering. Their next-gen tech is highly valuable to us and will no doubt come in handy down the road. Targeting the son of the owner would cause a great deal of destabilization that we can't afford. Moreover, his reckless edge is a sticking point for me and mine. Besides, Caterina was the lead on all of this. It's been her all this time, working in the shadows, undercutting my efforts. It was even she who murdered Santino. I want *her.*"

"Never," I seethed.

"Sure, you're resistant. You obviously offered this to me all in the name of protecting her. But, Joseph, you're under the illusion that you actually have a choice. I *will* take her. Now, I can do that without harming her, or I can inflict a great deal upon her. I can break her and build her back up to my liking. You *do* get to make a decision where that's concerned."

"In exchange for what?"

"Call off their attack immediately. Then get on your fucking knees and lay down your life. No games. No tricks."

"I won't let you corrupt my daughter."

"As I've said, where that's concerned, you don't have a choice. It's already done."

"The hell it is."

I stepped back and ripped open my tactical jacket.

His eyes shot wide, and he jerked back.

Even his operatives followed suit and shuffled back several steps without orders from him to do so. That was how shocked they were. And afraid.

Good. Really fucking good.

"You've lost your mind," Nathan choked, staring at the shit-ton of explosives that I had strapped to my torso. His eyes darted to the trigger than I'd just released from being hidden up my sleeve, and he swallowed hard.

"Given everything I've endured, you'd think it would have happened sooner, no?"

"You do this and we all die."

I lifted a shoulder. "I don't have a problem with that."

His men went to take aim at me, but he held up a single hand that had them holding off. "Don't be fools."

"I'll protect Caterina to my last fucking breath," I seethed. "And all of yours."

My finger brushed the detonator.

"Stop!" a voice rang out.

My whole body tensed.

And that reaction got a whole lot worse and harder to contain, when she came into view, flanked by her men.

There she was, over by the northeast exit, in her turquoise leather jacket and a pair of jeans, not even protected in proper gear, indicating she'd rushed up here.

Nico, Julian, and Milo were much the same way, just in their street clothes.

But Julian and Milo were holding grenades in both hands, a clear warning to Erebus and Nathan. Nico had a gun trained on Nathan's skull.

And Caterina had her knives.

My God.

It was insanity.

Why?

Why would she do this?

Why would she risk this?

"It doesn't need to be this way," she called to me.

"Of course it does. How long have you been here? Did you hear everything he said? His plans for you?"

"Yes."

"So, you see, then? You see why I need to do this?"

"I see why you *think* you need to. Because you have tunnel vision when it comes to me, and because you believe you need to prove yourself as my father. You don't."

"Of course I—"

"Not like *this!*"

"Caterina—"

"Prove it by sticking around! By being in my life! By developing a proper relationship with me! Not by sacrificing yourself when there's another way!"

When I hesitated, my finger still hot on the trigger, Nico cut in, "The assault on the operational hub is complete, Stover!"

"What?" Nathan roared.

I frowned. "How—"

"You don't think we anticipated this? That we didn't know where you were headed?" he put to me. "You underestimate your daughter."

She'd tagged me.

Likely with a liquid tracker, knowing how she—the protein shakes!

"It's over," Nico said, glaring at Nathan. "Your operatives weren't expecting us. We moved up the timeframe. They've all fallen. The hub is decimated to fucking ash. You're done."

They'd done it? They'd actually taken them down without falling in the process?

I couldn't—I'd thought—I *had* underestimated things.

I'd allowed my fear for her wellbeing to cloud so much.

To almost kill me.

To take me away from her yet again.

Fuck me.

"You won't survive this," Nathan seethed at Nico. "I'll come for you. The Marchetti Syndicate. The Benzino Family. Everything and everyone you fucking love!"

My finger wavered on the trigger.

"Not like this!" Caterina called to me.

"I can't just—"

"Trust us! Trust me!"

As Nathan lost his shit, realizing he was beaten, he kept spouting off threats of ruin and death, over and over, unable to do much else, because if he so much as signaled his men to fire, he knew I'd take out the whole place with the vest.

"*Dad!*"

Caterina's cry cut through it all.

Calling me by that name… *fuck me…* it was everything.

I turned to look out at her, our gazes locking.

And I fucking smiled.

"I hear you. I'm with you."

Relief flooded her features.

I backed away toward the door with them, Nathan

pacing in a fury and his men left impotent because of the threat I still posed.

The moment we were through the door, I was ushered several feet away by Caterina.

"Disarm it," she ordered me fiercely. "Right the hell now."

I took care of it, and then I pulled it off and away from me. "I'm sorry. I'm so sorry."

Her fierce, pissed expression cracked. "I know you are. It's okay now. It's all okay."

"It won't be all the while they remain," I warned.

"We've got that covered," Julian told me.

"What?"

Nico pulled out a sleek, metal cylindrical device. "With all the self-important talking Donahue was doing, it gave us time to wire the place."

"Impressive."

"Shouldn't have doubted us," Milo told me.

"It wasn't about doubt. It's them. They're—"

As if to prove my point, the door we'd exited through flew open, and then Nathan barreled out with several of his guards flanking him.

He caught sight of us quickly as he roared profanities our way, then took aim at Nico.

A shot fired, ripping right through Nathan's skull before he could even pull the trigger.

As he jolted and dropped hard from the instant kill, I caught sight of Milo's gun aimed his way.

He smiled at Nico. "Always got you, brother."

"Blow it," Caterina breathed, clearly unsettled by how close that had been.

We didn't need to worry about any more of that, though, as Nico set off the explosives that they'd rigged.

Balls of fire tore through the structure, debris blowing

sky-high, along with all those inside, and even those Nathan had just brought outside with him.

The place was utterly annihilated within moments, collapsing in on itself, windows, metal, and wood blown to shit.

I watched the four of them all draw together, wrapping their arms around one another.

"The bastard is gone. It's done," Julian uttered.

Through it, Caterina smiled and reached out to me.

I went to her and took her hand.

She pulled me against her, bringing me in close, making me a part of it.

"You're my dad. I want you to stay. Do you understand me?"

"I do. And, fuck, you don't know how much I've wanted that, too. For so long."

"Well, now, is our chance. Let's not waste it."

I smiled and hugged her to me. "Let's not."

"This marks the beginning of our freedom," Julian spoke, before crying out into the night, "Whoop!"

A chorus of celebratory cheers followed as his words sank in.

It was a hell of a thing.

No more just surviving.

There was a hell of a lot of actual living to do now.

I couldn't wait to get started with my daughter.

And her mother.

So much loss along the way.

No more.

34

~Caterina~

It had finally happened for Julian.

He'd been able to throw the party that he'd wanted.

Although it was encompassing several different celebratory matters now.

Carlo and Remo's engagement.

Our victory over the two families and Erebus.

And even me winning a massive contract with the Brimbank Waterfront development!

There was one more thing still to celebrate. I only had to hold on a little while longer where that was concerned.

The place was decorated with gold and silver streamers, the same going for the balloons. There were flower arrangements all over the place and Julian had sweetly picked my favorites, peonies, for that aspect. He'd brought in two fountains—one a champagne fountain and the other a chocolate fountain. There were suited servers all over the place dispensing the most luxurious foods as well as some fancy cocktails. He'd really gone all out.

It had been several weeks since the home invasion and

it had taken that long to repair the damage that had been done that night. Now that had finally been seen to, the party had been able to happen.

"Caterina," a familiar voice called, and I spun from staring out through the window of the foyer that looked out at the courtyard that was currently jampacked with vehicles, to see Dante striding up to me with Matteo.

They'd been meeting with Nico in his home office.

Nico Marchetti, now officially Boss of the new incarnation of the Marchetti Syndicate.

"The Boss tells us congratulations are in order," Dante spoke as the two of them reached me.

"You got a big portion of that development for Camlann Corporation. Impressive," Matteo added.

I smiled. "Yeah, it's a major step up, without a doubt."

"Well, you deserve it."

"You've long deserved all of this," Dante said, gesturing around us. His smile faltered, the mood dampening as he uttered, "I'm sorry, Caterina. I'm so sorry I couldn't do more to protect you from what you suffered through."

"Dante, you were my guard for many years. You protected me from a great deal. Three kidnappings, I believe."

"But not from *him.*"

Matteo hung his head, looking as ashamed as Dante.

"Circumstances being what they were, no one could have protected me from Santino," I told them. "You did the best that you could with what you were given. I don't hold you responsible for any of it. I don't blame you."

"Thank you, by the way," Matteo told me.

I arched an eyebrow.

"Nico told us what you did. Replacing what Santino

took from me and then some in my account. The same with Dante."

"Well, you were both caught up in a no-win situation. You deserve the chance to start over in whatever manner you like, a way without restrictions or strings."

"You've definitely given us that," Dante said. "We're both going to remain in the city. At least for now. We'll see you around, Caterina?"

"I'd like that."

With that, they both smiled at me, then headed on out of the mansion.

"Seems like that went well."

Before I could turn at the sound of the voice, an arm wrapped around me, and I was pulled against a hard chest, looking up at Nico in the next moment.

"Trying to literally pull me away from the foyer, huh?"

"I want you to enjoy the celebrations, *principessa.*"

"I will. I'm just——"

"Antsy? Excited? Maybe a little nervous, too, because it's been so long?"

"All of the above," I admitted.

"Well, hear me when I tell you that it's going to be fine. Better than fine. Perfect, warm, amazing, and everything you imagined."

"Wow, such lovely words and visualizations."

"What can I say? I'm in an excellent mood."

"I can see that," I said, stroking the collar of his crisp, white shirt that was tucked into a pair of black dress pants, and gazing up at his beautifully rugged features and how lit up he was. It was truly amazing to see that usual heaviness lifted off him.

I mean, there was definitely still a dark intensity, because that was Nico. But most of that was sexual, at least currently, as his fingers wandered over my little black dress while he held me possessively to him.

I snatched his hands. "Nuh-uh. Not yet."

"Not yet? I'm barely touching you."

I gave him a look. "You know exactly what you're doing."

"And *you* know that I'm holding myself back. Significantly."

I stretched onto my tiptoes, and breathed in his ear, "I'll make it worth your while once the party's over. I promise all three of you will have the night of your lives."

A delicious growl rumbled from him.

"Down boy," Julian's voice came.

Nico turned with me basically attached to him, to see Julian leaning against the wall in a casual stance, his legs crossed at the ankles of his sleek gray suit.

"I'm so close to making you shut this party down now," Nico told him.

"A couple more hours. Cat's present isn't here yet. And Stover's gone a long way to retrieve said present."

Nico grunted his displeasure at the wait.

"Not to mention you've barely mingled at all. You've been holed up in your office. First, meeting with Carlo and Remo, then your Capos, some new business associates, and then Dante and Matteo. Remember when we talked about work-life balance with Cat? You were included in that."

"I just took over as Boss, J."

"And you're just that fucking good. So don't give me that. I know you have the skills and the means to pull it off."

I chuckled at the look on Nico's face.

Julian definitely had him.

"Fine," he said. "Let's rejoin the party."

"Good, because I've just spent a hell of a long time holding court with your Capos to offset your lack of social interaction tonight. We're trying to keep things upbeat, so I've been keeping Milo away from engaging them solo. You know how he can get into that steadfast, way-too-serious business mode of his that can be a real damper on a party situation. I'll send him over to Carlo and Remo because nothing can dampen their mood. Also, he seems to have hit it off with Remo and the guy's promised to give him some Underboss tips."

"I love how you have a formulated plan for *social interactions*," I told Julian.

"Gotta give this party its best chance, darlin'. Along with the food and decorations, that's how you do it."

"And where will you be?" Nico questioned.

"Schmoozing your business connections, of course." He clapped Nico on the back. "I've got you, N. Don't you worry one little bit."

"And you're keeping to the zero posting rule?"

"Yes, Jesus. No posting any photos or anything else on my IG. Received loud and clear."

"Good." He clasped his shoulder. "And, thank you. I do appreciate it."

"I know you do."

Nico tucked me into his side. "Ready for this?"

"Ready as I'll ever be."

Social situations weren't my favorite things, but they were also necessary and an unfortunate part of running an empire.

We stepped back into one of the rooms overflowing with people, and I sucked in a steadying breath.

Here goes nothing.

THE PARTY HAD FINALLY WORN down.

It hadn't seemed like it ever would.

People had definitely had a blast.

Spirits were high.

Excitement was in the air with the new alliance and the new incarnation of the Marchetti Syndicate.

Everything was on a great track at long last.

I couldn't quite believe it.

It had been such a fight to get here, there'd been so much to overcome, yet here we were. We'd come through it.

"Hey."

I turned from looking out over a little wall by the patio, staring into the peaceful, dark night, to see Milo emerging.

"Hey," I returned, smiling out at him. "How are you doing? I know this sort of thing isn't exactly your favorite way to pass your time."

"It's not. But Julian was right. We did need to make a big celebration out of it. What we've all achieved is no small thing. And I did actually end up enjoying it." He came to me and made a show of whispering, "Just don't let Julian know I've told you that or he'll see it as a *go* to throw so many more of these things."

I chuckled. "I hear you there." I wrapped my arms around myself, feeling the chill now because I'd been out here for a good ten minutes or so. "Did you know that Nico had invited several key business figures here for me?"

He grinned. "Yep. We all knew. He doesn't want to actively interfere in Camlann Corporation, but he wants to be there for you. We all do. So this was the compromise."

"It was really sweet. I don't know how to thank you guys."

"You're already doing it," he said, reaching out and

tenderly stroking my cheek in a way that made my heart skip a beat. That was intensified when he shook off his blazer and draped it over my shoulders. "By being here with us, being a part of us. It's changed so much. And I love you for it."

"Aww, I love you too, Milo," I said, sinking into him.

I smiled as he rubbed my shoulders through his blazer, warming me up.

A throat cleared, and it had us pulling apart.

And then my breath caught as I took in the sight of Joe standing there, his hand clasping *hers*.

"Oh my God," I choked.

I'd known she was coming.

I'd been waiting all night for her to arrive.

But seeing her now, flesh and blood, right here after all this time… it was surreal.

She was dressed down, especially compared to how she usually was, in just a loose light-gray sweater and a pair of jeans, but she looked cozy and comfortable. Her eyes were bright and that downtrodden air about her was long gone.

"Mom," I croaked.

In the next moment, she was pulling from Joe and rushing to me.

Milo stepped away, and I saw Nico and Julian come out onto the patio, the two of them joining him, and looking on at the scene, just as my mom and I threw our arms around one another.

"I've missed you, sweetheart. I've missed you so much," she breathed into my hair.

"I've missed you too, Mom."

Long moments passed before we eased back a little.

She took me in. "You look well. Happy."

"I am."

"I can't believe it's actually over. I can't believe that

monster is actually gone, that the whole thing has been dismantled. Joey was filling me in. Everything has changed. All for the better. There's just so much—" She noticed the minor cuts and bruises that were healing and fading now from our last two battles but still noticeable up close. "Are you all right, my sweetheart?"

"I'm fine, Mom. Better than fine. Amazing."

"You have to tell me everything. I need to know how he was killed."

Bianca Leone was the sweetest and gentlest person ever, but what Santino had done to her over the years had cut her deeply. I wasn't surprised that she was asking for details, where his death was concerned. It was a form of closure that she needed.

"It was me."

"What?"

"I was the one who killed him."

She looked over at Joe. "You told me you didn't know who it was."

"Because it wasn't for me to say, angel."

Angel? I guess their long coming reunion was going well then.

"It was Caterina's story to tell."

"I understand, *but* these secrets and lone wolf tactics of yours will stop going forward if we're going to remain in the city together and try to rekindle things. Do you hear me, Joey?"

Wow. This was… a lot.

Rekindle things?

Her telling him off.

He actually looked nervous.

And he even answered her right away, telling her, "I hear you, Bianca. I'm sorry. It's going to take some time."

"I have no doubt," she rebutted, before turning her full attention back to me. "I'm sorry it fell to you."

"I'm not."

"No?"

I shook my head. "As sick as it sounds, I needed it to be me who put him down."

"Knowing that monster as well as I unfortunately did, there's nothing *sick* about it. You did what was needed for you *and* countless others who'd been oppressed and hurt by him."

"Thank you, Mom."

"Come here," she said, wrapping her arms around me. "Sit with me and tell me everything that's happened. And I want you to promise me that you'll meet with that therapist of Julian's regarding the loss you suffered during all of this."

I stilled and looked out at Joe.

"I thought it would help if she knew," he told me.

Well, he had actually made the right call there.

I looked back at my mom. "I will."

"Good." She eyed each of my men in turn. "Thank you."

"We'd do nothing less than what's best for Caterina," Nico told her.

"As I suspected before I left. And something that's been reinforced through what Joe has told me about what's happened while I've been away."

I looked out at Joe again.

It had actually worked. I'd actually managed to get through to him. Not just that night when he'd put his life in jeopardy in a misguided bid to protect me by sacrificing himself, but beyond that, too. He'd really heard me.

We could move forward much more easily now.

As my mom led me past the guys, I reached out to him and took his hand.

He beamed out at me as the understanding passed between us.

Having him here, having my mom here, all alongside my men, too, was incredible.

All of it was more than I could have ever hoped for.

Epilogue 1
~CATERINA~

Eighteen Months Later

I smiled down at my phone and the text message exchange I'd been having with my mom and my dad—yes, that was how I was finally referring to Joe.

We often communicated in a group chat now.

That was how often they were together.

They'd started dating again soon after the party at the Manor and things had been going swimmingly. They were even talking about moving in together.

With both the Leone and Marchetti mansion being torn down under Nico's orders—orders that had been well-received—and my mom not wanting to set foot back inside the former anyway, I'd given my apartment to my mom. My dad had been staying in one of Julian's hotels for a long while, but now it looked like they were both going to settle at my former place together.

Dad: Still on for dinner at Il Forno? All six of us?

Caterina: Still on, Dad.

Mom: You've reminded her three times in the last forty-eight hours, Joey.

Dad: So, you can tell that I'm excited then, huh?

Mom: No, really?

Caterina: Too funny. Dad, your meeting with Nico is tomorrow. Are you ready?

Dad: Got it locked down. Don't worry.

Caterina: Perfect. He's looking forward to it.

Dad: I doubt that. But I appreciate you trying to soften it for me.

Caterina: Trust me, you're growing on him. He wouldn't allow this otherwise.

Dad: I know. He doesn't give his trust lightly.

Mom: Understandable after what he's dealt with.

Dad: True, angel.

Mom: I'll talk to you later. Being paged. Guess my break's over. See you after my shift, Joey.

Dad: I'll pick you up from the hospital right after.

Mom: Perfect.

Calls from the boys caught my attention.

Caterina: Gotta go, too. Love you guys.

I smiled to myself as they responded in kind.

Then I stowed my phone in the inside pocket of my leather riding jacket.

The riding gear I was decked out in was something I'd been planning on putting to use tonight. But after what I'd discovered a couple of hours before heading down here from work, that had now gone out the window.

That discovery also meant that me, my parents, and the boys, getting together for dinner in a few days would be more than just one of our regular get-togethers with all six of us.

The rumble of motorcycles sounded around me, taking my attention, as the boys got ready and into position.

I could feel the excitement ramping up as I took in the three of them, mounting their bikes and pulling their helmets on.

We'd been holding true to our commitment to maintaining a healthy work-life balance.

And this, tonight, was just one example of living up to that.

Having fun.

Taking a step away from work.

Nico and Milo were running the Marchetti Syndicate and even reworking things in a much more legitimate direction. One such legitimate operation was Reincourt Construction, which Julian and I had partnered with them on in order to develop business outside the city and to expand. Nico was going to be meeting with my dad and bringing him on as his Chief Security Advisor for all things Marchetti Syndicate. Nico had already taken his secret company, *Cronos Group*, and turned it into a charitable foundation that had been working with the Carver Foundation to further its reach and expand into other charitable endeavors.

Julian was running Carver Group.

There was me with Camlann Corporation and working on the Brimbank project.

Julian and I had also gone further than our hotel *mega hub* idea and we'd created LC Entertainment together to produce many other like it beyond the City of Tolhurst.

The two of us were also still in therapy and seeing Roslynn regularly.

Even Nico had gotten help with undoing the compartmentalization he'd employed over the years when he'd basically been existing in survival mode.

We had a lot going on, but we'd been managing it well with our relationship and enjoying our lives.

That management was about to be pushed further, though.

Julian was extra happy tonight because he wasn't riding Milo or Nico's bike. He was riding his own again. His own, incredibly pimped out Harley. Milo had worked hard to have it rebuilt and replicated exactly as it had been.

I watched as he got going then had adrenaline shooting through me as he performed a wheelie to claps from me and the guys, but then took it further by executing a fucking headstand *while* doing that—a switchback headstand was what he'd termed it when he'd explained to me what he would be doing earlier. He maintained seemingly impossibly perfect balance on the bike while upside down.

When he came out of it, he landed perfectly back on the saddle.

"Holy shit!" I cried, whooping and clapping.

"Still got it, Sunshine!" Milo called out.

Nico was next, performing wheelies and drifting, then even standing up on the saddle while his bike was tearing down the road.

I knew it had been a long time since he'd done anything like this, but it wasn't showing. His love for it was. His wild side. The part that wasn't just rooted in darkness or extreme protectiveness.

As he came to a stop, I watched Milo place both legs on the handlebars while his bike leaned on the rear wheel while still riding.

It was spectacular.

"Whoop! Insane!" I yelled out to them down the back road.

Julian came to a stop beside me first.

He dismounted and pulled off his helmet.

"I'm thinking we delve back into some primal kink

after you've had your turn, darlin'. Hardcore primal in these woods right here. What do you say?"

Oh shit. A dirty thrill rolled through me at his words.

The timing, though? That was a whole other thing.

"I'm down for that," Nico said, pulling up beside his bike.

"Once you've had your turn, beauty," Milo told me, dismounting as Nico did, the three of them walking to me, all excited and elated.

As Milo went to hand his helmet to me, I took a step back.

And the mood abruptly shifted.

Oops.

This wasn't how I'd meant to do this.

I just hadn't been sure until I'd gotten the news earlier.

"That's not the best idea now," I told them.

"Why? What's wrong?" Nico asked.

As Julian and Milo went to join in, I held up my hand.

"Relax. Nothing is wrong, per se. I mean, there is something. But it's not bad."

"Cat?" Julian pushed gently.

"What's happened?" Milo asked.

I sucked in a breath, then it came bursting out of me. "I'm pregnant."

Nico blinked harshly. "You're sure?"

"I just came from the doctor. It's confirmed."

A huge, blazing smile spread over his face. "Fuck, *principessa.*"

"This is the best fucking news!" Julian cried.

Milo tossed his helmet on the ground. "Well, damn!"

And in the next moment, they were all over me.

Holding me.

Loving me.

Giving me everything I'd ever needed.

Epilogue 2
~NICO~

One Year Later

Sleep regression.

Who knew those two words could strike fear into even the most hardened?

We did.

We fucking knew it now.

I jolted awake as insistent screams reached me.

The slightest cry could awaken me now. I'd become so attuned to it. All four of us had.

I sat up, blinking rapidly to get my bearings in our bedroom.

The *renovations* had gone ahead, and we'd ended up combining my room and Caterina's old room into one massive space. And, yes, I'd given in and allowed Julian to put his own splash of flamboyant décor, mixed in with everybody else's mark on the room. Cobalt-blue shimmering paint adorned the walls. There was also a bold zebra-print shag rug that was centered in the space. The room was a mishmash of different styles that didn't quite

353

go together. But that was fine—at least when it came to our shared bedroom. *We* were a mishmash of personalities. And it worked between us in a large part because we were able to blend that together so well. So the room was somewhat of a physical testament to that.

I frowned as I looked to see that only Milo was in the bed with me now.

No. That wasn't supposed to be the case.

I mean, Milo was actually meant to be sleeping right now, because he'd taken the earlier shift. But Caterina and Julian were also supposed to be with him, not out of bed and dealing with the little nightmare next door. The two of them had a highly publicized ceremony to attend tomorrow, the opening of their first *mega hub* via LC Entertainment. They needed to be well-rested and at their best.

I eyed the monitor on the nightstand, finding the crib empty. Yet the little cries were still as strong as ever.

The situation wasn't calming down.

I pulled on my boxers, then rushed out of the bedroom, making a right turn for the nursery.

As I neared the door, Julian's voice reached me.

"Vicious things tangling in the night/ She was made for one hell of a fight/ Fuck it, she was born for this/ Born to be merciless/ Girl's got claws and she'll sure as fuck bite."

I stilled for a moment.

Was he seriously singing those lyrics right now?

They belonged to Levi's love, Colton Sharp, via his band, *Mythic Cry,* that had blown up to unbelievable heights lately. You could rarely turn on the radio without hearing one of his songs. To say he'd hit it big would be an absolute understatement.

I burst into the room, startling them.

Caterina was holding a warmed bottle of her breast milk as she lounged tiredly on the amazingly comfortable turquoise couch, while Julian was singing in his tone-deaf way and rocking our little bundle of screams over by the insanely extravagant golden crib.

"You're supposed to be asleep," I told them. "I had it."

"We were actually already up," Caterina informed me.

"Yeah. We were too wired about tomorrow to manage to sleep through the night."

"Hmm. Is that *her* excuse as well?" I asked, gesturing at our three-month-old in Julian's arms.

"Her excuse is that she's a baby," Caterina said, chuckling. "This sleep regression at her age is normal, the extra fussiness, refusing to go to sleep at all sometimes too."

"You made sure of that when you had her checked by three fucking doctors," Julian said.

Of course I had.

I'd wanted to make sure she was truly okay. I wasn't taking any chances where her wellbeing was concerned. Ever.

"Watch the language around her. It's bad enough you were singing that song to her."

"What? You don't want her to be tough and fierce when she grows up?"

"She doesn't need to be. Especially not right now. She just needs to be a kid." Something none of us were allowed to be. "Safe and happy and loved."

"And she is, Nico," Caterina told me. "She's so loved by us."

I reached out and Julian handed our daughter to me.

I adjusted her in my arms, holding her against me, and nuzzling her soft cheek as I stared into her stunning sapphire eyes.

Her cries started to calm a little as I stroked her fuzzy light brown hair.

"Bottle?" I called to Caterina.

355

She was there in the next moment, coming to us and handing it over.

"Here, little love," I spoke softly, brushing the bottle over our daughter's lips. She took it eagerly, clearly hungry.

"Ah… yes," Julian breathed. "The cries finally cease."

"Now that you've stopped singing."

"Hey, I was gonna bring in Milo, but you were adamant that he rest tonight. Cat's voice is as bad as mine. And who knew Milo had a voice like fucking silk? I'd never heard him sing before, or so much as whistle a tune in all the time we've known him."

Yes, that had definitely come as a surprise.

"Not even in the shower?" Caterina asked me.

"Not even then."

"Well, it's definitely come in handy with this little one."

I smiled and stared down at her in my arms.

Lucia Leone.

The perfect addition to our family.

Caterina had wanted to give her the last name *Leone*, the notion that she and Lucia would reinvent the Leone legacy, that Santino's version of it would perish fully in the process, eventually as though it had never existed in his image at all.

She was our chance.

She was our hope.

The love of our lives.

Our daughter.

She'd changed so much for us.

She'd brought out different facets of all of us.

She'd challenged us and also given us so much joy.

Every day, she changed and grew.

And I would relish every single day of the four of us watching her grow together.

"Everything okay in here?" Milo's voice sounded, and I

turned with Lucia in my arms to see him stumbling tiredly into the room.

"All good. Go back to bed."

"Nah," he said, coming over to us. "Who cares about sleep when there's this sweet little picture here, all of us gathered around this little beauty?"

I chuckled.

He certainly wasn't wrong there.

It *was* picture perfect.

Something none of us had believed we could have.

But we'd fought harder than anything to make it so, against ruthless enemies who'd threatened to take every fucking thing from us.

They'd all failed.

They'd all fallen.

And here we remained.

Stronger than ever.

A true family of our own making.

I looked out at them all and smiled widely. "I wouldn't have it any other way."

THE END

___

**Want some dark college RH?
Check out WALKING WITH MONSTERS.**

**Or dive into dark academy paranormal RH,
ELECTI ACADEMY.**

Coveted Kingdom Series

WHERE THE WICKED REIGN
VICIOUS LITTLE PRINCESS
THEY MAKE MONSTERS

Connected Series

VICIOUS THINGS & COVETED KINGDOM

VICIOUS THINGS
Brianna, Levi, Colton, Mason
THEY BREAK BEAUTY
WHEN KINGS FALL

COVETED KINGDOM
Caterina, Nico, Emilio, Julian
WHERE THE WICKED REIGN
VICIOUS LITTLE PRINCESS
THEY MAKE MONSTERS

WALKING WITH MONSTERS & TWISTED TORMENT

WALKING WITH MONSTERS
Aurora, Asher, Killian, Jonah
LOCK UP THE DARKNESS
SCARS RUN DEEP
BURN IT DOWN

TWISTED TORMENT
Skylar, Bastian, Caleb, Caspian

WRECK ME
HATE ME
CRAVE ME

———

IMMORTAL PASSIONS & IMMORTAL FLAME

IMMORTAL PASSIONS
Mia, Jaxon, Ryker, Lucian
IMMORTAL BURDEN
REIGN OF THE BEAST
FALLEN ANGEL
OUT OF ASHES

IMMORTAL FLAME
Ariana, Kai, Vorzyr, Nyx
HARBINGER
LEGACY
MANTLE

Leia King Library

WALKING WITH MONSTERS
LOCK UP THE DARKNESS
SCARS RUN DEEP
BURN IT DOWN

TWISTED TORMENT
WRECK ME
HATE ME
CRAVE ME

VICIOUS THINGS
THEY BREAK BEAUTY
WHEN KINGS FALL

ELECTI ACADEMY
WICKED HEIRS
CURSED HEIRS
FALLEN HEIRS

COVETED KINGDOM
WHERE THE WICKED REIGN
VICIOUS LITTLE PRINCESS
THEY MAKE MONSTERS

IMMORTAL PASSIONS

Leia
KING

About the Author

Where Damaged Heroes and Badass Heroines Collide.

Leia writes edgy and emotional stories across multiple genres. She enjoys crafting flawed heroes with a dark side and strong women who hold their own.

WEBSITE
INSTAGRAM
PINTEREST

Printed in Dunstable, United Kingdom